Wild Sorrow

Sandi Ault

BERKLEY PRIME CRIME, NEW YORK

South Sioux City Public Library
2121 Dakota Avenue
South Sioux City, NE 68776

THE BERKLEY PUBLISHING GROUP
Published by the Penguin Group
Penguin Group (USA) Inc.
375 Hudson Street, New York, New York 10014, USA
Penguin Group (Canada), 90 Eglinton Avenue East, Suite 700, Toronto, Ontario M4P 2Y3, Canada
(a division of Pearson Penguin Canada Inc.)
Penguin Books Ltd., 80 Strand, London WC2R 0RL, England
Penguin Group Ireland, 25 St. Stephen's Green, Dublin 2, Ireland (a division of Penguin Books Ltd.)
Penguin Group (Australia), 250 Camberwell Road, Camberwell, Victoria 3124, Australia
(a division of Pearson Australia Group Pty. Ltd.)
Penguin Books India Pvt. Ltd., 11 Community Centre, Panchsheel Park, New Delhi—110 017, India
Penguin Group (NZ), 67 Apollo Drive, Rosedale, North Shore 0632, New Zealand
(a division of Pearson New Zealand Ltd.)
Penguin Books (South Africa) (Pty.) Ltd., 24 Sturdee Avenue, Rosebank, Johannesburg 2196,
South Africa

Penguin Books Ltd., Registered Offices: 80 Strand, London WC2R 0RL, England

This is a work of fiction. Names, characters, places, and incidents either are the product of the author's imagination or are used fictitiously, and any resemblance to actual persons, living or dead, business establishments, events, or locales is entirely coincidental. The publisher does not have any control over and does not assume any responsibility for author or third-party websites or their content.

Copyright © 2009 by Sandi Ault.
Cover illustration © by Aleta Rafton.
Cover design by Diana Kolsky.
Interior text design by Tiffany Estreicher.

All rights reserved.
No part of this book may be reproduced, scanned, or distributed in any printed or electronic form without permission. Please do not participate in or encourage piracy of copyrighted materials in violation of the author's rights. Purchase only authorized editions.
BERKLEY® PRIME CRIME and the PRIME CRIME logo are trademarks of Penguin Group (USA) Inc.

PRINTING HISTORY
Berkley Prime Crime hardcover edition / March 2009
Berkley Prime Crime trade paperback edition / January 2010

Berkley Prime Crime trade paperback ISBN: 978-0-425-23263-7

Library of Congress Cataloging-in-Publication Data
Ault, Sandi.
Wild sorrow / Sandi Ault.—1st ed.
p. cm.
ISBN 978-0-425-22583-7
1. Wild, Jamaica (Fictitious character)—Fiction. 2. United States. Bureau of Land Management—Fiction. 3. Pueblo Indians—Colorado—Fiction. 4. Murder—Investigation—Fiction. I. Title.
PS3601.U45W57 2009
813'.6—dc22 2008048318

PRINTED IN THE UNITED STATES OF AMERICA

10 9 8 7 6 5 4 3 2 1

For Sherry, Bev, and Rick–

such wild-hearted children, then and now.

Author's Note

This is a work of fiction, and the characters, many of the places, and some of the events herein are figments of my imagination. That being said, I have taken some license in highlighting in this story a very real and very sad chapter in our nation's history when—until quite recently—generations of children from Indian tribes were forced to attend Indian boarding schools. In these institutions they were mistreated, robbed of their culture, and deprived of the comfort and support of their traditions, their language, and their families. The effects of this heartless and brutal policy still reverberate through Native America and through the conscience of our nation, where this war made on innocent children awaits our awakening, our accountability, and amends so that all of our hearts can heal.

I write of rituals from several Native American cultures, especially those of the Native Puebloans, of whom I am most fond and with whom I am most familiar—however, out of respect for their wishes and their right to keep and to define their own culture, I have mixed and changed these myths and rituals and created some fictitious ones, leaving *a hole in the top of everything* so the spirits still move freely.

It's cheaper to educate Indians than to kill them.

—THOMAS JEFFERSON MORGAN,
United States Commissioner of Indian Affairs,
speaking at the establishment
of the Phoenix Indian School in 1891

◂ 1 ▸

The Predator

The wind howled like a broken-hearted woman who had given up on life. I had not meant to come this far, but it was too late now. I had followed the blood, expecting to find a wounded animal. But not this.

It was ten days before Christmas. Before dawn, a shepherd had fired a shot at a shadow that lurked in the scrub, while his sheep huddled into a knot in the arroyo where he'd brush-penned them for the night. He'd wounded the predator without getting a clear view of it, and could not identify what it was. The tribe had reported three sheep kills since they brought their flocks down from the mountains for winter grazing on the high mesas above Tanoah Pueblo. Rumors rose up that wolves, newly reintroduced in the region, were the cause of the attacks. But I suspected a mountain lion, and I rode horseback on the rangelands west of the pueblo with my wolf, Mountain, loping alongside, determined to find out. It was my job—I'm a resource protection agent for the Bureau of Land Management assigned as a liaison to the pueblo. My name is Jamaica Wild.

I followed the tracks of a big cat through the afternoon—losing the trail, doubling back and finding it again as it led out onto a windswept, desolate canyon rim. A storm was building to the west, the billowing sky the color of steel and filled with heavy foreboding. I felt the moisture in the air, the temperature diving. Rooster, the young sorrel I rode, turned skittish, feeling the oncoming tempest. But the wolf didn't seem to notice. He led—darting along with his nose to the ground as we tracked the trail from blood spot to blood spot—stopping when he found sign and scanning the area with his senses. I scanned, too, but I was also calculating time and distance and the torment in the skies, the clouds growing more menacing with every moment.

The ruin stood high on a knoll, visible from a mile away. As we approached, the sound of the gale rushing across the high mesa split into a chorus of voices as it swept along the jagged, stacked-rock walls, over the lips of long-abandoned kivas, and through the crumbling stone shells of the once-tall towers that marked an ancient village.

I looped Rooster's reins around a stone on the ground outside of the ruin wall. Mountain watched me for cues—wolves hunt in packs. "You stay with me, buddy," I whispered. "You stay with me."

I drew my rifle from the saddle scabbard and clicked off the safety. I made my way around the wall until I was downwind, Mountain moving low and close beside me. We climbed over a breach of collapsed flat rocks and I studied the interior of the pueblo ruin. Several subterranean stone circles clustered together in a corner. I walked cautiously toward them, across a hundred-yard carpet of pot shards peppered with nuggets of red chert. I felt the crunch of brittle pottery beneath my boots as the freezing wind blasted my face, tore at my hat brim and coat, and wailed over the walls, creating three distinct pitches, all of them piercing and plaintive.

As we approached the rim of the first sunken circle, I signaled the wolf to stop. I crouched low and edged forward, peering over the round rock lip. Six feet below, a scrub juniper and a pile of toppled rock created a barrier near the interior wall. A mound of earth nearby indicated the ground had been dug out beneath. Mountain pushed forward to the kiva rim, sending a loose stone along the edge shooting down into the center. Before I could raise up and ready my rifle, two faces peered out from behind a limb covering the doorway to the den. Cubs! Two little mountain lions, no more than a few months old. As the wind blasted us, it carried their cries—these babies were hungry.

I grabbed Mountain's collar, pulled a handful of jerky strips from my pocket, and pitched them into the kiva. The wolf was curious, but did not resist my hold as I led him away. I kept Mountain close as I explored the rest of the ruin. But there was no sign of the she-lion. I searched the perimeter for blood spots, then moved outward in concentric circles. No trace.

From the high ground near the ruin, I surveyed my surroundings. The winds suddenly subsided, creating an eerie stillness. The air pulsed with gray-green light and electric anticipation. To the west, a wide, winding crack in the earth created a long, snaking canyon fed by an insufficient river. Arroyos leading out from the canyon fractured the high plain to the north. To the east, the way I had come, I could no longer see the blue silhouette of Sacred Mountain and the range that sheltered Tanoah Pueblo. To the south, set in a swale below, a massive old adobe compound seemed to be melting back into the earth.

I mounted up and rode down the slope, the wolf following—the sky sinking around us like a heavy black blanket, the sound of the horse's hooves pounding like a drum on the dry desert dirt.

A high adobe wall, cracked and eroding, surrounded a U-shaped compound of buildings. Plywood over the windows had withered, splintered, and separated into gray ribs reminiscent of prison bars. There were no roads nearby—only a stretch of dirt track grown over from disuse that led downslope and dead-panned into a low area long ago washed out by spring floods boiling out of the canyon. As I approached the arched mission gates in the wall, I heard a faint howling sound like the crying of children coming from inside. Or was it the cat?

A brass plaque on the wall read:

San Pedro de Arbués Indian School
established 1898

As I read this, the cloud deck quaked with bellowing thunder. Tiny white pellets of ice began to strike my hat, my coat, making small, dull ticks, the rhythm growing faster and more intense until there was a barrage of unbroken clattering and a white carpet covering the ground. Rooster bridled, his withers quivering, and he threw his head to the side and looked at me with one wild, obsidian eye, his nostrils inflating and collapsing in a frantic rhythm, his ears back. All at once, he reared and stood on hind legs, pounding the dried wood of the gates. I started to slide, clinging to the reins—which yanked Rooster's head back—and he responded by bucking violently. As he threw himself forward, I felt his hindquarters rise like a surging storm wave, and then my own backside left the saddle as I flew up and forward, hard into the gate and the path of Rooster's heaving hooves.

My shoulder slammed into the iron hinge that spanned the width of the wood. I slid to the ground, splinters shredding the sleeve of my coat and scraping my skin, and I landed on one knee and hand in a bed of cactus. But I forced myself to roll to the side just as Rooster's powerful front hooves boomed beside my ear, exploding a weathered slat, trapping his foreleg in the hole he had just made. The rhythm of his tirade interrupted, his front foot snared, Rooster's weight surged forward, off balance, and he crashed through the right half of the gate, his big body like a long-legged locomotive speeding toward me, his massive red rear yawing to the left and threatening to pin me against the side of the gate still standing.

I was down already; there was no time to rise and run. I dove under his belly as the horse came at me. The metal stirrup struck my forehead with a thwack, and I hit the ground just behind him as Rooster rammed into the gate, an explosion of dirt, shards of wood, and snow pummeling my body.

Mountain had stayed well away from the action. He came to me now and sniffed at my face. "I'm okay, buddy," I said as I got to my feet, feeling my forehead where the stirrup had hit. Rooster was down on one side, lying in the center of the entrance, both gates flung open by the force of his slide. He looked at me over one shoulder and then struggled twice to right himself, finally springing to his feet. A shard of wood extended from his right foreleg, and I cooed to him as I approached, patting his rump, running my hand along his side, catching hold of the reins and petting his nose. I pulled out the big splinter and the horse flinched, but he let me examine the area afterward. The leg seemed good, and as I walked him to test it, a granular snow drove down around us as if the clouds had opened a too-full chute and dumped a winter's worth of payback all at once. A boreal cold accompanied this downfall, and Rooster's breath froze in a cloud around his face.

"We gotta get inside," I said, leading Rooster into the yard of the school, where I tied his reins to a hitching post inside the wall. The wolf raced ahead of me, into a blinding white blur. I followed, and he led us right to the doors of a chapel across from the entrance. A slat had been nailed across the double doors, but it was loose, and I easily pried it away. "This looks good, buddy," I told Mountain.

I pushed on one side, and the heavy door groaned and screeched, its bottom scraping and then jamming against the hard floor, permitting barely enough opening for me to slide through. I took a moment for my eyes to adjust, brushing the snow from my shoulders and sleeves, and then Mountain wriggled through the gap and rammed into the backs of my knees, sending me sprawling toward the floor. I thrust out my hands to break my fall. That was when I felt cold flesh.

The body beneath me was frozen, blue-white, and stiff. Two sightless eyes stared through me; a round mouth opened onto a deep, black cave. I screamed and sprang to my feet, backing to the door, where Mountain gave a nervous whimper.

From here, I could see the whole scene, my eyes having adapted to the minimal light. An elderly Anglo woman lay dead on her back with legs spread wide, a dust-covered black dress reaching below her knees. A collar of twisted sage and feathers decorated each ankle. Her hair had been razored off at the scalp, her face painted with two yellow lightning bolts. A sign hung from her neck. I had to move close to read it. Scribbled in red crayon were the words *I am not an Indian.*

◂ 2 ▸

The Howl

As I made my way back to Rooster, snow pelted my face—not just flakes of snow, but a blasting curtain of icy gobs that stuck to my nose and eyelashes and pasted the front of my coat with white ice in a matter of seconds. The winds had picked up again, and they were bearing down a blizzard on us. I looked down at Mountain, who was slinking beside me, and saw a thick coat of white frosting his head, neck, and back. "We have to stay here tonight," I shouted into the wind, as I pulled my sidearm from the holster beneath my coat and slid it into my pocket. I untied the horse, who now looked like an enormous white sheep from the quilt of snow he wore.

I led Rooster through a blinding whiteout to the door. Once I had tied the reins to the door handle, I opened my saddlebag and grabbed a flashlight and my LED headlamp. I drew my handgun out of my pocket, then slid through the narrow opening and looked around, carefully sidestepping as Mountain came through so that he wouldn't knock me over again. I strapped on the headlight, feeling a pang as the elastic tightened over the place where the stirrup had struck my forehead. We stood in a big, empty nave, its small, high windows emitting little light. There was nothing but cold adobe walls and a hard stone floor.

I used my flashlight to examine the cadaver. On one side of the deceased's neck, I saw a dark line in the flesh. A tail of thin gray hair lay loose just above her head, where it had been sliced away from her scalp. Two low-heeled black shoes had been tossed to the side, no doubt removed so that the sage bracelets could be slid over her feet. I noted again the dust on the woman's black dress, and yet the chapel floor did not seem dirty. I spotted Mountain sitting nearby watching. He cocked his head at me.

"Wow," I whispered. "This old woman had somebody real mad at her."

Mountain followed me close as I looked around the chapel. In addition to the entry, there were two doors: one on the outside wall at the front and another on the opposite side at the back. I went to the one near the entrance, readied my gun, and pulled on the handle. Unlike the entry, this door opened with little effort, exposing me to bitter, arctic cold. A small square belfry stood empty, save a large drift of snow.

At the back of the church, I tugged on the arched door and it gave a deep groan, then a wailing sound that whistled down a long hall with doors along each side, which I presumed were the school's classrooms. I guessed that this wing led to the other big building in the U-shaped compound, probably the living quarters for its residents. I closed the door again, sure that whoever had left the old woman's body here was long gone.

I needed to get Rooster inside before the blizzard worsened. I pushed and shoved on the chapel's entrance doors, but just the one would move, and only a few more inches before its sagging hinges drove the bottom of the heavy wood slab into the stone floor. I tried to tug Rooster by his reins so he would muscle into the barrier, but seeing the obstacle before him, he pulled away instead. Finally, I pressed my back into the old door, bent my knees, and gave it all I had. There was a grinding rasp, then the sound of wood cracking as the lower hinge ripped from the frame. I straddled the door, heaved upward, and managed to lift it slightly and drag it back enough to lead Rooster through. Once inside, I attempted to push the door closed again to keep out the frigid air, but the hinge had warped and would not comply. The door stood ajar, snow driving through the opening, and within a matter of minutes, a drift began to build on the inside of the entry.

At the rear of the chapel I hobbled Rooster to keep him from straying. I removed my saddlebags and inventoried my provisions: jerky, two energy bars, some dried fruit, dog cookies, a small bag of oats for the horse. There were matches, toilet paper, a first aid kit, and a good knife. My bedroll, kept dry in a stuff-sack, had an extra set of clothes rolled inside. But my canteens were low—if we stayed more than a night, I'd have to find a way to build a fire and melt some snow.

After I unsaddled the horse, I dressed the small wound below his fetlock, where the wood shard had penetrated, with some antibiotic ointment and a gauze wrap. I shook the bag of oats and offered a handful to Rooster, but he snorted and drew back.

Mountain stood close, watching my every move. "At least there's one good thing about spending the night here," I said to the wolf, to whom I often talked, since he was my live-in companion. "It will give

Rooster's leg a chance to rest." It was so cold that my breath was visible when I spoke, and the layer of ice still frozen to my coat made it heavy and brittle. I held up a stick of jerky. "You want something to eat, buddy?"

The wolf snapped his head to one side, as if the sight of the meat offended him.

I couldn't have eaten either, if I'd tried.

Since I'd taken my gloves off, my fingers ached and had begun to stiffen. In the cold darkness of the big, empty chapel, the wind gusted in gales, and with each one, a terrible groaning noise emitted from the bell tower. Mountain began to howl as if he could not bear the sorrow of the sound. This was more than I could endure. I went to explore the source of this horrible noise. I stood in the square adobe turret and looked up, the light of my headlamp projecting a few feet above my head. Lashed to iron spikes driven high into the walls, heavy ropes were tied around the old iron bell to keep it from moving, and it strained against the silencing bonds with every squall. As if to demonstrate, a bone-chilling bluster set the ropes to singing, and the hideous groaning sound reverberated against the slick walls of the belfry.

I knew I should roll out my bedroll and try to rest, but I could not bring myself to do it. First, there was the cold—a heavy weight of deepening chill that seemed to sink into the joints. Then there was the hate lingering around the remains of the woman whose final hours had clearly been spent in humiliation. But there was something more: I felt haunted by the sorrows that had seeped into the walls of this place. Even if I tried to sleep here, there would be no peace with that wailing wind.

I decided to explore the premises. Mountain followed as I beamed my flashlight ahead of us, and we pursued the pool of lemon-colored light down the hallway. Inside the first room on the right, several boxes slumped against a wall. The top one contained a cache of old items, including several group photos of the Indian children who had resided at the school.

The first, an aged, sepia-toned print, showed three rows of small boys, nine in each line: the first row seated, the second kneeling, and the third standing in regimental order. They wore brimmed high caps, round-collared coats buttoned to the neck, knickers, socks, and lace-up boots. Every item of their apparel appeared to be gray. No boy could have been more than six years of age, and not one of them had even a hint of happiness in his face. I felt such sadness as I looked at the photo that I set it aside, hoping the next would be a happier scene.

But it was not. The second photo bore the inscription *Sewing Class*. Eighteen young girls wearing identical sackcloth dresses, dark boots, and stockings sat like automatons in their chairs, which were aligned in a semicircle around baskets on the floor heaped with cloth. Each girl had her sewing in her lap, and looked down at it dutifully. Behind the students, three white women watched sternly over their charges, and five older girls sat at antique-looking sewing machines. On the wall hung a portrait of the Virgin Mary, a length of wire tacked to the top of the frame, allowing it to tilt downward so that the Virgin looked down upon the little children. Dark shades covered the windows; the only light in the photo came from a partly open door. A rack of newly made garments lined one wall. The children were manufacturing clothing.

There were photos of small boys blacksmithing, a picture of students hoeing weeds in an impossibly parched garden, group shots of small soldiers posed in perfect military formation in front of the chapel doors I had just damaged, older girls working in the laundry, and a nighttime glimpse of little tots in white nightgowns kneeling in prayer beside makeshift cots with threadbare blankets on them.

The last photo showed a priest in a long black frock surrounded by twenty or so thin, dark boys perhaps eight to ten years old. The group stood in the front yard of the school—I recognized the chapel with its bell tower. When this picture was taken, two large wooden crosses adorned the top of the chapel's front wall. One of the boys held a football—at last, a sign that the children were permitted to play! But I was relieved too soon. As I studied the photo further, I saw a small group gathered on the sidelines. A little boy who sat in a wagon had no feet. Another leaned on crutches. Beside him, a pale, emaciated boy with one arm in a sling had a disfigured face covered with boils and sores.

As I studied this last photo, the sound of a disturbance came from the chapel. Rooster whinnied and brayed, and I heard his shoes clattering on the stone floor. Mountain raced ahead of me as I made my way out of the classroom and back to the nave.

The sorrel strained against his tether, rearing and huffing, his eyes fixed on the chapel entry. I followed his gaze. In the spare glow of my headlamp and flashlight, I saw the big cat just inside the door, encroaching on the deceased's remains. The cougar was thin and ragged, a large place in the meat of her back thigh black with blood. She stood her ground, clearly out of desperation and hunger, and she opened a huge mouth full of powerful, pointed teeth. From deep in her throat, a deafening *gnaaagh* rang against the walls and reverberated across the room. Mountain charged forward, the hair along the ridge of his back standing spiked, and he gnashed his teeth as he growled and snarled. The cougar hissed and lowered her head, unwilling to concede defeat. The wolf postured, pulling his lips back hard and showing his teeth, lowering into a crouch, only a few yards from the cat.

"Mountain, no!" I yelled, moving toward him as I pushed my hand into the pocket with the gun. With the other hand, I kept the flashlight trained on them. I swallowed hard, tried to calm my voice and yet still be heard over the hissing and growling. "Mountain, stay," I said. "You stay."

The two opponents began to circle slowly around the body on the floor, the lion moving clockwise, and Mountain squaring off by shifting directly opposite her. The cougar gave another powerful warning *waul,* and rotated her huge head to look at me. Mountain lunged across the corpse and toward the cat, who drew up and uttered such a deep, rumbling growl that I could feel it in my gut. Just a foot from her face, the wolf snarled and snapped, and the cat recoiled from his gnashing teeth, one of her paws poised to slash.

The ear-splitting crack of the gunshot caused them both to freeze, and while the sound was still ringing against the walls, the cougar slithered out the door. Mountain dropped into a crouch and he trembled with fear. I lowered the gun from its skyward aim and blew out my breath. "It's okay, buddy," I said, my pulse still racing. "It's okay."

But a sleepless night ensued as the living stood watch over the dead—during which time I was plagued by the heartrending voice of the howling wind. It was the sound of wild sorrow.

◂ 3 ▸

Morning

When the first gleam of alpenglow began to shimmer on the horizon, I saddled Rooster and brought him outside into the dense, cold air. I walked him around the schoolyard, studying his gait. His leg seemed well enough to go the short distance I would need to ride to regain radio contact. The night winds had pushed snow into drifts against the west walls, and patches of white clung to low depressions, but most of it had blown across the mesa toward the mountains to the east.

While Mountain scampered around methodically marking everything in the area, I assembled a pile of large stones and a weathered sign and used them to secure the doorway so the cat could not reenter the chapel. The air was so frigid that even lifting and carrying the heavy stones did not make me break a sweat. When I returned to Rooster to mount up, he had a slick coat of frost on his rump.

I rode east under a thick, dull sky that had nearly strangled the light out of the sunrise, back toward Tanoah Pueblo. As I went, I watched for tracks of any kind that might have led to the school. But the winds had disrupted the soil, leaving the loose dirt of the desert ravaged.

An hour later, I saw the ATV on the horizon. Two men approached at high speed. My field superintendent, Roy, sat in the driver's seat, and before he could kill the engine, Kerry Reed, my forest ranger boyfriend, flew out of the other side and up to me. "Babe, are you all right?" He took my shoulders in his two hands and looked into my face.

"I'm okay," I said. "My horse took a big splinter, but he seems fine."

"Your coat. It's all torn." His green-flecked brown eyes were full of worry.

"Yeah, I hit a gate. Rooster threw me."

By then the Boss had gotten to us. "We'd have been here sooner but I forgot they had fenced that big federal training facility. Had to go around it." He took Rooster by the reins and examined his fetlock. "How in hell did you end up all the way out here?" Roy said from under the horse.

"I was tracking a cougar," I said. "Another attack on the pueblo flocks."

He raised up. "Well, why didn't you let someone know?"

"I didn't think I would end up so far out, but when I knew we were closing in on her—"

"Her? It's a female?"

"Yes. With two young cubs. She's wounded, and she looks half-starved."

"You must've got a good look at her, then."

I nodded. "She visited last night."

Kerry brought water for Mountain from the ATV, and a thermos of hot coffee. He poured some in a cup and handed it to me. I held it between my palms for a moment and watched the steam curl from the surface.

The sound of an engine whined from the east as another ATV approached, rocking and dipping over the rough terrain, disappearing into arroyos and then surfacing seconds later. Soon FBI Agent Diane Langstrom unfolded her long-legged form as she climbed out of the seat and gave me a dutiful smile. "We have got to quit meeting like this," she said.

In the chapel, Diane circled the corpse with a camera, the flash shooting sparklike rays of white light into the dimly lit space. She snapped a lens cap over the camera's eye. "With the body frozen, it will be hard to determine the time of death."

Roy, Kerry, and I watched as she got down on all fours and sniffed the victim's open mouth, then drew back. She lifted the hem of the dusty black dress and peeked underneath. The men turned away, pretending to examine the chapel's architecture.

Diane looked up at me. "The body's been moved since the victim died. There's signs on the tops of her legs that the blood pooled there, as if she'd spent the first hour or so after death facedown. I don't see any indication of sexual assault, but we'll let the medical examiner decide; she's on the way. These marks on the neck are from a rope. See the crosshatch pattern of the fiber? Nylon rope."

"Hanged?" the Boss said, looking up at the vigas that spanned the roof.

"No, strangled. If she were hanged, there'd be a sort of upside-down V pattern where the rope pulled up on either side. This is straight around. She was strangled, and from the side, because it's worse here, on the left—the rope cut right through the flesh of the neck. Somebody made sure it took. I'm going to use my sat phone and make a call," she said, springing to her feet and dusting off her hands. "This is a hate crime. We got a special unit for that."

While we waited for the medical examiner to arrive, we split up to look for tire tread marks, footprints, or tracks in the surrounding ground surface, but it proved fruitless since the previous night's high winds had disturbed the topsoil, and patches of snow still covered some of the recesses. Plus, before I had been aware that it was a crime scene, I'd explored much of the area both on foot and horseback with the wolf alongside. I didn't mention that Mountain had trounced the corpse in his encounter with the cougar.

I approached Kerry as he crouched on the ground outside the compound wall, examining a pot shard. He looked up the slope to the ruin. "This must have washed down from up there," he said, rising to his feet. Mountain came over to see what he held in his hand, sniffed the shard with disinterest, and then trotted away. Kerry looked at me. "Babe. What were you doing all the way out here by yourself?"

I shook my head. "I was doing my job."

"You need to buddy up when you're this far out of range."

"Buddy up? We don't even have enough staff in the winter to man the phones!"

"Well, you can call me if—"

"And you'll stop working at your job and come help me do mine?"

He turned his head to the side and looked at me, a furrow across his brow that nearly joined his brown eyebrows in the center. "It's just common sense. You shouldn't be out this far alone.

Even an amateur hiker knows not to venture out by himself into the wilderness."

I held up my hand. "That's enough."

He stepped toward me and tipped my hat brim back. "You have a bad bump there on your forehead."

"Yeah, the stirrup."

He chuckled and gave my shoulder a squeeze. "I don't even want to know."

Roy strode toward us, pumping his arms. "Jamaica, how long since you fed Mountain?"

"He wouldn't take any jerky last night, so . . . yesterday morning."

"Well, I had a big old deer sausage one of the guys gave me and a breakfast burrito I had picked up on the way to work, and that wolf got in the ATV and ate every bite. The whole sausage. Enough for four or five meals. And the burrito, too."

Mountain slunk up beside me, noting the tone of Roy's voice.

"I'm sorry, Boss. I should have kept him with me."

"Damn right you should have. That was enough sausage for a big party! I was looking forward to having some of that."

"I'll buy you some sausage when we get back to town."

Roy huffed out a breath and waved me off. He started to go back to the ATV, but turned and looked at me. "Whatever happened to that cell phone I issued you?"

"I've got it."

He nodded his head, then gave a little snort. "Ever turned it on?"

"Yeah . . . I, yeah."

"What's that number again?" He cocked his head slightly.

"The cell phone? I . . . I don't know it."

"You turn it on and use it. Today."

"It won't work out here, Boss. There's no cell phone coverage half of the places I go."

"So turn it on and use it the other half. I'd just like to be able to keep track of you at least some of the time."

"Actually, half's probably an exaggeration. I bet I don't have cell phone coverage more than ten percent of the time when I'm on the job."

Roy reached a hand up and toggled his cowboy hat slightly to reposition it on his head. "Use the cell phone. That's an order." As he walked away, he muttered, "Damn, it's cold out here! I didn't get any breakfast. I'm hungry."

◂ 4 ▸

The Silver Bullet

Diane Langstrom and I had worked together on several cases, from cattle mutilation to murder, and we'd become friends over the course of our last investigation. She was an avid practitioner of martial arts, a crack shot, and as good a person to have at your back as anyone could want.

We watched as Kerry rode away on Rooster, headed back to Taos, with Roy idling the ATV behind him.

"This guy that's coming from the hate crimes unit," Diane said, "they call him the Silver Bullet."

"Why?" I asked.

"His name is Sterling—Agent Sterling. He's a legend in the bureau. I've been dying to work with him. I've heard stories about him ever since I trained at Quantico."

"What kind of stories?"

"There are droves. He's nailed serial killers, kidnappers, even solved cases that had gone completely cold. He's incredibly fast and highly intuitive. He starts where all the leads have played out for others, and he goes from there. He just thinks differently, thinks of things no one else would. They call him in when they're all out of options."

"So he only does hate crimes?"

"No, he's done everything. But right now, he's head of the hate crimes unit in this region, and that's a lucky thing for me."

I thought of the woman on the stone floor in the chapel. It was hard to think about luck in a situation like this. But I also knew that Diane's detachment from the horror of this crime was a vital element for her survival and success in her work. You couldn't let it get to you, or you wouldn't last—you were no good to anyone. I wasn't as adept at this as my friend. I'd seen plenty of death—more than my share. I never got used to it.

We'd walked out a few hundred yards to a flat place on the mesa, near where Diane had left her ATV when she arrived. We cleared some brush to make a heliport, then tied several long lengths of yellow Crime Scene tape to the ATV, which Diane parked on the perimeter on the west side. The lutescent tape fluttered in the morning breeze, creating a marker for the pilot as well as a gauge for wind speed and direction.

"The Silver Bullet could sure give my career a boost," Di said as we worked. "I've been stuck here in Taos without any opportunity for advancement for three years now."

"What can this guy do? Can he get you a promotion?"

"He's got long coattails. Everyone who works with him moves up. I could get out of here and get someplace civilized." She tossed a stone away into the brush. "Look at my hair," she said, coming toward me. "Look at this side here." She pointed to the place in front of her left ear. "I had to cut that way back because it was burned. And check out my eyebrows. They're singed, too."

I inspected her face. "What happened?"

"My oven blew up on me. I told that worthless landlord it wasn't working right, and he had some creepy cousin of his named Benny come out to fix it. But all he did was ogle me and fool around with the stove like he knew what he was doing, which he didn't. The next time I went to use the oven, I opened the door, and flames shot out."

"Wow. You're lucky you didn't get burned."

"That's just one example of how it has been for months now. I leased from this guy, I paid him first and last month's rent and a deposit, and I've had nothing but trouble with him. The fridge either freezes all my food, or everything spoils. And the front door won't even shut properly. I've come home and found it standing open. I have to slam it so hard just to get the darn thing to stay closed that the front window rattles in the frame. And this guy has said he'll evict me if I make any more complaints. He doesn't care if I'm happy, there's a long list of poor schmucks who will give him a deposit and first and last month's rent, and he triples his money every time he gets a new renter."

"Isn't there an agency that regulates . . ."

"I've checked. It's hard to enforce tenant rights in New Mexico. I read the statutes, and they are nine-tenths about the right to evict. The only thing I could do would be to take the guy to court."

"Maybe there's a better place to rent while you figure all this out."

"Nah, I've looked. There's not much out there, unless I want to live in a trailer. And I can't afford one of those new condos. But it's not just the rental situation. Taos is the only third-world country in the United States."

I was quiet. The thing I loved about Taos was how time seemed to stand still, how the past refused to give in to the present and held steadfast to ancient customs and rich cultural distinctions. Taos was timeless, and fiercely so.

Diane's sat phone rang. "Give me that lat and long," she said to me, nodding toward the small yellow GPS we'd used to calculate our exact location.

I read the coordinates to her. Within minutes, we could hear the hum of the chopper coming; then we saw it buzzing toward us from far away, like an oversized mosquito bearing down on its target. As soon as the wolf recognized the sound, he broke into a run, away toward the high ground near the ruin.

I ran after him, calling to him to stop, but he scooted up the slope with his tail between his legs. I finally caught up with him when he tried to hide in a low area next to a big sagebrush. He was shaking violently, huddling into the small hollow. The sound and wind of the helicopter were enough to scare anyone. But only a few months before, Mountain had been airlifted by a chopper during a wildfire when he'd been severely injured. I could still remember how he looked then as he hung suspended in the air from the rescue belt—weak and frightened, as if he were about to let go of life. I approached the shallow pit, crouched down next to his head and shoulders, and leaned over him in a protective way. I put my arms over his back and sheltered his head. He shook with fear, his body trembling like a tuning fork.

When the chopper's blades stopped beating and began to shift from a high-pitched whine to a sputtering drone, the wolf got to his feet. I grabbed hold of his collar, thinking he was going to flee again, but he stayed beside me, still quivering, his body pressed tight against my leg. We walked partway back down the slope, then stopped and watched as the heavy cloud canopy to the east parted, and the morning light burst through a gray cowl, bestowing the helicopter with a shimmering silver halo.

The door of the airship opened. A man dropped to the ground, light on his feet, stooping to avoid the slow-spinning blades overhead. As he stepped toward us, he straightened. A thick crest of shining silver hair topped a suntanned face and a tall, powerful physique. Agent Sterling wore black—from his shades to his boots. He looked like Adonis. Behind him, the medical examiner climbed out and someone from inside the bird handed her a black bag. The ME trudged toward Diane, clutching her hat to her head with one hand, holding her bag in the other.

But I could not take my eyes off the Silver Bullet. And neither could Diane.

While the FBI and the medical examiner went to examine the body, I returned to the ruin to check on the cougar offspring. But the den was abandoned—the she-cat had moved her cubs in the night during the storm.

After he'd seen the body, Agent Sterling wanted to talk with me. "Tell me your name again?" he asked, removing his shades as we stood in the dim light of the chapel.

"Jamaica Wild. I'm a resource protection agent for the BLM."

He smiled, his teeth white against his tan face. "I know who you are. I just wanted to hear you say your name. So what brought you here?"

"I was after a wounded cougar."

"Tell me about how you got in here," he said with a flip of his hand.

"We got caught in a blizzard—"

"We?" He moved his head slightly toward me, tilting it to the side as if he hadn't heard me correctly.

"My wolf, my horse, and I. We needed shelter. The slat over the double doors was loose."

Sterling walked out the door and looked to one side. He pointed with the sunglasses in his hand at the piece of wood on the ground. "Was that the slat?"

"Yes."

He squatted and scrutinized the wood. "Did you make these pry marks here?"

I bent down to look. "No, I pulled it off with my hands. It was loose."

"And the door?" He stood up and pointed with his sunglasses again. "Did you do this damage to the door?"

"It was the only way I could get the horse through."

He nodded, pressing his lips together. Then he walked across to the entry gates. "And these gates? Did you break them for the same reason?"

"That was an accident. The storm made Rooster skittish—"

"Rooster is the horse?"

"Yes."

"And the wolf, what's his name?"

"Mountain."

"Gorgeous animal."

Sterling waited, but I didn't reply. Someone who kept a pet might have said "thank you" with pride of ownership. But Mountain was not my property, nor was he my pet. He was my best friend, my companion, my family.

After a few seconds of silence, the agent spoke again: "What kind of a woman lives with a wolf?" He didn't look at me at first, but then turned and locked his dark brown eyes on mine.

"Is this about the investigation?" I asked.

He continued to hold my gaze and gave a fleeting grin. After a moment, he looked back at the chapel and said, "This crime scene is pretty well trashed."

"I know. I'm sorry. I didn't know it was a crime scene until after the damage was done."

He popped his shades on, raised up his chin, and smiled. "I like a challenge."

◂ 5 ▸

Facts of the Matter

Daniel Kuwany wanted to believe that the predator he'd shot was a wolf. "They say wolves are coming down at night now. The people hear them howling, especially the village priests when they go out to pray on the rooftops." The shepherd eyed Mountain with suspicion. "Is that wolf there a pet or something?"

I had hooked Mountain's lead to my belt with a carabiner so he couldn't run the sheep. "Something like that," I said.

Kuwany licked his fingers as he finished the rest of the meat-filled tortilla he'd been having for lunch. Grease stained his shirt cuff where the mutton juice had oozed down his wrist.

"The animal you wounded was a cougar," I said. "A female with two cubs to feed. The three of them are starving. That's why she's been coming close to the pueblo, raiding the sheep."

"How do you know?" he asked.

"I saw her. And her cubs."

Kuwany, who had been sitting over a weak fire trying to force it to thrive on sage limbs and dried chamisa, jumped up and grabbed his rifle. "Tell me where they are, and I'll go shoot them."

"They're not there anymore. They were at the ruin out by the abandoned Indian school."

"That's a bad place." He carried his rifle with him and went to a brown plastic tub, took off its lid, rummaged around, and came back. He held something between his fingers and offered it to me. "Take this," he said, gesturing for me to open my palm. He had completely forgotten his fear of Mountain and was now standing just a few feet from the wolf.

I opened my hand.

Kuwany dropped a stub of root into my palm. "You better take some of this, or you'll get ghost sickness."

I looked at the little stub of woody tuber. "Osha?" I asked.

"You know how to do it?"

"Yes."

He set his rifle down and picked up the blackened enamel coffeepot that was sitting on a rock beside his fire. He poured some of the dark liquid into a brown-stained, plastic coffee mug. "Take a bite of it now. Wash it down with this." He handed the mug to me. "Then you better keep the rest of it."

My medicine teacher from Tanoah Pueblo, Anna Santana, had taught me about osha and its many uses, including protection from ghost sickness. As I had been trained, I pressed the root to my forehead and closed my eyes—a gesture of both invitation and listening to the wisdom of the plant, which helped it to work its healing power. Then I bit off a piece from the end and chewed the fibrous chunk so it would release its medicine from the pulp.

Kuwany watched me intently.

When I had softened the chaw, I took a big slurp of the coffee and swallowed the gob, which had tripled in size. "Thank you," I said, swallowing again.

"If that cougar was living where you said, it could be a ghost."

"She wasn't living there. She was living at the ruin up the slope, near the canyon rim. She just came in the school while we were there. We spent the night there during the storm."

Kuwany's eyes bulged. "You spent the night in that place?"

"We had to have shelter from the blizzard."

The shepherd picked up his coffeepot and threw the rest of the liquid into the fire. With his boot, he spread the embers out and kicked dust on them. "I got to move the sheep," he said. He went to the plastic tub and put the coffeepot inside.

I poured my coffee on the fire and offered Kuwany the mug. "Thanks for the coffee and the osha."

"You keep the mug," he said. "I don't need it."

"No, I'm all done. It's empty." I set the cup down and started to go.

"Children died out there," he said to my back as I was walking away.

I turned to look at him.

"They got treated so bad that even some of those ones that lived, their souls left their bodies and couldn't never get back in, even after those kids came home. Some kids tried to get away, but they never made it home. That place is evil. We don't go near it. I bet that wasn't no cougar. I bet it was a ghost."

"You believe the children who died are ghosts now?"

"No. Not the children. The soul-eaters. If I see a cougar or a wolf around here"—he looked down at Mountain—"I'm going to kill it." He picked up his rifle from the ground and turned and walked toward the sheep.

I arrived late for a meeting at the BLM. Roy was in the middle of briefing the field staff on the growing problem of all-terrain vehicles—ATVs—on BLM land. "Folks, we've been directed to crack down on this problem," he said as I came in the room. I took a chair in the back, moving as quietly as I could.

Mountain, who had just drunk voraciously from the bucket we kept for his water dish, plopped down on the floor beside me and gave a loud groan. Everyone laughed.

"Jamaica, I'm giving you a mandate as the Taos field office's resource protection agent to find and cite anyone illegally using an off-road vehicle on BLM land. I want to send a message to the public that it won't be tolerated. It's doing irreparable damage to the environment, and we've got to put a stop to it."

A terrible smell began to migrate upward from where Mountain lay on the floor. Several people wrinkled their noses, others waved their hands in front of their faces, and one woman said, "Phew!"

Roy got a whiff of the stink and said, "Eddie, that would be the aftermath of your deer sausage from that buck you got. That doggone wolf ate the whole log in one sitting. I didn't even get to try a bite of it."

After the meeting, I put a call in to Department of Game and Fish agent Charlie Dorn to report the wounding of a female cougar with dependent cubs. Since the shooting had occurred on the Tanoah reservation, neither Dorn nor I had jurisdiction, but if it had happened elsewhere, Charlie assured me it was a violation of the law, even for a hunter with a lion tag. I offered to talk to any nearby private landowners about setting humane traps for the lions so we could rescue the injured cougar and her cubs. Before I could do that, I needed to find out who the landowners were.

Roy came up to me as I was filling out an incident report on the events of the previous day and night. He fished a slip of paper out of his shirt pocket and handed it to me. "That's your cell phone number. Better turn it on and plug it into your car charger. I gave that number to that FBI gal, Langstrom. She's going to call you after she gets the medical examiner's report."

It was late in the afternoon by the time I got to the Taos courthouse to investigate ownership of the lands abutting the Pueblo Pena parcel.

As I was entering the courthouse, a man wearing an army camouflage uniform brushed past me on his way out, bumping into my sore shoulder. He rushed on without turning back, and I stopped inside the door, wincing as I clutched my upper arm to quiet the pain. I noticed a couple waiting in the lobby. She wore a strangely mismatched ensemble: a blue baseball-style jacket over a beaded white dress and heels. He looked uncomfortable in a suit that was much too large for his slender frame. They glanced up eagerly when I came in, but then gave each other a look of distress, as if they had been expecting someone else.

My map had indicated that the segment of public lands where the Pueblo Pena ruin and the abandoned Indian school were located was landlocked on three sides. With the help of the county clerk, Nina Enriquez, I learned that a fenced federal training area abutted the south side of the section, the Tanoah Pueblo reservation lands bordered it due east, and a large spread owned by fifth-generation rancher Scout Coldfire and his wife, Lorena, rimmed the north. To the west, the canyon and the high desert beyond was all public land, most of it remote and inaccessible. Nina, who had been about to close the office for the day, looked up the Coldfires' phone number for me before she locked the door to count the day's revenue. "Boy, am I ready to go home today," she said. "I had people in here all afternoon, one after the other. One guy had me look up five or six different properties because he was looking for an easement. Another one didn't understand why we raised his taxes when he added two thousand square feet to his house."

As I was leaving the courthouse, the woman in the white dress, still waiting in the lobby with her beau, came up to me with a frantic look on her face.

"Our friends did not arrive. It is almost time for the courthouse to close, and we cannot wait any longer. Please, miss, will you be a witness for us?"

I opened my mouth to speak, but could not think how to reply. I was exhausted from a night without sleep; my arm and shoulder hurt from the bruises, scrapes, and splinters I'd received from being thrown by the horse; the bump on my head where the stirrup had smacked me was throbbing. I still felt disturbed by the nature of the crime I'd discovered, and I'd managed to put in a full day of work without complaining once. And I had another obligation to meet that evening before I could get into my Jeep and drive home to my little cabin, the request of this couple notwithstanding.

My hesitation only upset the bride-to-be more. Tears welled in her eyes. "Please, miss?" she said, so softly that I read her lips more than heard her words.

Judge Valerio opened the door from a small courtroom. "Jamaica! I didn't know you were here. How are you?"

"I'm okay, Judge Valerio, thank you."

He turned to the young man and woman. "Well, are we going to have a wedding or not? It's time to go home."

They looked at me.

"Can I get some water and take Mountain a drink first? He's eaten some salty meat and he's really dehydrated. The water I keep for him in my car is frozen."

Valerio smiled. "Oh, I see. You're going to be their witness? Good! Well, just bring Mountain in and give him a drink, and he can be a witness, too! I'd like to see that wolf, I haven't seen him since he was a pup. I'll have my clerk look for something he can drink out of."

"I have a dish," I said, heading out the door to the parking lot.

Back inside, Mountain drank all the water in the collapsible dish and looked at me imploringly for more. "Sorry, buddy," I said, "I don't want you to bloat. You've already got a challenge with all that deer sausage to digest." While Judge Valerio remarked repeatedly how big and beautiful Mountain had become, I silently prayed that the wolf wouldn't send up a stink during the wedding ceremony as he had at the BLM.

In the small county courtroom, Mountain and I and the judge's clerk attended the wedding of the two young people who were desperate to marry that day. As I stood next to the bride, the wolf sat beside me, attentive to Judge Valerio's every word. At the end of the brief ceremony, the clerk and I stepped to a table to sign the certificate as witnesses.

Without warning, the bride yelled, "Get ready!" I looked up just as she tossed her bouquet directly toward me. I failed to react for an instant, then hastened to grasp for the small spray out of some vague sense of propriety. But my fingers only managed to touch the tips of a few fragile petals, and the bouquet tumbled to the floor at my feet. Mountain dodged the incoming object with a start, then sniffed at the little bunch suspiciously. Satisfied that the bundle was harmless, he dropped to the floor with a *plumpf* and yawned.

The newlyweds rushed away to their honeymoon supper while

Judge Valerio and I exchanged a few parting pleasantries. It was dark when the wolf and I stepped out into the cold night, and the judge's clerk locked the glass door of the courthouse lobby behind us. My Jeep was the only car in the unlit visitors' parking lot at the back of the justice center. Colonies of mammoth cottonwoods bordered the lot on either side, their wrinkled limbs lifted up toward the stars. Remnants of last night's windblown snow lay piled against the giant trunks at their bases. As I was loading Mountain into the cargo area in the back of the car, a white pickup swerved into the lot at too-high speed and drove around the perimeter of the parking area, bass notes booming from blown speakers in the back of the cab. I watched the truck as I lowered the hatch on the Jeep, then slowly turned to follow the vehicle as it circled me. When the pickup started its second circuit around the lot, I opened my coat and unsnapped the snug on my sidearm. The truck stopped in the next parking lane over, and the thundering bass notes ceased, too. The passenger-side window lowered. I stepped back so that I was protected by the rear corner of the Jeep, one hand on my automatic. A man waving an open, quart-sized bottle of beer yelled, "Hey, is the wedding over?"

I sat in the driver's seat for a few minutes with my forehead against the cold steering wheel, reminding myself I hadn't had any sleep the night before, and that anyone might have gone on the defensive in the same situation. Just as I was beginning to feel some of the adrenaline subside, a shrill, piercing peal sent a shock wave up my spine. I jumped in my seat, then froze, unable to process the meaning of this unfamiliar alert. In a moment, the sharp sound repeated and I located its source. I picked up the offender, stared into its one large eye, and registered what I saw. I inhaled, pushed the green dot, and spoke. "Resource Protection, this is Agent Wild . . ."

◂ 6 ▸

Aunties

"We've identified the body." Diane's voice sounded clipped through the cell phone's speaker. "Agent Sterling's going to release the name of the victim to the media. We missed the five o'clock news, but they'll pick it up for the six in Albuquerque. The deceased was a woman named Cassie Morgan, apparently an unmarried seventy-seven-year-old with no known kin."

"That didn't take long."

"No, we got lucky. Morgan's housekeeper reported her missing just today. When we went to check for missing persons reports on an elderly white female, it was right there, a perfect match. Evidently the cleaning lady comes once a week, and Morgan's bed had not been slept in since the last time she was there; everything was exactly as it was on the previous weekly visit. We went out to Morgan's house, talked to the housekeeper. She was unwilling to go to the morgue and identify the body, so we obtained dental records. There was a bill from a Taos dentist in Morgan's files.

"And listen to this: Cassie Morgan was a former matron at the Indian boarding school. The housekeeper told us that much, but she wouldn't say more. So I called that guy at the radio station who knows all the local history—you know, the same guy who writes that column in the newspaper about the customs of northern New Mexico? He was reluctant to say much at first, but finally he told me that Cassie Morgan was remembered for depriving, humiliating, and beating the Indian children."

"Man," I said, more to myself than to Diane. "What a broken world this is sometimes." I felt my spirit standing at an emotional crossroads, not knowing which way to go. On the one hand, the shocking image of Cassie Morgan's desecrated body came up like bile, the killer's fury still clinging to the corpse long after the abominator had left the scene. I should feel some sympathy for someone so wronged. And yet the things I had seen and sensed in the abandoned school were even more horrific to me. If the woman who died had caused the sorrows that still clung to the walls of San Pedro de Arbués Indian School, then the temptation was to feel some satisfaction at her death. This last thought caused me discomfort. I clicked off the connection without even saying good-bye.

Tired as I was, there was no way to get out of the commitment I had made to help the Tanoah women from Anna Santana's clan make up Christmas baskets that night. Before going to the pueblo, I shopped for goods to put in the baskets at a little market on the north side of Taos. When I told Jesse, the grocer, that I wanted something special to give, he helped me pick out some small, sample-sized bags of piñon coffee.

"Where you been?" he asked, as he put the little coffee bags in a sack. "You look like you got all banged up." He pointed at the torn sleeve of my coat.

"I was out all night tracking a mountain lion."

"In that storm? How could you track in a storm like that?"

"I couldn't. When the storm hit, I had to take shelter out by that ruin, Pueblo Pena."

"Oh, that's no good."

"It was better than being out in the weather."

"Yes, but do you know what Pueblo Pena means?"

"No." I handed Jesse some cash for the purchase.

He took time to carefully count out my change from the register. As he was putting the money into my open palm, he looked up from my hand to my eyes. "It means Place of Sorrow."

I picked up my sack. "I'd say that's about right. Thanks, Jesse."

"I hope you will forgive me for saying this, Señorita Wild, but you don't look so good."

"I'm just tired."

"You must get some rest then, my friend. Would you like for me to get you a bone for El Lobo? I got some nice beef knuckles."

"Thanks anyway, but Mountain doesn't need to add to the deer sausage he stole from my boss this morning. If he eats anything more today, I won't be able to ride home with him in a closed-up car. And it's too cold to drive with the windows down."

At Tanoah Pueblo, several bonfires blazed in the plaza at the center of the ancient walled village. Dark silhouettes of figures wrapped in blankets surrounded the towering fires smoking with the perfume of *trementina,* the spicy-smelling sap of piñon wood. Behind this scene rose the massive four-story, stair-step structure that was the oldest and most distinctive element of the pueblo. Its adobe face glowed mango-colored in the firelight against a backdrop of black mountains and deep indigo sky.

I drove past the wall and down a narrow dirt lane to the home of my medicine teacher, Anna Santana, who had instructed me from the beginning of our relationship to call her "Momma Anna." Nine aunties from her clan had gathered at her house that evening and were ready to begin work.

"I saw bonfires in the village," I said, after I'd greeted Momma Anna.

"Some those men, they happy tonight," she said. "We got work do." She pointed at two high columns of stacked plastic laundry baskets.

And work we did. We spent over an hour filling thirty baskets with all sorts of goodies for the poor and elderly families at the pueblo. Crocheted hot pads, hand-thrown pottery Christmas ornaments, packets of elk and buffalo jerky, strings of dried chiles and garlic, sacks of candies, jars of homemade chokecherry jam, cans of peaches, and the small bags of piñon coffee I'd brought were sorted into the humble containers. When we had filled each of them more than halfway, a colorful piece of cut cloth was draped over the top, and then tied under the basket's rim with a long piece of twine.

While we worked, the aunties chattered, mostly in Tiwa.

Yohe, one of my favorites, suddenly broke into English. "My son see on TV over at casino. He came fast my house, tell me good news."

"What good news?" I asked.

"Tst-tst!" Momma Anna warned, wagging a finger at me—perhaps because I had just asked a question, which was considered rude among the Tanoah.

Yohe answered me, in spite of this. "Mean old teacher leave this world."

There was a chorus of grunts from the women gathered, a ritual I had witnessed before when the women were releasing something unwanted, cleansing their spirits by breathing out repeatedly with a low, percussive *unh!*

Yohe went on after this: "Lot of us have many bad time, that one."

"You mean the woman who was matron at the Indian boarding school," I said, careful not to say the name of the deceased.

No one answered, but many of the women were nodding their heads in agreement.

Suddenly, one of the aunties answered Yohe as if I had not even spoken: "You were not there that long, Yohe. They took me there when I was five, away from my family. I had to give up my name. They called me Rebecca. They cut my hair, and if I spoke Tiwa, they washed my mouth out with chlorine and lye and it burned for days. I was there so long, I forgot what my mother and father looked like. The headmaster wouldn't let the young ones go home for holidays because he was afraid we wouldn't want to come back. I remember crying because I was so lonely for my family, and that mean old matron made me stand in the hallway all night. She tied my hands and feet together so if I fell asleep I would fall and hurt myself. When they finally let me come back home, I had forgotten who I was, and I didn't even want to be at Tanoah Pueblo anymore. I didn't want to be an Indian! I had to work hard to learn my own language again, to get to know my family. I almost left here and tried to be white because they made me hate who I was, what I am!" She began to cry, and several of the other women went to her and comforted her.

Another auntie spoke. "They never have enough food, too many mouths to feed. I hate that soupy thing they make us eat, taste like dirt water. I am hungry all time, even now, I am still hungry from that."

One woman laughed. "Oh, at least you don't have to sleep in same bed with stink girl."

Yohe said, "I not sleep nobody. I wet bed. I am so lonely, afraid, I make water at night, not even know."

The women all shook their heads and made little commiserating noises.

Yohe turned to me. "I get sick eye, they send me home. Almost go blind. They want me out so they will not get it and go blind, too."

Momma Anna spoke. "You home this time, Yohe. That next other time gone. We all home today."

"Not all," Yohe muttered under her breath. "*Unh.*"

All the aunties helped carry the baskets from Momma Anna's main room into a cold mudroom along the side of her kitchen. The women made approving comments about how attractive the baskets looked, and how happy they would make the recipients. Then, one by one, the ladies wrapped themselves in their blankets and went out the door, bidding one another a good night.

As I was leaving, Momma Anna made a request. "Maybe you help take basket to people, Christmas Eve."

"Sure, I'd be glad to."

"Many basket. Maybe you drive."

"Yes, I'll drive."

"Yohe drive next other time. This time, candy cost more."

"Oh, she's out of gas money?"

"Not too far to walk home from here."

"I can give her a ride. Which way did she go? I'll go pick her up and take her home."

"No. That Yohe's gift. Candy, no gas."

• • •

I got in the Jeep and turned the key in the ignition. The headlamps illuminated Momma Anna's little adobe house with its apple tree in front, a stack of cut wood along one side. I knew that Momma Anna depended on the wood for heat and to fire her pottery, and on the apple tree for fruit. She also counted on the small, desperately tended summer garden in the back for food—which she ate fresh, and canned and dried for the cold-weather months. I had accompanied her as she gathered wild spinach and harvested piñon nuts for family meals. The men at the pueblo hunted annually to make sure that the elders had meat, and Anna Santana dried some as jerky in addition to cooking it fresh in posole and chili and stew. She made a little money from the sale of her handmade pottery, dreamcatchers, and jewelry to buy the rest of the things she needed from the market in Taos. I had been to the homes of several of the aunties involved in tonight's Christmas basket project, and all of the women lived well below what the rest of the country would consider the level of poverty. And yet, this did not seem to affect the aunties' willingness to give generously of whatever they had. They had saved and schemed, worked and cooked, and somehow managed to come up with bountiful Christmas baskets for those whom they perceived to be in real need.

As I drove past the village plaza again on my way out, the bonfires had burned down, but a gang of men huddled around one small fire they were keeping alive. Their shadows hovered like dark spirits on the adobe wall of the pueblo behind them. The group suddenly burst into loud laughter over something one of them had said. I saw a bottle passed between two of the men, even though alcohol was forbidden on the reservation. The recipient jumped to his feet, and his silhouette—distorted in the flickering firelight—looked more like a coyote than a man. He held up the bottle as if it were a lance or a tomahawk and his strength came from its power—and he gave a whooping war cry.

◂ 7 ▸

Bad Wolf

I was bone tired and aching as I made the forty-five-minute drive from Tanoah Pueblo to the remote cabin west of Taos where I lived. I prayed all the way that an elk or coyote wouldn't dash in front of my car, as they were wont to do. To stay awake, I promised myself a hot shower when I got home, a warm fire in my woodstove, and then a good night's sleep.

But it was not to be.

For the third time in as many weeks, the electricity was off at my remote little abode, which was nestled against forested foothills. I rented this place, which was almost entirely off the grid. No phone, no television reception, no Internet—and though some or all of these might be available via satellite, there were not enough residents in the area to make it worth anyone's while to develop these services for so few. All this was fine with me. My first six years at the BLM,

I had worked as a range rider, riding fence lines and patrolling the backcountry either on horseback or in a four-wheel-drive vehicle. I had learned to sleep out under the stars, travel light, and live next to nature for seven or eight months of the year.

But for a year and a half now, I'd been assigned as liaison to Tanoah Pueblo, which was nearly surrounded by BLM land. I had to interact with people every day, frequently show up dressed in a uniform. When the power went out at my cabin, that meant I lost kitchen and bathroom facilities because my water was drawn from a cistern by an electric pump. During the previous power outages, I had told myself that the situation was temporary, used an area in the woods behind my house as an open-air latrine, roughed it until the electricity came back on. I had hauled water in buckets for washing up and for cooking from La Petaca, the shallow, icy stream above my cabin, about an eighth of a mile away in the forest. I can cope better than most with inconveniences of this nature. But this was getting old.

Since I had not been home for two days, my cabin was so cold that it was probably a good thing there was no water in the pipes. I cleaned the ash out of the woodstove, laid a new fire, and tended it until it got going. Then I grabbed the big plastic bucket, a tube to siphon, and a little ax to break the ice, and headed up the slope toward the woods and La Petaca. Mountain ran ahead of me, eager for an outing after spending so much of the day snoozing in the back of my Jeep.

I chose a good place on one side of the stream where there was solid, high ground next to a fairly deep little pocket that trout liked to frequent during the spring and summer flows. These little recesses might have been the reason for the name of this seasonal stream. *La Petaca* meant "tobacco pouch," probably named for the brownish water that pooled in tiny coves on the edges of the current at the center. I squatted on the cold ground and began chipping at the ice with my ax. I could hear Mountain sniffing and snorting and snapping twigs as he explored around me. As I struck the ice with my ax, I felt a throbbing ache in my shoulder where it had slammed into the gate. My head hurt both from lack of sleep and the welt from the stirrup. I pounded the ice again and again, creating a rhythmic sound with the impact: *chank, chank, chank, chank*. The cadence seemed to offer momentum to my thrusts, so that all I had to think about was keeping the beat—not how the blade was barely scoring the ice, how the ice was so thick that it wasn't breaking, how it might be that the shallow stream was frozen completely through, or even how much it hurt to strike each blow. It was only the tempo that mattered, keeping time, every crack ringing out in the night in the silent woods.

And then I stopped. The woods *were* silent. I rose to my feet. "Mountain? Mountain? Mountain!" My voice echoed against the ice. Then, stillness.

I dropped the ax on the ground and started for the last place I'd noticed the wolf rooting through the undergrowth. I called again, "Mountain? Mountain!"

Instead of the usual crashing of brush as the wolf responded to my call when he had wandered a little far, there was not a sound beyond my own breathing, and the pounding of my heart in my ears. "Mountain!"

I searched and called for the wolf for two hours. This had never happened before. Mountain might jog off after some critter, but he always returned within minutes, and never went far. There was not a sign of him anywhere. I returned to my cabin feeling like my gut had twisted over something as hard and cold as the ice over La Petaca.

Fear and worry crowded my chest until I could barely breathe. With anxiety coursing through me, I forgot my fatigue and paced the floor of the one big room of my cabin, unable to sit or lie down.

It crossed my mind that the experience of spending such a cold and miserable night with a dead body may have upset Mountain almost as much as it had me. But this was so uncharacteristic of the wolf—wolves lived and traveled in packs, and I was Mountain's pack! He had never left me before, and he never wanted me to leave him, for any reason. I had lost a lot of my personal belongings to his abandonment anxiety–driven rampages in my cabin when I'd tried leaving him for short periods of time. And now he had suddenly run off without regard for where I was or how he would get back to me!

When I finally forced myself to sit down in front of the fire, I soon dozed off. The sound of the wolf scratching at the door jarred me awake instantly and I shot to my feet and raced to open the door. But Mountain was not there. I shook my head to wake up, grabbed a flashlight off the kitchen counter, and walked outside. Ten yards away, Mountain stood over something, his ears up, his tail wagging wildly with excitement.

"Mountain!" I said, moving toward him. "Mountain, I've been so worried! Where have you been? Come here."

The wolf lowered his head and grabbed at something with his teeth. Something big.

"Hey, buddy. What have you got there?" I lowered the light from the wolf's face and shone it on the object on the ground, trying to discern what the unfamiliar shape could be. This thing was coated in dirt, matted with bits of duff and tiny twigs and thorns, brown and white, almost as large as Mountain, but flatter. Wide at one end, and narrowing to . . . *a hoof!* It was the leg, the entire hindquarter of a cow.

While this last registered, I heard the distant sound of a car engine. Then headlights shone like two eyes looking at us from afar, as the vehicle turned down my long dirt road, a drive leading only to my cabin. Mountain and I turned our heads in unison and watched the car approach.

There is at least one good thing, and probably more, about having a forest ranger boyfriend who works evenings and frequently stops by your cabin after he gets off work, often very late at night. Kerry got out of the truck and came to see what was illuminated in his headlamps. "He must have dragged that thing from wherever he got it. It probably weighs well over a hundred pounds, at least. Good-sized calf or mature beef, I would guess," he said.

Mountain delighted in the attention his captured prize was attracting, and he pranced around the carrion, sniffing it and nudging it with his nose, as if to dare it to move.

I shook my head. "But where did he get it? He couldn't bring down a cow by himself. He wouldn't."

"It doesn't seem likely. For one thing, have you ever seen Mountain hunt?"

"Mice, sometimes, in a field or when we're hiking."

"Okay, so he's no hunter."

"He likes to play with coyotes and run around with them."

"Yeah, but that's play. He's not hungry enough to want to hunt."

"Not unless it's something like a mouse—something that stimulates him with fun and excitement."

"Well—fun and exciting—that's not a cow. Probably the animal got sick and died. Or coyotes took it down if it was hurt or slow. Even coyotes wouldn't be likely to take down a healthy steer." Kerry bent down to give the remains a closer look. He waved a hand over it, scooping air toward his face, sniffing for signs of decay, then probed at it with a finger. "No, this cow didn't die tonight. It's been dead long enough for this meat to be frozen. It could have happened recently, since it's been freezing for days, just not in the past few hours."

The wolf wagged his tail and grabbed hold of a flap of hide on the thing. Tugging and jerking, he dragged it a foot or two, working hard to pull the heavy weight across the ground.

"It must have taken a ton of effort for him to drag that here," I said.

With Kerry's help, I got a lead on Mountain and forced him to leave his prize and come in the cabin. Once we got the wolf inside, Kerry gave me a hug. "I can't stay. I just stopped by to tell you that I have training the next few days in Albuquerque," he said. "I'll be back late on Friday night."

"I've got the weekend off," I hinted, smiling.

"I'll come see you on Saturday, then."

"I'll miss you," I said, meaning it.

"I'll miss you, too, babe." He reached down and gave Mountain's ears a tousle, but the wolf was too obsessed by the thought of the bovine booty outside. While I held Mountain by the collar, barely containing him as he struggled to escape, Kerry went out the door to put the carcass in the back of his truck and haul it away.

I tried to distract him, but Mountain was not fooled. He stood at the window looking out as if he could actually see from the light into the darkness, and he yipped and howled and paced from the window to the door for nearly twenty minutes. I tried to get him to come to me, and I even got down on the floor, prepared to snuggle him and sing to him, which was usually a comfort for both of us. I knew he was tired. He had to be tired. I was tired.

But the wolf was angry, and he pulled up in the corner farthest from me and lay down on the floor, his back to me. Within minutes, he curled into a wolf donut, his nose tucked under the thick fur of his tail, and went to sleep.

◂ 8 ▸

What It Means to Be Hungry

When I left my cabin in the morning, I drove to the first place where I could get cell phone coverage. I pulled over in my Jeep to call the power company on the new and unfamiliar device that I had decided to call "Screech Owl" because of its insistent, shrill ring. The receptionist left me on hold for a near-eternity, then transferred me to a voice-mail message system. I left a report that my power was out, the cell phone number, and a description of the location of my cabin. In northern New Mexico, there are still plenty of places without addresses. In fact, they haven't entirely sorted out who owns all the land because of a complex tier of Spanish land grants that began in the 1500s. These grants have been redrawn and rewritten every time the territory of Nuevo México changed hands—and when it became a state, the mess got worse. It has created some complex real estate laws, and a few interesting loopholes as well. When a squatter started up an illegal homestead in an inaccessible place along the Rio Grande, he managed to evade legal action for so long that the BLM just let him have the place. His address became "Brown Trailer, Agua Azuela, NM," because there were no roads on that side of the river to use for an address. When you go to someone's house for the first time, your instructions might be, "Take the road by the house with seven windows, follow it to the big willow, and turn up the hill toward the bottle house," because there are so many roads without names, and so many distinctive houses built without codes or covenants. My mailing address was a home carrier route number, followed by the number on a metal box at a unit of postal boxes up by the highway, over three miles away from my cabin. If anyone around there referred to my place, it was usually "that old cabin up near La Petaca."

I left Mountain in the back of the Jeep when I went to the governor's office at Tanoah Pueblo. A tall man stood in front of a counter that nearly spanned the tiny entry room. He was wearing a tan blanket with pale mauve stripes, his long silver hair loosely plaited into two thick braids. He studied me before speaking. "May I help you?"

"I'm Jamaica Wild with the Bureau of Land Management. I'm liaison to the pueblo. I came to ask about setting a meat lure and some traps on Tanoah land in order to capture a wounded mountain lion and her cubs."

The man drew up his chin and narrowed his eyes. "I cannot make any decision for the tribe, miss. I am just here for tourist."

I looked out the open door at the empty, snow-patched, dirt plaza, the seldom-used aspen-log hide-drying racks, the closed blue and turquoise doors of the apartments in the mammoth adobe structure. "Do you have many tourists this time of year?"

"No," the man said. "That is why they ask me to be here for this time. I am not good at talking much." He broke into a wide smile. "I have seen you before."

"You have? I don't remember you, I'm sorry. I'd like to know your name." I was careful not to *ask* for his name, as the Tanoah looked upon a question as a demand for information. The tribe spoke Tiwa, and their native tongue contained no direct way to say *no*. Instead of learning to speak against things, they had developed a complex and subtle system of civilities that made them a generally peaceful people. I had learned that their language was the strong seam that held the fabric of their culture together.

The old man looked at me approvingly, noting that a white girl—and a yellow-haired one, no less—had demonstrated a respectful manner. "My name Sevenguns."

I smiled. "Sevenguns. I like that name."

"Me, too," he said, moving to the corner and picking up a long wooden pole, which he used to poke at the flaming embers in the kiva-style adobe fireplace. Even though it was cold outside, he seemed fine with leaving the door open, perhaps in order to welcome hoped-for tourists bringing a little revenue to the tribe's coffers. His fire gave off a considerable amount of heat, and the thick adobe walls retained and reflected the warmth. He continued to tend the little blaze he had provoked and said, "I will talk with the governor about traps. The war council make all the decision about pueblo land. Maybe about a week, you come back and I will know."

"I can't wait that long. The she-lion was wounded by one of your shepherds. She's thin and starving, and if she dies, her cubs will die. They don't have a week. I'll talk to the rancher up north; maybe he will let me put traps on his land."

The old man stopped poking his fire and studied me. "Where you want to put a trap?"

"Out on the mesa where the reservation abuts the Pueblo Pena parcel, not far from where that old ruin sits on the rim of the canyon."

The Indian searched my eyes as if he were studying a map. His expression never changed, but I felt as if he had taken a lightning-speed journey along some line of thought our conversation had evoked.

To be sure he knew where I meant, I went on: "There's an old, abandoned Indian boarding school near there."

Sevenguns began to nod his head slowly, and he kept nodding.

A long silence followed, and I knew better than to speak and break the fragile intimacy created by it. I stood still, slowed my breathing, kept my eyes respectfully somewhere around Sevenguns's chin, and yet not averted. The old man continued to study my face, and though his nodding had slowed, his head still bobbed up and down ever so slightly.

"Lot of people this time do not know," he finally said, "what it means to be hungry."

I tipped my face to one side and looked directly into his eyes, encouraging him to go on.

"When I am a boy at that old school, I am always hungry. Always hungry. I still remember that in here." He held one hand to his middle and began to rub in a circle as if his stomach still ached for food. The other hand held the long wooden pole that he had used to stir the embers of the fire. It reminded me of seeing a storyteller holding a staff at a ceremony the previous summer. Momma Anna had referred to the eloquent man at that event as being "good with talking stick."

I knew better than to utter a word now that Sevenguns had opened a door into a tale from his past. I even tried to keep my breathing quiet so that I would not distract this grandfather who seemed poised to tell a story.

"They boil everything: potato, rice, vegetable. They boil meat, not enough meat to make good taste in a stew. One time my brother work in the kitchen, and he say they put a mouse in the soup, you know, say it is more meat and will boil until it is clean. I believe him." Sevenguns's eyes seemed to be looking off into the past and seeing all that he was describing. "I am so hungry that I look in my bowl for that mouse, but I eat the soup anyway. I eat everything I can get, and I am still empty here." He patted his stomach. Then he looked at me, as if he expected me to make a comment.

I felt a dull aching in my own gut to hear this story. "I have been to that school," I said. "I could tell it was an unhappy place."

The old man nodded again. "Every day, we get up, and it is dark, you know, and the prefect make us stand on a cold floor while he walk around and look for wet bed. If someone wet the bed, he get a beating right there. We stand and wait, and my feet are so cold on that floor. We wash, we march to church for prayer, and my stomach is growling. Then we get breakfast: mush or bread. Mostly mush. Sometime we get a cup of milk, mostly on Saturday. They have a few chickens there, you know, but the priest and the prefect and the teachers eat all those eggs.

"We go to work next. We do all kind of work. Big boys, they work in the barn and they also blacksmith. They build the fence and they plaster the school wall with mud. In summer we tend garden and those priest they want to grow potato—but you know potato do not like to grow there and they only grow small and hard like a rock. Sometime we are so hungry we eat a hard little potato right out of the ground with dirt on it and then later we have stomachache from eating them raw. We also have some apple tree over on one side of the school and need to bring water up from the river in the wagon for those tree. That is a good job, go out in the wagon get water.

"They have bread and butter for lunch, sometime pickle or beet. Big boys steal butter from little boys. When I am a little boy, I still remember that bread my mother bake. She bake bread every morning, you know, and that bread is warm and soft and taste like the sun melt in my mouth. Not this bread. They have hard, cold bread, taste like bird dropping. If you don't have your butter, you cannot eat it, the taste is so bad. Many times, I keep my butter but get a black eye or loose tooth from a big boy who want it." The old man stirred the fire again, and added a small log.

Through the open door, I could smell the delicious scent of bread baking in the *hornos*, the beehive-shaped outdoor adobe ovens the Tanoah women still used every day. I wondered if this was what triggered Sevenguns's memories of food, and of bread in particular.

The old man picked up a chunk of cottonwood root from under the counter. He stood the log on one end, pulled a small knife out of a sheath on his belt, and began carving the soft wood, his eyes focused intently on the work. "We have lesson in afternoon. I am lucky boy when I get bigger. I am very good at catching things, you know. I can figure out how to make a trap or hook. So they do not make me do lesson many times. I catch the rabbit in winter, catch the fish in summer, and also the walking bird. They get spoiled meat or sometimes canned meat or just bones from the government. They boil that in soup to make it kill the germs. But they do not kill all the germs. Lot of children get sick, many die. Some, they send home sick so they will not die there, but they still die, and we hear about it later, and we are sad to know it.

"The priest and the teachers, they do not eat the stew. They use the fresh meat that I catch, you know, and we can smell that meat roasting and they give us a cold potato for our supper. I go to bed dreaming of that meat with my belly gnawing on that little cold potato, and I am so hungry that I ache."

Toward the end of this tale, a Tanoah man wrapped in a sky blue blanket came through the door carrying a parcel, but Sevenguns was so engrossed in both his carving and his story that he did not notice. Beneath the hood made by this newcomer's blanket, I could see a tobacco-colored face marked with deep lines from his nose to the corners of his mouth, and three furrows across his prominent, high forehead. I couldn't tell whether he was pained or angry. He stood respectfully waiting for Sevenguns to finish speaking. But when Sevenguns came to the part of his tale about boiling spoiled meat and sick children dying, the man in the blue blanket grew agitated. He repositioned the package from one arm to the other. He threw the tail of his blanket over his shoulder, rearranging it around his face. He shifted his weight, rolling onto the balls of his buffalo moccasin soles as if he were preparing to sprint. He looked out the door, then back at Sevenguns, then at me, and quickly down to the floor when he saw that I was watching him.

Sevenguns, once his story was finished, looked up and noticed the new presence in the small room. He looked at me and said, "This guy name Rule Abeyta. He live on Winter side of pueblo, over there." He pointed across the tiny río that ran through the village, dividing the old part of the pueblo into two main multistory structures, which were referred to as Summer for the south side, and Winter for the north.

Rule Abeyta nodded, but he did not speak.

"How do you do?" I said. "I'm Jamaica Wild. I work for the BLM."

Before he could respond, an earsplitting clang boomed from the nearby bell tower. Rule Abeyta ducked his head as if to avoid a blow, nearly dropping the package he'd brought. The bell pealed again, heralding the daily morning mass. Abeyta quickly recovered, took three steps across the room, and shoved the package into Sevenguns's hands. "They left this at the gate for the governor," he said. He nodded in my direction as he turned to leave, his eyes cast down to avoid meeting my gaze as he walked full-speed out the door.

I watched him as he hurried away across the plaza. "Wow. The church bell really startled him," I said.

Sevenguns nodded. "Many our tribe have a scar inside from that time, you know. It is not good, that school. Tanoah of many age—my father, his father—many are wounded from that time at that place. Rule Abeyta is like that. They ring a bell at that school, up in that tower there, and it mean chore time, or it mean we have to pray now, or lesson time, or it time for someone get a beating, or they make us all stand and look while they have a trial and some little child they make a decision how to punish him. That bell ring and we march, we get up, we sit down, we kneel down, that bell ring and we are like children with no soul, you know? We just do.

"When they close that school, some people from Tanoah Pueblo tie that bell out there with big rope. We push sage up in that bell until it cannot make a sound, we tie it down so it cannot move. It must be silent so it never sing again that sad song that make children slaves."

I felt such sadness that my body felt heavy, and I wanted to sit down by the fire, to not move, not think. I hadn't had much sleep, and I knew I was tired, but this story reminded me of the way I had felt in the abandoned school. After a long silence, I said, "Thank you, Grandfather, for telling me about that time."

He nodded.

"I thought you said you weren't good at talking much."

He smiled. "Maybe today I am good."

It was my turn to smile.

"You want to catch that cat, put something that move."

"I was going to hang meat. The cats are starving."

"Cat is not raven. Cat want food that move, not food already dead."

You'd be surprised, I thought to myself. Then I said aloud: "This cat knows what it means to be hungry."

◂ 9 ▸

The Coldfire Episode

I went to talk with Scout and Lorena Coldfire, ranchers whose spread abutted the BLM land near the ruin and the abandoned Indian school. Scout, whose family had owned and ranched the land there for five generations, turned out to be a font of wisdom about the locale. Over coffee and some delicious homemade cookies, he told me all about the historic land disputes in that area between the Spanish and the Indians, and later the Anglos—including his ancestors.

"That ruin out there looks just like a castle from a ways off," he said. "You can see it from miles around, perched up high on that rim like that."

"That's where the cougar had her den," I said. "There must not be any human traffic in that area, or she wouldn't have put the cubs there."

"I don't think anyone goes out there," Scout said. "It's landlocked on three sides. And if someone had to come in from the west, that'd be pretty tough. It's a long piece to the nearest road out that way. It would be days of harsh badlands hiking."

Lorena, who had been in the middle of baking when I arrived, returned from the kitchen with another plate of cookies fresh from the oven. "I think I'm probably the only person who goes out to that old school," she said. "I take food and flowers to the graves of the children in the cemetery behind the school every year on the Day of the Dead. But I've never seen anyone else coming or going out that way, or any signs that anyone ever has." She picked up the coffee carafe to pour me another cup and found it empty. "Just a minute," she said. "I've got a fresh pot brewing." She headed back to the kitchen.

Scout picked up one of the warm cookies. "Well, come to think of it, someone goes out there every once in a while. I think it's the Indians. Did you know there's a stone staircase carved into the cliff wall right there near the ruin?"

"You mean steps?" I said. "Or hand- and footholds?"

"Oh, it's real crude, just the pecked-out places to put hands and feet, like you said. It's weathered enough, I don't think many people know what it is."

"Does it go all the way down into the canyon?"

"Sure does. I think the Indians from long ago must have carved that staircase into the rock so they could go down to get their water from the river. It has to be. I don't know how else they'd get water up there if they didn't."

"You said you'd seen signs of people out there?"

He got up and went to a small secretary and took out a piece of paper and a pen. "Let me draw you a map." He started sketching as he spoke. "If you go right straight out to the west from the ruin, there is a place where some big rocks sit right on the edge. Most people wouldn't think much about it but the rocks are blocking a little pathway, and you can't see it very easily. But if you can slip around those boulders—there's a pretty steep grade to it—but there's a narrow little path there that lets you down just twelve feet or so to a shelf just below the brow of the canyon rim. It's not a wide shelf, maybe six feet at best, and it's under a lip, so you can't see it from up on top. But that's where the stone staircase leads down from. And there's two small shrines there—just little cairns of rock, but I've seen them decorated with offerings from time to time."

"What kind of offerings?"

"Oh, you know, the usual things."

"Like feathers? Prayer bundles?"

"Yeah, stuff like that."

Lorena came back with the coffee. "Do you have a big dog out in your car?"

I stood and looked out the window. Mountain was standing up in the back of the Jeep, looking out one side and then the other. "He's a wolf," I said. "He's been in my Jeep most of the morning. Would you mind if I let him out? I'll put him on a lead."

Lorena set the carafe down. "A wolf?" She hurried for the entry and grabbed a coat from the hook by the door. "I can't wait to see him. Come on, Scout, there's a wolf out there!"

Later, after Mountain had met the ranch dogs and peed on every bush and post on the ranch house lawn, I explained to the Coldfires that unless we trapped the cougars, they probably would not survive.

"My father and grandfather would have rejoiced at the prospect," Scout said. "Fewer mountain lions to take our beef."

"Are predators attacking your cattle?" I asked.

"Not often. And I'm not my father or grandfather, either. I'm starting to get that we need to leave room for wildlife. Of course, that's to a point. If I start losing cattle, I'm going to—"

"Oh, we haven't lost any for a long time. I wonder if we shouldn't let her put out her traps for the pumas," Lorena said.

"What about if you do get them in your traps? Where will you release them after you're done with them?"

"I'm going to call the Department of Game and Fish agent for this area, Charlie Dorn. We will talk to him about that."

"Oh, yeah, we know Dorn. He's a good guy. He helps me keep my ponds stocked, and he arranged for some folks to do an owl study here one time—they released a pair up in those foothills."

I didn't tell the Coldfires, but now that I had been to their property, I believed the wounded cougar and her cubs were more likely to have moved there than onto the high mesas of the reservation. The Coldfire land offered safety in its wooded areas and rocky clefts where there would be sheltering caves.

"I'm sure the cougars have left the den at the ruin permanently because of all the recent noise and activity there," I said. "I don't think that little family will survive if we don't trap them and try to save them. The cubs are too young to hunt alone, and the she-lion is wounded. And she was awfully thin."

Lorena and Scout looked at one another. I knew we'd reached the point where I dare not be the next one to speak. When I was young—before an accident had taken his arm, and drink had taken his soul—my father, a Kansas farmer, had frequently demonstrated the principle he called "the next person who talks buys it." When dealing on the price of a tractor or a dozen eggs, he knew that when both sides had stated their case, the next person who spoke would be the one to give up ground.

"I'm just wondering: how would you get them to come to the traps?" Lorena asked.

Cha-ching!

I drove my Jeep cross-terrain along the Coldfire Ranch boundary where it joined the BLM Pueblo Pena parcel, looking for a good spot to set traps. I stopped near a spring that had formed a small ice pond no more than ten feet across. Sheltering berms formed a crescent shape around the seep. Although Scout Coldfire had stated that the only way the ancient Puebloans could have gotten water up to the ruin on the canyon rim was by bringing it up from the river, I recognized this place as an archaeological site. The ingenious ancient ones had learned to build check dams on plateaus to collect rain and spring snowmelt, and huge earth mounds like these to protect modest springs and encourage the scarce water to pool. They had irrigated the arid land in the most hostile places and created scarified crop fields. I knew this watering hole would be an attraction to the cougar, and since it was near to the ruin, she probably knew about it and had used it as a water source. It seemed a good place to set some traps. I was careful not to spread my scent along the ground, and I didn't let Mountain out to do so either. I got my field glasses out of the Jeep and scoped the site.

I heard the whine of an engine in the distance. Turning my binoculars toward the sound, I saw an ATV puttering along slowly about a mile away on BLM land, traveling in the direction of Pueblo Pena and the Indian school. I threw my field glasses in the passenger seat, fired up the Jeep's engine, and drove. I knew the turf was too rugged for me to get far, but that ATV was barely idling along, so I hoped I could get near enough to get a better look at it before I had to turn back.

I sped out onto the scrubland and managed to close a half mile of the gap between us before the driver of the ATV must have spotted me coming. That buggy tore into high gear and suddenly veered away from the ruin and out onto the high plains to the north. I knew from my previous day's survey of the surroundings that the ground to the north was riddled with arroyos. But nonetheless, I gave chase, knowing full well I didn't have the machine for it. The ATV raced across a dangerous, high-desert obstacle course, and I pursued, barreling up and down the landsliding slopes of red dirt arroyos, my Jeep taking to the air and Mountain and me along with it. We rocketed over sage-covered berms and rattled over ripple rock outcrops, the wolf jostling around in the back trying to keep from crashing into one side of the cargo area and then the other. I pushed the Jeep to its limits, calling out a litany of warnings to Mountain as I went, "Look out, buddy. Brace yourself! Get ready! No, get down. Hang on." I talked to the Jeep, too, as we blasted up out of a gully onto a slender, soft-dirt ridge that skirted the brim of a craterlike depression. "Come on, baby! Come on!" I struggled to keep the wheels from dipping to either side and drawing us down into a roll. Mountain stood up in the back and lowered his head to look out the front window, keenly aware that we were on the hunt. We shot over the slickrock, careening at a teetering angle on the sandstone edges and ledgy slopes leading along a low white brow at the end of the canyon. Here, the river played out and panned into a wide, waterless streambed blanketed by a foot-thick base of dry quicksand. All through the chase, the ATV had barely eluded me at every turn, but now that we were down in the wash, it scooted through the silt, while my Jeep's wheels spun, churning into the dry sand, losing traction.

After several tries, I managed to get one wheel onto rock and the four-wheel drive gained enough purchase to propel the car slowly forward onto some rocky soil on one side of the dry gulch. But while I struggled to keep the Jeep from bogging down in the sand, the ATV raced away and out of sight around a bend.

I pulled up onto some solid ground and got out, letting Mountain out, too. A stand of slender, bare willows stood waiting for spring, when this dry riverbed would swell with life from the snowmelt. A mile in the distance, high on the top of a vertical cliff, Pueblo Pena looked—as Scout Coldfire had said—like a castle in the air.

◂ 10 ▸

Latchkey ATV

It took me the rest of the afternoon to get back. I called Roy on the Screech Owl and reported the incident with the ATV. "It's suspicious that the ATV seemed to be headed to Pueblo Pena and then veered away when I pursued," I said.

"You're right about that, especially since a vehicle like that would be the most likely means for transporting a body out there to that old school. Did you get a look at the rig, maybe get a model, an identifying plate, anything?"

"No. I didn't get that close. I couldn't tell you much about the ATV, except that it seemed bigger than most. And it was so dusty, I couldn't tell if it was dark green or black."

"That's too bad. You be sure to report the incident to the FBI."

"I will," I said. "I'll call Diane as soon as we're done."

"Good," Roy said. "I just hope it wasn't a latchkey ATV. This danged ATV issue is so rampant that the Santa Fe office has coined that term because so many kids are coming home from school and amusing themselves by tearing around on public lands on their three- and four-wheelers."

"I don't think a schoolkid could drive like that."

I heard a sigh on the other end of the phone. "I hate to ask about your Jeep."

"You'll be relieved to know that I haven't wrecked or seriously damaged it, but there may well be some scratches and dings from the chase."

Roy chuckled. "Well, that's good for you. Because I can usually count on keeping the body and auto glass shops in Taos in business just from your handiwork alone."

"Hey, that's not fair!"

"You know I'm right. Call Langstrom. You need practice using the phone."

I called Diane and told her about the ATV chase.

"Tell me again about the other vehicle," Diane said.

"It was larger than the average ATV, I think. It had something like a cargo box on the back. Dark color. Maybe black."

"Those are called UTVs. They're bigger and more powerful, sort of like a cross between a small pickup and an ATV. Did you see the driver?"

"No," I said. "I never got that close."

Knowing I would have to prime the pump for the cistern when I got home that night, I stopped at Jesse's small market to buy some jugs of water. Just to be sure, I bought extra. I was the only customer in the store, so Jesse and I exchanged chitchat about the weather and the upcoming holidays at the register. "Hey, did you hear about that old lady who used to teach at the Indian school?" he asked.

"I did." I nodded, looking down into my grocery sack. "I heard about that."

"I knew her, you know. A little bit, anyway. She ordered her groceries from me."

I hesitated. Then I asked: "What was she like?"

"Señora Morgan? She was kind of cranky, you know. She had a real nice house, though, real nice."

I lingered at the register, hoping for more. A silence fell between us. Finally, I said, "Anything else you can tell me about her?"

He looked one way and then the other, as if someone might be listening in. Then he leaned over the register and said, softly, "You see, I delivered there every two weeks, always the same thing: a case of wine, four lamb chops, two pounds of sausage, two dozen eggs, a bag of potatoes, a bag of carrots, a chicken, and a roast. You must not let my wife know I told you that. *Ay!* She would kill me. We don't talk about the customers. Especially if they order wine."

"I won't mention it, Jesse." I thought about Sevenguns and the story he'd told about the children getting sick and going hungry while the teachers ate all the eggs and the meat he trapped and shot.

Jesse interrupted my thoughts. "Hey, I still got that leg joint for Mountain. If you want, I can go get it for him."

"That would be nice, Jesse. I have to go out to the pueblo, and he can worry on that while he's waiting in the car."

Later, when Jesse had given Mountain the bone and was lowering the hatch on the back of my Jeep, he said, "I should say something good so I don't have to go to confession for talking about the dead. Señora Morgan always paid her bill right on time," he said. He looked satisfied with himself for having paid his penance.

"Well, that's one good thing."

"And another thing. I think she was maybe a good Catholic. There was a sister at her house the last few times I took the wine and the groceries."

"A nun? From your church?"

"Not from my church, no. I never met her, but I can tell you she was not from the church here in Taos. If she was from my church, I would know her."

◂ 11 ▸

Deserters

Two years ago, Momma Anna had adopted me as her student almost immediately after meeting me at an art show, and had begun instructing me in the ways of her people, which she called "Indun Way." Initially, when I came to visit her, she talked to me very casually about the customs of her people as she cooked or made pottery or jewelry. She often enlisted my help in many of the labor-intensive tasks that she and the other women of her clan performed, such as collecting clay for making pots, making jerky, and large-scale cooking and baking for feasts. And she included me in family gatherings and some rituals, when it was not forbidden to do so by the tribe.

When I visited her alone at her house, I often took notes in a notebook. Momma Anna had told me one time that writing things down was my way of learning. When I let her know that I had tried once before to write a book, she astonished me by encouraging me to record the stories, the recipes, and the customs she shared with me for a book about her people. This was especially surprising since she had told me about another author who had written a book about the people from three Tiwa pueblos. His book had been driven out of print, his house burned, and the Puebloans who shared information with him had been banned from their tribes. When I asked Momma Anna about this contradiction, she told me that she feared that the old ways were dying out and that many of the rites and traditions she still practiced would pass away with the elders, gradually eroding the culture and homogenizing it. The Tanoah children were torn between the world outside the pueblo and the tribal ways, and the result was that much of the life Anna Santana had once known was vanishing. Since I loved to write, my job was to attend, watch, listen, and take notes.

But Momma Anna had also warned me that the book I was preparing was not to be published until after she had passed beyond the ridge, as the Tanoah were fiercely secretive about their culture, and there would be repercussions to anyone who shared these things with an outsider. In the past few months, Momma Anna seemed to have developed a sense of urgency about my training, encouraging me to participate more often in the feast days and customs.

The holidays at Tanoah Pueblo involved days of elaborate preparation. Momma Anna had insisted I must come with her this day at sundown to the home of a friend. The modest apartment was on the Summer, or south, side of the village, and its door faced onto the central plaza. Here inside the wall, there was no electricity or running water, as the tribe insisted on keeping life in the old ways in this historic part of the pueblo. The only heat in this tiny dwelling came from a fire in the corner fireplace and a wood-burning kitchen stove in an adjoining room. Two gas lanterns hung from heavy spikes driven into the vigas that spanned the ceiling. The lamps hissed and radiated amber pools of light. When Momma Anna's friend invited us into her home, she cast a plump shadow on the whitewashed wall that seemed to be welcoming us a second time once we'd stepped inside.

Anna spoke to our hostess in Tiwa and gestured to me, saying, "Ja-mai-ca."

The auntie held out her hand to me and permitted me to take it. I bowed slightly, but did not speak, which was the formal salutation from a young woman first meeting an elder at Tanoah Pueblo.

"My name Sica. Sica Gallegos," she said in a deep, smoky voice. "My *Indun* name Blue Cloud."

Once we had finished the greetings and introductions, Sica said she would bring us tea. She turned and limped toward the kitchen with such a hobble that I worried each time she stepped on her left leg that she might tumble over. She returned holding two cups, and the liquid sloshed over the rim each time she limped on the shorter leg. She gave us each a half cup of tea. Momma Anna opened a plastic grocery bag and pulled out a bundle of cream-colored wool cloth, smoothly woven with bright red and green designs along the hem edge. It reminded me of the ceremonial kiltlike wraps the Tanoah men wore when they danced the deer and buffalo dance. "This special made for Holy Family," Momma Anna said.

The two women took the cloth to a square folding table that had been set up under the only window in Sica Blue Cloud's home. They arranged the fabric such that the red and green pattern design showed prominently across the front and two sides. Momma Anna asked me to stand back and help them assure that it hung evenly. "Holy Family come here," she said, sweeping her hand across the plane of the table, "before the solstice. Stay until Day of Kings."

Sica Blue Cloud nodded, smiling. "My family give them home."

"Next other time, maybe my family," Momma Anna said.

One of the aunties had explained this tradition to me the night we had made the Christmas baskets. A group of *bultos*—carved wooden statues of the Nativity, including the Holy Family—were moved from the pueblo church to one of the family homes at Tanoah Pueblo, and the bultos would reside there until the Epiphany. This was a great honor for the chosen family. Food and drink were left for the bultos each night, prayers offered, and many visits to the home made by members of the tribe who wished to pay their respects to the shepherds, the three wise men, and especially Joseph, Mary, and the baby Jesus.

While they were adding elements to the table, such as straw for the stable and cotton to represent snow for the surrounding landscape, the two old women gossiped in Tiwa.

Sica turned from her fussing over the table and looked at me. I had been studying a few framed photos on an adobe ledge in the otherwise-spare room. Sica wobbled to a basket in the corner and picked up a folded blanket and handed it to me. To many of the elders at Tanoah Pueblo, this was the same gesture of hospitality as the offer of a seat on the sofa in a contemporary home. Momma Anna often taught me lessons as she did handwork on her jewelry or dreamcatchers while seated on a blanket in her front room. It was an old custom to keep a house without furniture, and few of the elders at Tanoah Pueblo adhered to it anymore. Momma Anna had told me that when she grew up, her family ate their meals, told their stories, and played winter games on a blanket in their home and never wanted for more.

I unfurled the blanket and sat down cross-legged on one corner. Sica Blue Cloud looked at Momma Anna and smiled approvingly, and they returned to their chatter. I heard the word "schoolteacher"—the only bit of English in a steady stream of Tiwa—and I knew they were talking about Cassie Morgan and the news of the former school matron's death. After a few minutes, the two women came to join me on the blanket. Sica brought a little stool from the kitchen, then leaned against the wall and slid down carefully, using the stool as a place to put her hands as she supported herself on the way down. When she sat down, her left leg extended at an angle, straight out from her hip across the floor. I could see a huge knob below her knee through the fabric of her dress. Both women were quiet for a moment, and then Sica began speaking to me. "You know I am old, but I still remember that one who died. She was a long time coming in my dreams, long time."

Momma Anna grunted, "*Unh.*"

Sica went on: "One time, two Apache boy come to that school, they are wild as jackrabbit, get in lot of trouble. One bite the teacher ear, make her bleed. The next one jump on a teacher back and pull her hair and she scream, run around like a horse try to buck him off." Sica put fingers over her lips to suppress a giggle, remembering the sight. But then she sobered, and she pursed her lips and looked down. "They whip those boy in front of everybody, make us watch. They beat them many different time, sometime one, sometime the next one, sometime both boy at same time. Then those Apache boy escape from that school. They call them 'deserter.' They ring the church bell, make us get in line, stand outside at night. They say, 'You tell, you can go back to bed,' but no one tell where those boy are." She threw up her hands. "I do not know where those boy are, but I am happy they are not there. The priest call the Apache boy 'deserter' many time, and he say we stand all night if we do not tell. We stand out there in the cold, and this time, some those teacher and other one search all the way back to Tanoah Pueblo, maybe even up in the mountain. But they do not find those boy. After sun rise, they make us go to work, no food. The little one cry but we tell them hush and we are hungry, too. Some older boy say the two Apache boy, they find way to climb down into canyon, stay by the river, wait three day until full moon. Then those Apache boy will make their way home by moonlight.

"We go to bed hungry that night. They give us some little food next day, still make us stand long time, say we must tell where the deserters. Nobody talk, and pretty soon we are back to work. Three day and moon is full. We think Apache boy can see good now, go home. We are happy and whisper good luck at them.

"That night, I hear lot of noise. Pound on wood and door slam, then I hear lot of people move around. I get up and go to the door—they call where we sleep 'dom-ee-toy.' I go to door that dom-ee-toy, look out on school yard. I see man they call headmaster and next other man come out store room—they have room there where they go down under ground and food stay cool, like potato, apple, onion, shelf with jelly, beans. Those two men they try shut door to that store room, they bang with rock, they slam door, it will not shut no more. Then they take rifle and go through gate, head up to canyon rim with those gun."

Sica Blue Cloud Gallegos began rubbing the swollen knob on her left leg, and she grew quiet.

I looked at Momma Anna. Her eyes were squeezed tightly shut, and she was shaking her head *no,* back and forth, over and over, as she worked the turquoise beads of her rosary in her hand.

I thought the story had ended, but Sica continued. "That one who die this time, that bad woman. She find me stand in door. She take a broom and hit me. She hit me and hit me, knock me behind my knee and I fall down, and she hit me on my leg and my back until broom break, then she yell at me, go back to bed. But I cannot get up. I cannot walk." Sica rubbed her leg again where the bulge rose from below the knee. "I am bleed and I cannot stand, but she yell and grab that broom. I drag myself to my cot, hope I not get beat for blood on sheet, but my legs are bleed from that beating and I have to bite sheet to keep from cry out, my leg hurt so bad. I roll top of that old sheet and I bite on it and I can feel my leg wet with blood. We hear two shot fire, gunshot. All the girl in that dom-ee-toy, they wail, but that bad woman come back and say she got a next other broom to use on every one who make sound. We never speak about Apache boy no more, but our hearts are hurt for them, every one cry inside for them.

"I cannot walk, they try tie my leg to a board, but my bone keep break. Maybe three time. I cannot work, they send me home. I am lucky I don't have to stay there."

Like Momma Anna, I found myself shaking my head with disbelief, and I drew my hand to my mouth and bit on the side of my fist, grimacing at the pain of this tale.

As Sica was finishing the story, the door opened with a creak, and an icy draft of air swept through the opening and across the floor with a breathy, high-pitched wail. A man with a big smile stepped in carrying a folding chair, some cut pieces of thin plywood, and a small hammer. He leaned the chair against the wall and set the other items on the table, then closed the door with a soft thud. As he came forward to greet the women, Sica's face bloomed with delight, and she reached up to take his hand. Sica said, "Jamaica, this my nephew Eloy."

Eloy smiled at me as he kissed his auntie on the head.

"Eloy like my own boy. He stay with me, just little child, when his mother sick."

Eloy tenderly helped Sica to her feet. "You took good care of me,

Auntie Sica." He nodded to Momma Anna. "Hello, Grandmother," he said. This was a sign of respect that a younger member of the tribe used to greet an elder he knew at Tanoah Pueblo.

I stood up and offered a hand to Momma Anna and helped her up. Then I turned to Sica's nephew. "I'm Jamaica Wild."

"Eloy Gallegos," he said, giving a polite nod.

"I know I've seen you before . . ."

He wrinkled his brow, waiting for me to finish my sentence. Then he offered: "Perhaps here in the village? I visit my auntie frequently."

"Possibly. I'm the liaison for the BLM, so I'm out here at the pueblo quite a lot for work—"

Sica interrupted: "Eloy build stable for Holy Family." She smiled.

Eloy gestured toward the things he'd brought in. "I brought a chair so I could work at the table. I don't know why Auntie Sica still insists on sitting on the floor. I've offered to bring her some furniture, but she won't take it."

Sica put her arms around her nephew, smiling as she patted him on the back. "He's a good boy," she said.

"Okay, Auntie," he said, giving her a smooch on the forehead. "You want me to build you a little stable? Let's get started."

◂ 12 ▸

Disempowered

Once again, it was late by the time Mountain and I got home to the little cabin, which was dark and cold. When I opened the front door and flipped the switch for the lights and ceiling fan, there was still no power. I stood in the entry and closed my eyes. I counted to ten, taking deep breaths and blowing them out to dispel the anger. Then I thought of Sica Gallegos and her humble, gas lamp–lit home, and I found it hard to feel sorry for myself. Fortunately I had the water in the car that I'd bought to prime the pump. I could use some of it for cooking and washing. I hauled the jugs inside as I told Mountain, "No running to La Petaca tonight. Tonight we are going to bed early and getting some sleep."

I lit some candles, then started a fire in the woodstove and put the big cast-iron kettle on one side of the top, full of water to heat for washing up. I put another kettle on the other side for tea. While they heated, I took a shovel up to my designated latrine area, and labored to dig a deeper trench in the frozen ground so I could use the facilities another day or two if need be. While I worked, Mountain surveyed the area around the cabin, his nose to the ground, looking for any sign of his side of beef. He searched methodically in a circular grid, widening his ground at every revolution until he reached the edge of the woods, where I had carved out my trench.

When we returned to the cabin, I brought in a cooler from the little shed out back and unloaded the contents of the refrigerator into it to set outside in the cold. The milk was marginal, at best, having been shut up in a refrigerator that hadn't worked for more than two days. But Mountain's supplies—some partially frozen ground lamb, elk bones, and venison in the freezer—had kept the butter and cheese somewhat cool. With the bears hibernating for the winter, I figured I could set the cooler on the shady side of the house and it would be all right. Just to be sure, I placed a big rock on top of it, and came back inside to figure out what I could make for supper. When the washing water was warm, I poured it into a big stainless steel bowl I'd set in the kitchen sink, and I took another pot to the woodstove to heat water to cook some noodles I'd found in the cupboard.

I prepared to bathe using the water in the sink, stripping down and taking some time to soothe the scrapes and bruises on my arm and shoulder with the warm washcloth. I pulled my hair up into a ponytail and sponged gently at the knot on my forehead, then washed my bangs, and finished by using the precious water for a warm sponge bath that felt close to heaven. While I was standing at the sink with the front of my hair dripping, completely naked, I heard a loud *bump!* Mountain suddenly hurled himself at a window on one side of the room, making a loud *thwock* and nearly breaking the glass, as he gave an earsplitting bark followed by a low, threatening growl. I heard another *thump!* I snatched the towel lying on the counter and wrapped it around me and tucked it in at the top. Then I reached into my big bag on the table, pulled out my handgun, and grabbed the flashlight by the door. In spite of Mountain's attempts to butt me aside, I squeezed through the door without letting him out, slipped around to the side of the house where I'd heard the noise, and aimed my flashlight down the log wall. On the ground lay the open cooler, the contents ravaged, packages torn open, butcher paper flapping in the night breeze. Mountain looked out the window at me, his ears up, eyes wide open, on full alert. On the rocks above the cabin, I heard coyotes yipping, counting coup.

I opened a window in the bathroom slightly and another one over the kitchen sink to pull fresh air through the house so I could work by the light of a propane lantern. It was a week before Christmas, and I still had to finish making gifts for Kerry, Roy, Momma Anna, and an old *curandera* I knew named Tecolote. For Kerry, I was making a deerskin vest that had pockets for his camera lenses and accessories, since he was an avid photographer. For Momma Anna, I had already finished a large elk hide bag with appliqués of horses sewn onto the front. For Tecolote, I had used deerskin and the wolf's hair that I had saved from his spring and fall sheds to make a small, soft pillow. Tecolote lived so simply that this would be a true luxury. For Roy, I had two possible ideas: I had braided some horsehair that I could make into a hatband for the trademark cowboy hat he always wore; or I had made an outline of his favorite knife and could make a leather sheath so he could wear it on his belt. I had one big, gold elk hide left. I spread this across the kitchen table so that it hung over on all four sides. The skin was large, smooth, and nearly perfect. As I stared at it, I thought of the northern Plains Indian tradition of using the contemplative time of winter to create images on hides depicting the year's leading stories, and allowing these symbolic accountings to accumulate into a spiral of annual pictographs. These became incredible painted story hides called winter counts. Together with the oral element of storytelling to explain and enhance these images, the winter count served as history, art, philosophy, and myth for the cultures that produced them.

Were I to create a pictograph of my own experience in the past year, I certainly would count finding Cassie Morgan's body as one of the leading stories. But hers was not the only body I had found this year. Another image I might paint on a winter count hide would be the spectacular vision of the twin spires of Chimney Rock with the moon rising exactly between the two steeples, and a wildfire blazing up the slopes. A burning man might be another image from my summer assignment on an incident management team deployed to that wildfire. Last year's leading story for the winter count might have featured a man trampled by buffalo—something I'd watched happen, helpless to do anything about it. And I could go back farther, with still more life and death tales.

Smitten with the idea of making a winter count with my last hide, I decided it would be the horsehair hatband for Roy. I went to the long, narrow closet on one side of the pass-through between my cabin's one main room and the small, shed-roof bathroom that had been attached well after the cabin was built so the landlord could rent the place. As I rummaged through my closet looking for painting supplies for the hide and a silver conch to use for the hatband, I came across the shoe box containing my mother's poetry, something I hadn't looked through in a long time.

Perhaps the sad stories of the Indian children away from the comforts of home and family had something to do with it, but I took the box down from the high shelf and brought it back to the table so I could peruse the contents by the light of the gas lantern. Besides the poetry, the box contained the one photo I owned of my mother, taken when I was just an infant. I studied the color image: a blonde-haired girl who looked a lot like me, her long, curly locks flowing wildly across her shoulders. She was sitting on the steps of our Kansas farmhouse wearing a flimsy, flowery blouse that must have shocked the staid families in the farm community where we lived. She held a bunted infant in her arms and smiled directly into the camera lens, a gorgeous smile of youth and hope with a hint of mischief. In her amber eyes, I could see the sadness that was like a signature scent lingering around her person—something most people would miss when they saw this attractive woman in the photo. But that sadness was what I remembered most about my mother—even though I was only a small child the last time I saw her. She left when I was four, and if I tried hard, I could still recall the sound of her voice, but little else.

I ran my finger along the edge of the photograph, as if I might be able to connect through my fingertip with a time when I was nestled against my mother's bosom, held tightly in her arms, her radiance and beauty surrounding me. In the picture, I was only a tiny, blanketed shape, a stretch of pale, smooth forehead, one eye, and a button nose peeking out from the swaddle.

I put the photo back in the box and rifled through the poems. I picked up a short one jotted on a torn piece of paper.

Pale morning moon
Over prairie farmhouse.
Meadowlark sings
In the afternoon.
Why am I here?
Because I belong.

Not to a place, but
To this moment.
I belong to me,
Not just to a prairie.
I belong to this moment.
Like the bird's song belongs
To the meadowlark,
I belong to me.

I knew instantly I wanted to give a copy of this to Diane. I thought perhaps I could burn it into a piece of deerskin to use as a bookmark, but my leather burner needed electrical power, so it would have to wait. I set the shoe box on the nightstand beside my bed, to keep it handy for when the electricity came back on.

A sudden knock at the door surprised me, and Mountain jumped up from a deep sleep and went on full alert. It was late, almost midnight, and I was in my pajamas. I drew my handgun for the second time that night and went to the door to answer the summons. I looked through the peephole and recognized a neighbor from down the road. I opened the door a crack, keeping it wedged against my foot so Mountain couldn't get through.

"Yes?"

"I'm your neighbor, next place over." His voice was hard and had a bitter edge.

"I know."

"I lost a steer, and I'll tell you straight out: I suspect your wolf for the kill."

As he said this, Mountain stuck his nose in between my knee and the door and gave a loud snort. He wheedled and pushed, trying to wedge the door open, but I kept my foot in place behind it, the door wobbling back and forth with our struggle. The neighbor looked down at the wolf and curled his lip in a snarl.

"If I ever see that wolf on my property, I'll shoot him. You got that?"

I blinked, stunned. "Listen, he wouldn't take down a steer by himself. In fact, he wouldn't take down a steer at all. Wolves hunt in packs, and he's not hungry, so he wouldn't go through the work. I just had a hungry pack of coyotes raid my cooler out back where I'd put my food to keep it from spoiling. It had to be them, and even then, the steer had to have gotten stuck or been sick or hurt for coyotes to—"

"Miss," he interrupted, holding up a hand with the index finger pointed at me, "we've all been pretty tolerant up to now with you having that danged wolf as a pup. But now that he's grown, he's a menace. And I meant what I said." He jabbed the finger toward Mountain, who was watching through the opening of the door with his ears down. "I'll shoot him, sure as I'm standing here." He turned to go, then turned back. "You know, it's as dark as a tomb at your place. Why don't you turn on some lights?"

◂ 13 ▸

The Lures

Shortly after dawn, I met Charlie Dorn at the Coldfire Ranch to help with the setting of the traps. Dorn had arranged for a state Department of Transportation crew to bring a road-killed deer for the lure. We worked to get the traps into place, wearing thick rubber boots and rubber gloves that had been prewashed and were relatively free of human scent. Charlie used a reciprocating saw to cut the deer into three parts so we could put meat in each of the traps. "I doubt we'll get those cubs unless the den is somewhere close," he said. "If they're as young as you said, they don't go out hunting with Mama yet."

"What will we do then? The cubs will die without their mother."

"Let's just see what we get, and then we'll go from there. With the mama cat wounded, the cubs probably aren't getting much to eat anyway."

My heart ached for this desperate family of mountain lions. Cougars formerly ranged far and wide on this continent, but had been extirpated in all but fifteen states—and in those, they were still shot, poisoned, trapped, and sport-hunted to the brink of near-extinction. These elusive and mystical cats were one of the last vestiges of wildlife, and their offspring had a survival rate only near fifty percent in the best of circumstances.

When Charlie and I had placed the meat lures, I went to my Jeep and brought out the pelt of a quail, which the Tanoah often called the "walking bird" because of its tendency to run and apparent reluctance to fly. When I found feathers like these, I generally gave them to Momma Anna for use in her dreamcatchers, but I remembered Sevenguns's advice about cats being attracted to live prey that moves, and so I hung some feathers in each trap to flutter in the breeze and hopefully attract the attention of the cougars.

When we had finished, I headed back toward Taos. Once in range, I pulled over and used the Screech Owl to put in another call to the power company. But I was forced to leave a voice-mail message again. I made a terse recording, saying I had been without power now for several days, had left previous messages and not gotten any response, and wanted a call back immediately to let me know when the technician would be at my place. I left the cell phone number and hastened to add the directions to my place as well. A few minutes after I'd hung up, the Screech Owl went off with a shriek.

"Are you the one from the BLM?" a man's voice said.

"Yes. Are you from the power company?"

"Something has happened to an elk on the BLM land north of Tanoah Pueblo. Forest Road 109, back in two miles on that road. There's a meadow there with woods all around. The elk is down in that meadow."

"What's happened to the elk?"

There was no answer.

"Is it a cow or a bull?"

Silence.

"Who is this?"

I heard a click, then nothing.

I called Dorn. "Charlie, I just got a strange call. Some guy said that something had happened to an elk two miles back in on Forest Road 109."

"Probably an elk-versus-car report."

"I don't know. This guy sounded strange. Not like he was reporting hitting an elk. Besides, I know that forest road. It's too primitive to drive more than a few miles per hour on it. There's no way you could hit an elk on that road unless the animal decided to lie down and watch you as you slowly ran over it."

"Well, I'm on the way to the shop to drop off these boots and gloves and this saw. Let me unload them and I'll come right out."

I went to investigate the report, bumping slowly down the old forest road, which was little more than two tracks in some grass and brush. The trail led up into some foothills near thick forest. I kept one eye on the rearview mirror and another on the rutted dirt track ahead of me, thinking this could be a bad place to get lured into and trapped—an irony after I had just helped to create those same conditions for the cougars. At the top of a little rise, I could see down into the bowl of a meadow surrounded by gentle slopes leading up to dense woods on all sides. There, in some short grass near a small pond, was an elk cow. She was down.

I looked in every direction. No vehicles, no sign of people. A haze of cold hung in the pines that surrounded the meadow, and a patch of clouds had drifted in front of the sun, leaving the ground in shadow.

I grabbed my rifle, checked to make sure I had some ammo, took another look around in all directions, and began to hike down into the field. As I walked, I turned my head, sweeping my eyes to the left along the ridge where the road came in, across thick stands of timber, and then to the right where the woods deepened and the road continued on. I turned and looked behind me, walking backward as I did, scoping the land behind me, taking a sure bearing on my Jeep in case I had to run for cover or make a getaway. But it was at least a hundred yards to the elk, and after a certain point, I knew I was committed to that destination.

When I approached the cow from the back, I slowed. I could see a dark, red-black pool on the grass below her. She tried to raise her head when she heard me approach, but she was too weak. She had lost a lot of blood. I came carefully around her head, staying a few feet away so as not to frighten her. The sight before me was so appalling that I cried out—and at the same time my stomach started to heave. I felt rage rising with the bile that fought to come up. I wanted to kill whoever had done this.

The elk's front legs were roped together above the hooves; one back foot was tied to a stake driven into the ground. Her loose back leg trembled uncontrollably. Her belly had been slit open. Before her on the ground lay her unborn calf, coated in a gelatinous skin that must have been the cow's placenta—the baby had been pulled from her body. As I looked closer, I realized that the calf, too, had been brutally eviscerated. The cow breathed wet, heavy breaths and stared at me with an eye that telegraphed terror. Something that *walked* like me had done this, something that *smelled* like me, that *looked* like me, something *the same as* me. And now, what was *I* going to do to her?

I choked back a sob as I raised the rifle. But it was anger—at whoever had done this—that helped me to steady the stock against my shoulder, to tip my head to the side as I aimed at the elk's brain pan. I swallowed, then took a deep breath and let it out. After I pulled the trigger, I screamed, "Aaaaaaaaaaahhhhhhhh!" My voice echoed along with the gunshot in the empty meadow and against the stands of forest around me.

I went to touch her to make sure she was gone. A dark circle right above and behind her eye glistened black. Her thick neck was still warm. She didn't move. I inspected her baby. The calf, too, was warm to the touch. This had happened right before I arrived, in spite of the phone call earlier. Someone had downed the cow somehow and then timed it so I would get there . . .

A crack of gunshot interrupted my thoughts and I dove to the ground, then crawled behind the elk cow's back to take cover. I couldn't be sure exactly where the shot had come from, but as I watched the woods, three men emerged and began running toward me, carrying rifles. Behind me, I could hear a vehicle coming down the road. I glanced back and saw Charlie Dorn's green truck as it lumbered over a rise and then disappeared back down into a dip in the road. He would be here in minutes.

The three men were making good time as they ran directly for me. I would have to make a move before Charlie arrived. I decided to take the offensive. I pointed my rifle barrel and took dead aim, zinging a shot right past the man in the middle, slightly above his head. "BLM Resource Protection. Drop your weapons and put your hands up!" I yelled. *Please, Charlie, get here quick!* I thought.

I watched as the three men did as they were told.

"Step back from your arms!" I yelled again. "Take three big steps back, no more."

They did.

"Put your hands on the back of your head and keep them there. Do not speak, do not turn around, just stand there and keep your hands on your head!"

I took another glance back down the road, but didn't see Charlie yet. I had to see this through by myself for now. I got up, my rifle pointed at the three men. I walked around the elk and farther down into the field toward them.

I didn't speak again until I had kicked their weapons to the side. I jerked my head back toward the elk. "Did you do that?" I screamed, my voice giving away my fury.

The men shook their heads no, but they did not speak. Their eyes were wide, either with fear of what I might do or with surprise at having been caught.

"Why did you shoot at me, then?" I heard Charlie's truck and I glanced quickly sideways and saw him pulling up beside my Jeep.

"We didn't shoot at you, miss," the man in the middle said. "We were running because we heard one shot from one way and then another from another way, and we didn't know who it was or where it came from."

I snorted. "You have weapons here, gentlemen. You expect me to believe that?"

By this time, Dorn was sprinting toward us, and he held his rifle at the ready.

The man in the middle spoke again. "We been shooting targets all morning. We're out of ammo. We're parked over the next hill"—he pointed farther down the forest road—"and we were headed that way when we heard a shot and then a woman screaming. We didn't know who it was, but we were coming to see if we could help. It sounded like somebody was in trouble. Then we heard a second shot. So we decided to get out of there, and we started running out. We were just trying to get to the road as fast as we could when you shot at us."

Dorn looked at me, his brow puckered.

"I fired a warning shot over their heads. They were coming straight at me, right after a shot had been fired at me."

He pressed his lips together and gave a nod. "All right, fellas, let's see what you got in your backpacks," he said.

The men claimed to know nothing about the mutilated elk. They were carrying bags of spent shells and paper targets in their backpacks. We scrutinized their identification and gun licenses, and then I hopped in Dorn's truck with him, and we followed the three men, idling slowly along behind them as they walked up to their truck, a quarter mile farther down the forest road and around a bend. We checked their truck, got their license plate number, and let them go home. They seemed to be telling the truth.

While Charlie was looking over the elk cow and her calf, I went back to my Jeep with my rifle. There was a package on the driver's seat, wrapped in white butcher paper. Without picking it up, I pulled the paper away at the top. I drew in a sharp breath, and I thought for a moment I wouldn't be able to breathe again—my chest had knotted up and stalled. Nestled inside the waxy white paper was the bloody heart of the elk calf, with a note which had been printed on a flap of the wrapper with a red crayon. It read: *Este pobre muchachito lo dejaron abandonado*. I translated the words one at a time: *This poor child was left abandoned.*

◂ 14 ▸

Chill

I drove back to the tiny village of Cascada Azul, just outside the gates of Tanoah Pueblo, to gain cell phone service so I could call Roy. I used the Screech Owl and reported the incident through shivering lips and chattering teeth, trying hard not to let Roy know it. I had a sudden case of the chills, and I couldn't stop shaking.

"What in the hell?" he barked into the phone.

I shook my head and gritted my teeth, but didn't answer. I yanked up the zipper of my coat, pulled on my gloves, but I didn't think it would matter.

"What kind of jackass would do something like that?"

"It would have to be someone really cruel. Someone who enjoyed hurting . . . life. Charlie found a foot-noose trap. They must have caught the elk in a foot-noose and then snared her front legs. They timed it so I would get there while the cow was still alive."

"Damn. It sounds like the work of some psycho. Can you think of anyone who might have it in for you for some reason? Have you busted anybody for illegal hunting this season? Anybody hunting in the wrong place, or maybe someone who got a pregnant elk?"

"No. I'm not a game warden. I hardly ever bust a hunter."

"I know. I'm just trying to find a handle on this. Why a pregnant elk?"

"I don't know, Boss. It was . . . it was just so cruel." I whispered that last.

"I'm coming right out. I want you to get on out of there, have Dorn wait for me. I don't like this, Jamaica. You need to mix up your routine, take the rest of the day off, maybe stay with a friend or in a motel for a few nights."

"I'm going to call Diane Langstrom and report this to her, too."

"Yeah, good idea. We call the FBI on cattle mutilation, so this is no different. Only it seems like it's more about you than the elk."

"It could be nothing, but the note was written in r-red c-crayon," I chattered.

"What? Are you all right?"

"I'm just cold. I think it was also r-red crayon that was used to write the words on that sign that was hung around the neck of Cassie Morgan."

"Oh." He was quiet a moment. "Okay, be sure to tell Langstrom that, too. Maybe you should stay with Dorn, then, until I get there. I don't want you out there by yourself."

"Boss?"

"What?"

"Did you give this c-cell phone number to anyone else?"

"Just your FBI friend, Langstrom."

"No one else?"

"Not a soul."

I jotted the caller's number down from the Screech Owl's call log and gave it to Diane when I phoned to report the incident to her. Then I sat in my Jeep in the lot of the little gas station in Cascada Azul with the heater blasting, trying to chase the chills away. Roy got there first, and I got out to talk with him. A few minutes later, Diane pulled up. As she got out of her car she said, "Guess where the call came from."

"The power company?" I said.

Diane shook her head no. She pointed at the pay phone booth listing against the side of the building.

"What?" I asked, disbelieving what I'd seen.

"That's it. That pay phone right there. That's your number on your caller I.D."

While Roy went to join Charlie to examine the elk, Diane stayed with me and took a report. We sat in the front of her car. After she'd heard my story and asked a few questions, she said, "Listen, Jamaica, it sounds like somebody set you up to take you out."

I sat still, my eyes making REM-like movements as I tried to fathom what was happening. I knew what Diane had said was true. "If those three men hadn't run out of the woods—"

"Exactly. And then you said Dorn drove up. You foiled the shooter, whose plan was to take you down. The elk was the lure."

I shook my head no. "But I—"

"Look, you need to get past the shock and surprise here and start thinking on your feet again. Let's start with the phone call you got about the elk."

"That's the part I don't get. The only people I have called on that phone are you, Charlie, Roy, and the power company. I left my number at the power company right before I got that call about the elk. Nobody else has that cell phone number."

"Okay, then we gotta check out the power company, and we can do that. But you need to think. Why is someone gunning for you? Who would want to kill you?"

I thought for a moment. "Maybe this has something to do with the ATV driver yesterday."

"My thought exactly. What was he—or she—doing out there by the ruin and the old school? And didn't you say the vehicle was idling along really slow?"

"Yeah, really slow. Until the driver saw me coming."

"So whoever was driving that ATV thinks that you saw him. Or her."

"But what if I did? I could bust them for driving an ATV off-road on BLM land. But that doesn't seem like enough reason to want to kill me."

"Murderer returns to the scene of the crime?"

"Yeah, maybe. And thinks I'm onto him or her. So what was the ATV doing out there, possibly for a second time?"

"Idling along slow . . . maybe looking for something?" Diane said.

"They wouldn't have been worried about covering their tracks—the wind took care of all the tracks. Maybe something else?"

Diane nodded. "Keep thinking. In the meantime, maybe you ought to come stay with me for a few nights. If someone at the power company is involved, they know where you live."

"But . . . Mountain."

"So, bring him. Hang on a second and let me call the Silver Bullet."

As I thought of Diane's offer, I wondered how the wolf would handle staying in a house in town. But the idea of electricity, hot showers, and flush toilets was irresistible. I started running down a list of things I'd have to pack for a few days' stay.

Diane flicked her phone closed. "The Bullet is going to have someone go to town on the power company, and by the time he's through with them, they'll have all their files alphabetized and we'll know everything about everyone there, right down to their sock size. He'll find out where all their people are now and have been all day. Agent Sterling said for you to call the sheriff and have him send someone out to back you up at your cabin while you get Mountain out and whatever things you need."

"Okay," I said. "I'll go get Mountain now. Then, while I'm out that way, I have an errand to run. Do I need a key to your place?"

"No," she said. "Remember? I have a heck of a time getting the front door to stay shut, and it won't lock even if it does. You know where it is, right?"

I nodded.

"Okay, then. I have to go check out this elk now. Whenever you get there, just make yourself at home. *Mi casa es su casa*."

When I called the sheriff's office, the dispatcher told me that there were no deputies available for a nonemergency assignment. Evidently an RV had overturned on the highway south of Taos, completely blocking traffic, and every available deputy was needed on the scene. I headed for my cabin, suddenly realizing that if someone were out to get me, they might harm Mountain. I drove at top speed, telling myself all the way that the wolf would be fine, that everything was going to be all right. As I turned off the gravel county road onto the long dirt drive that led up to my place, I felt an unaccustomed sense of fear, my eyes searching every rock and tree, scanning the forest behind my cabin, looking for any sign of danger in this place where I normally found peace and comfort.

Instead of hooking around and facing my Jeep out, as I normally did when I pulled up to the end of my drive, I checked my rearview mirror to make sure no one had followed me in, then parked the car facing the cabin. I turned off the motor, eased my automatic from the holster, and sat watching the house for any action. After a few moments, I got out of the Jeep, but I didn't bother to close the door. I raised my gun, pointing the barrel upward, and I braced the grip with both hands. Looking right and left, I made my way as quietly as I could across the porch. I saw Mountain looking out the window at me, wagging his tail, and I felt a weight drop away from my chest. I let out a huge sigh of relief, then looked once more to either side just to be sure. I opened the door. I was so happy to see that the wolf was all right, I almost didn't care that my cabin had been pillaged.

Mountain had been busy demolishing an assortment of my personal belongings. Angry that he didn't get to go with me that morning, and then eventually anxious over being "abandoned," he had chewed through a tube of body cream, smearing the contents of it across the hardwood floor in a trail from the bathroom to his lambskin rug beside my bed. He had also shredded a shower sponge, leaving a web of pink nylon netting stretched across the cabin floor. The wolf had turned over my laundry basket and rummaged through the contents, choosing those items that smelled most like me to bring to his bed, where he rolled on them, and—in the case of two pairs of my panties—chewed through them.

His destructive tendencies due to his abandonment anxiety were a long-standing problem that had developed soon after he took up residence with me as a tiny pup. But his behavior had improved over time, as he began to trust that my rare short absences would eventually end with my return and our reunion. For months now, an occasional few hours alone in the cabin had not resulted in a destructive episode—but today, he surprised me by reverting to his old habits. Given the events of the past few days, I decided to make little of his misbehavior. I set about cleaning up the mess while he huffed nervously and wagged his tail, his ears down, hoping for me to forgive him.

"It's okay, buddy," I said, as I took a damp rag to the floor and swabbed up the goop. "After I get this mopped up, we're going to go see Tecolote."

His ears stood up, recognizing the name I had spoken. He stopped panting and looked at me with excitement.

"Yes, we're going to see Tecolote. And then, after that, we're going to go on a little urban adventure."

◂ 15 ▸

The Milagro, the Saint, and the Bruja's Gift

The tiny hamlet of Agua Azuela nestled in the mountains above a cerulean stream that fed into the Rio Grande. The ancient village centered around a deep fold in the earth where seventeenth-century Spanish settlers had built an adobe church, then a wall around it for protection against the Apache and Comanche raiders. The few dozen homes of the local weavers and wood-carvers were dotted around the *santuario*. Beyond this, Anglos had begun to build larger homes tucked into the foothills, but the center of the community remained small and humble, and the one-lane dirt road that led through the village ended at the gates in the churchyard wall.

In the hills above the chapel, up a slender goat path, lived an old curandera named Esperanza. The villagers sought her out for removing warts, for healing from sickness or depression, for salves for wounds or scrapes, and for counsel on matters beyond the reach of the church or the medical services at the clinic down in Embudo. They called the old *bruja* Tecolote, which was the word for owl. Esperanza had engaged me with her visionary powers and trance-inducing teas and spells almost from our first meeting. She had given me aid and exhortation twice in life-or-death matters, and although her advice was often cryptic and confusing, I had learned to trust it.

Mountain and I hiked up the snowy slope along the goat path to Tecolote's tiny casita, and we found her—as we always did—waiting on the *portal* for us, as if she had known we were coming. She huddled in her woolen shawl, smiling, and when Mountain saw her, he bolted up the path and onto the *portal* to greet her. "Ah, Montaña," she said. "What a good, big boy you are! You are getting to be a *lobo grande*, no?" She patted the wolf vigorously on the rump, and he nosed at her apron. Tecolote cackled. "Okay, I see there is no way to fool a good, big boy like you. You know Esperanza has a treat for you!" She reached into her apron pocket and removed an object that looked like a ball of gooey twine. The wolf grabbed it eagerly and retreated to a corner of the *portal* and began tugging at one of the thin strands on the outer surface.

"What is that?" I asked, almost afraid to know.

"Those are *los tendones y los intestinos*. It's very good for him now, when he needs to stay home, not run off in the night."

This, too, was typical of Tecolote. She seemed to know things she had no plausible way of knowing. "Is it going to give him a stomachache? Because he just ate a lot of deer sausage the other day, and—"

She held up a gnarled hand to stop me. "Shhhhh, Mirasol." This was the name she called me. It meant sunflower in Spanish. "*El lobo* needs this, I assure you. Now, come inside. I made tea."

Tecolote's tiny adobe casita consisted of only one room. On one side was the hearth, which she used for cooking and heat, and above it was a thick adobe slab known as a shepherd's bed, upon which thin cotton bags filled with straw served as a mattress, and a thick woolen blanket was folded for her cover. I had never seen a pillow or sheets on this bed, nor could I see a place in her austere abode where they might be stored. For this reason, I felt sure that Esperanza would prize the deerskin pillow I had made and stuffed with the soft downy fur from the wolf's spring and autumn sheds.

I sat in one of the two stick chairs at the rough-hewn plank table while the bruja poured water into cups from a cast-iron kettle that hung from an iron hook directly over the fire. She set a small, deep bowl with no handle on the table, and the aroma of Indian tea, a wild plant that grew on the hillsides here in the spring, wafted from the steaming cup. I was thankful to recognize this potion, as it meant I was not being served a *cura*, which might have caused me to hallucinate or fall into a trance, as I had unexpectedly done in the past.

Tecolote took the chair opposite me and set her own bowl of tea before her. "It is good to see you, Mirasol," she said, smiling, her few brown teeth crooked against pink-white gums.

"It's good to see you, too, Esperanza. I brought you something." I opened my backpack, which I had set on the floor by my chair, and pulled out the small deerskin pillow. *"Feliz Navidad,"* I said.

Tecolote's eyes widened. "Ohhhhh!" she exclaimed, genuinely surprised and delighted. "Oh, Mirasol! What a beautiful *almohada para la cabeza!"*

"Yes, it's a pillow for your head. Merry Christmas."

Tecolote took the gift from me and held it at arm's length in her two hands. "It's so soft," she said. "It will be good for dreaming." She jumped to her feet and put the pillow on top of the folded blanket on her hard slab bed over the fire. She patted it to fluff it with her hand, then picked it up again and pressed it to her face. "You put a wild thing inside," she said.

I smiled. For once, I knew something Esperanza did not.

The old woman looked at me, cocking her head to one side, so that I could see the large hump on her back over the other shoulder. "You are not going to tell me?"

I smiled again and shook my head no.

She pushed her nose into the pillow and inhaled deeply. She lowered the pillow with a twinkle in her eye. "It is your hair."

I had to bite my lip to keep from spilling the truth. This was the only time I had ever had anything on the old bruja.

Tecolote drew her head back and looked down her nose at me, and then she smiled. "Ah," she said. "Ah." She turned and put the pillow back on the blanket and patted it again, then ran her hand over the smooth deer hide. I could tell she was overjoyed with the gift.

"You haven't guessed yet," I said, wanting the fun to continue.

Tecolote turned to the *nichos* in the wall to one side of her hearth, where she kept candles lit and small carved statues of saints known as santos. "I don't have to guess, Mirasol. I know."

"You're just saying you know," I teased.

She turned to face me with a little bundle in her hand. "You have given me something very precious, Mirasol," she said, her eyes engaging mine tenderly. "You have filled the *almohada* with the *pelo* of the one you love."

I smiled again. "*Sí,*" I said. "It's the wolf's hair. Isn't it soft and downy?"

She nodded. "*Sí,* it is very soft, very soft. As it turns out"—she smiled—"I have a little something for you as well." She extended her palm.

I took the bundle, which was made of woolly red cloth. It was tied with a piece of sinew. I took my knife off my belt and cut the tie and unfolded the cloth. Inside the red wrapper lay a tiny silver heart which seemed to have cracked into two pieces, with a jagged split right down the center. The two sides of the heart had been secured together with what looked like three turns of miniature silver barbwire. I pressed the tip of my finger on one of the petite barbwire points and felt a pinprick. I looked up at the curandera and smiled. "Is it a charm?"

She nodded her head. "*Sí,* it is a *milagro*."

"A miracle?"

"You are given a milagro for your particular ailment. Go into the church, say a prayer, pin the milagro onto a saint, and ask for a miracle to happen."

I felt my pulse quicken. This was one of Tecolote's patterns. She was giving me instructions that I didn't wholly understand, but I knew from experience that I soon would. The old bruja had mentioned "ailment," which meant that she saw something sickening or troubling me. Often her "sight" extended into the future or the past, and was not terribly time-specific, though typically dead-on in its accuracy in all other respects. I waited for Esperanza to say more, but she didn't.

"What church should I go into?" I tried. "The one here in Agua Azuela?"

Tecolote took our cups from the table, filled them with more tea, and then returned them.

"A church is a church," she said.

"What saint, then?"

She shrugged. Then she picked up her bowl and took some tea, slurping loudly.

"Speaking of saints, do you know of this one: San Pedro de Arbués?"

Tecolote stopped slurping and peered at me over the rim of her cup. She set it down on the table. "How do you know him?" she whispered.

I told her about my dismal night in the Indian boarding school, about the body of Cassie Morgan, and the howling wind and the sadness I felt seeping from the walls of that place.

"A long time ago, that one, he was a persecutor of *los judíos*, which many people over here called Los Marranos—that is a term referring to pigs."

I made a small gasp. "And they made him a saint?"

"He was a part of el Santo Oficio, the Inquisition. They used to force *los judíos* to convert, you know, against their will. It was very sad. This was near the time when the conquistadors came here. They did the same thing to *los indios*. It is a black stain living on the heart of the Church. They have not repented for any of these things, and so the stain lives and the heart slowly is dying."

"No wonder they named that horrible place after him."

"They say he was assassinated, and many people over here believe he was a torturer and assassin himself."

I felt a heaviness sinking over me. "Speaking of torturers . . ." I went on to tell the bruja about the mutilated elk cow and calf and the note with the calf's heart in my Jeep.

The old bruja listened to my tale without blinking an eye. When I had finished, she raised a bony finger with a yellowed, curving hook of a nail on the end. "Do you know what you must do, Mirasol?"

I shook my head.

"You must listen to the trees and you must also watch the sky." She wagged the finger back and forth for extra emphasis. "I advise you to treasure every gift you receive. Even if the thing, it seems small or insignificant, you must treasure it."

I looked at her, bewildered. How could this have any bearing on people leaving desecrated bodies in horrible places, or luring me out to the wild with tortured animals to take shots at me? I was shaking my head in confusion when the bruja went on.

"And, Mirasol: consider your own childhood for the lessons and strength it offers you even now." She struggled to her feet and picked up our teacups, even though mine was still full. She took them to the hearth.

Taking her cue, I got up to leave. Mountain was standing in the open doorway, wagging his tail, having devoured his gummy gift.

"If I don't see you before then," I said to the old woman, "Merry Christmas, Esperanza."

"I wonder," Tecolote said, "if you would be willing to do me a small favor?"

I didn't answer, wondering the same thing myself. Tecolote was not the type of person to whom you wanted to issue a blank check.

"I wonder if you would mind taking a gift to the sister at the mission church at Tanoah Pueblo?" She went to the doorway and reached behind the open door, where she had propped a gunnysack against the wall. She pulled out a long cardboard carton printed with faded colors and handed it to me. It was an old box with a cellophane window in the lid, through which I could see a puppet-doll dressed like a cowboy in jeans, a checkered shirt, boots with *HD* written on the sides, and a bandanna. The name of the doll was emblazoned on the lid in green lettering across the top: HOWDY DOODY. It was a vintage, unopened doll, probably from the 1950s, still in its original packaging.

"You want me to take this to the church at Tanoah Pueblo?"

"*Sí*. There is a sister who works there. It is a gift for her."

It seemed a harmless enough request. "Sure," I said. "This is probably very valuable now, something this old and never opened."

"It would have been very valuable when it was first made," she said. "It would have been *very* valuable then."

South Sioux City Public Library
2121 Dakota Avenue
South Sioux City, NE 68776

◂ 16 ▸

Suffer the Little Children

On the way back to Taos, I saw a Tanoah man limping alongside the road wearing a thin, tattered coat that was open in front, despite the cold. I recognized the fellow as I came closer. He was a known Taos drunk who had lost fingertips and toes to frostbite from exposure when he passed out inebriated more than once in previous winters. Because of the missing toes, balance was a problem for him, and he could not walk normally, which only enhanced his reputation as an alcoholic. I slowed as I passed him, then pulled onto the shoulder ahead of him to wait, partly because I knew the man to be harmless, but also because the BLM encouraged a Good Samaritan policy. Tom Leaves His Robe, a Vietnam veteran and a member of the Cloud Runner Clan at Tanoah Pueblo, staggered toward me, hurrying to accept shelter from the cold and a lift into town.

He opened the passenger door, leaning down to look in at me.

"Can I get a ride to town?" he asked. Then he glanced warily at Mountain, who had stood up in the cargo area of my Jeep and was eyeing the man with curiosity, his head bent low and forward in order to see better.

"Yeah, we're headed into Taos. Where are you going?"

"I got to go to my AA meeting. At that little church in El Prado."

I reached back and grabbed hold of Mountain's collar. "It's okay, Mountain," I said to the wolf. And to the man: "Come on, get in. My wolf won't hurt you."

The Indian slid tentatively into the passenger seat, watching over his shoulder as he did.

Mountain was on guard. He studied the new arrival, raised his nose and smelled the air and then sniffed at the man's long black and silver braid of hair, the threadbare collar of his coat.

Tom winced and dropped his head forward. "He is going to bite me!"

"Don't worry," I said. "Wolves are naturally shy of people. Mountain's already decided you're all right. He's just curious now."

Still leaning forward in the seat, Leaves His Robe reached across his body with his left hand to pull the door closed. Pinned between his right palm and three stubby, deformed fingers, he clutched a roll of yellow legal-pad sheets that were stained with blue ink and small, round water spots that looked as if they had been made by tears. "Did you give me a ride before, when I was drinking?"

"A couple of times. I want you to fasten your seat belt, okay?"

He twisted in the seat and grabbed the buckle with his left hand, then pulled it across his torso. After a few seconds of fumbling to latch the belt, he looked at me from under his dark eyebrows. "I don't drink no more."

I reached out a hand and helped snap the seat-belt buckle in place. I noticed that he didn't have his normal eighty-proof odor. "Going to AA now, huh?" I said.

He nodded. "Been sober seven months."

"That's great, Tom." I put the Jeep in gear and started driving.

"I had a lot of help. I could not do it alone. I got to go to my AA meeting to meet my sponsor. Today, I do my fifth step."

I had heard about fifth steps, a kind of peer confession that unburdened the soul. "Well, that's good, Tom. I can get you to the church."

"They told me I don't have to drink again if I don't want to."

I glanced at Leaves His Robe but didn't speak. I turned back to look through the windshield out across the giant rent in the land made by the Rio Grande. The earth had split in two and formed a deep, narrow gorge that cut across the high mesa west of Taos.

"Do I owe you money?" Leaves His Robe asked.

"No."

"I don't remember much about what I done. I used to drink to forget."

"Well, you don't owe me any money."

"I wanted to forget all the bad things," he said. "I done a lot of bad things. Some bad things happened to me, too—way back when I was a kid. I been trying to forget."

"So, did you forget? Is that why you're sober now?"

He turned and looked out the passenger window. "No, I tried to forget them," he muttered, "but I could not. Now I got to live with things how they are. I just don't got to drink no more."

"So, what's different now? I mean, if you can't forget the things that made you drink, how do you know you won't drink over them again?" There was an edge in my voice as I remembered my father, his shame-filled remorse during hung-over mornings, his countless broken promises that he would stop drinking.

"It is over now," Tom Leaves His Robe said. "It is all over. My sponsor says I got to make amends for what I done when I was drunk. People I hurt. That is why I ask you if I owe you money. If I do, I got to pay it back. And my sponsor says I got to talk about what happened. So it don't eat me up inside. He said maybe it will help somebody else, to talk about what happened to me."

I glanced at the Tanoah man, and his dark eyes met mine. I saw courage and sincerity and I felt ashamed that I had projected my anger at my dead father on what appeared to be a heartfelt attempt on this man's part to reclaim his broken life. I was almost afraid to ask. "What happened to you, Tom?"

"I had a hard time when I was a little kid. They used to come round up kids in the fall and take them to that school out there. When I got to be the right age, my mom tried to hide me, but they kept coming, and one day they found me and dragged me away. They would not let me go back home. I cried, I wanted my mom, my family. I wanted to go home. They cut our hair, they beat us to make us do things. It was real bad."

I shook my head with dismay. "I've been hearing a lot of stories about that school lately," I said.

Tom Leaves His Robe began to twist at the sheaf of yellow papers, his hands trembling. "It was bad the first few years, and I was real little. Small for my age. The big boys were mean to me." He cleared his throat and looked out the windshield. "Do you think you could turn the heat on?"

I adjusted the heat and turned up the fan. "For a little bit. I keep it cold for Mountain. But let's get you warmed up."

"Thank you. My coat don't close. The zipper is broke."

"How long were you at the boarding school, Tom?"

"Most all the time when I was a kid. I went to the army when I got out. That was in 1959."

"I'm sorry you had it so rough. But I'm glad you're sober now."

"When I was nine, the prefect made me sleep in his room."

I gasped, my mouth falling open.

Tom turned his head away from me and looked at the floor next to the passenger door. I heard him sniffling, and saw him trembling. I reached into the center console and pulled out a tissue. I placed it on his lap.

He didn't look at me, but he picked up the tissue and blew his nose. "He liked to beat me first with that thing they call cat claw. It had a lot of leather straps with metal spikes. He liked to do that first."

I blew air from my lips, as if there were pain from this story in my own chest that needed to be expelled. "Did you report him to anyone?"

Leaves His Robe still did not look up. "They would not let my mother come to visit me. And they would not let me go home. That woman who ran that school, I told her, and she told him I told her. He got me good for that. They had to sew me up after he done that."

I pulled over on the shoulder, my eyes full of tears. I could not seem to suppress the flow of sadness that poured from me, and I was crying. I put a hand on Tom's shoulder and gave it a squeeze. "I'm so sorry that happened to you, Tom," I said, through my own tears. "No one deserves that."

He looked at me. "You want me to get out here?"

"No! I just . . ." I put the Jeep in gear and pulled back onto the highway for fear he might get out of the car out of shame or embarrassment. "I just wanted to—"

"You should not feel so sorry for me. I done a lot of bad things over there in the war. I was real mad, and I done some real bad things. I just wanted to forget those things I done. My sponsor—he is a lot younger than me, but he went to the same school, so he understands."

We rode the rest of the way into town in silence. As Tom Leaves His Robe got out of the Jeep in front of the church, he suddenly pointed to a man going into the vestibule. "That one there. He is my sponsor."

I recognized Rule Abeyta, the Tanoah man from the governor's office who had flinched and then hurried away when the mission church bell rang.

"He and I—we found a way. Now, it is all over and I am free."

I turned around after dropping Tom Leaves His Robe at the church on the north side of Taos, and headed toward the setting sun and the Coldfire Ranch. Out on the high mesa, far enough away so that there would be no contamination from my scent, I stopped the Jeep and got out with my binoculars. A thin rim of vivid, vermilion light pulsed along the western horizon, the sky above an alluring azure aura as stunning as a gem. One small star winked through the blue, announcing the coming of night. My breath fogged in the cold, and I raised my field glasses to check the traps we'd set for the cougar and her cubs, the ground there already in shadow.

The traps were empty.

◂ 17 ▸

Luminarias and Landlords

When Mountain and I arrived at Diane's house to spend the night, our hostess was making up a bed in the spare room. I unrolled the wolf's lambskin on the floor, and set his pack and mine on the bed. "I didn't bring much," I said. "I hope we aren't putting you out."

"Nonsense. Glad to do it."

"I'm hoping it won't be for long. Mountain is going to miss the woods and being able to run. Besides, with Agent Sterling in town, you probably had plans."

"I was thinking I would hear from him tonight. It hasn't panned out yet, but the night is still young." She winked at me.

"Any news on the power company?"

"We got a list of their employees. Sterling sent it to Albuquerque, and they'll run the names through the FBI's database tomorrow. We should hear back in a few days."

"A few days?"

"I'm sorry. The data guys had already gone home by the time we got the list today. They'll start on it tomorrow, but I couldn't expedite it because it's technically just an animal mutilation crime at this point, and that's not a high-enough priority for overtime. Maybe we'll get lucky and they'll finish it fast."

I shrugged. "I guess we wait, then." I opened Mountain's pack and took out two collapsible dishes. "I have to get this wolf his dinner."

"Let's fix ourselves something to eat, too. My skunk of a landlord said he had someone out to fix that oven today. We can bake a couple potatoes, and I'll make a salad."

While Diane sliced cucumbers and tomatoes, I scrubbed two large spuds and pushed the tip of a paring knife into their sides, then placed them on the lower rack of the oven. I opened the broiler door at the bottom and watched as the pilot light danced in the back of the cavern for a few seconds, and then a procession of peacock blue flame flared along each of the two burner tubes. "It seems to be working," I said as I closed the metal door. I grabbed a bell pepper and began slicing it into thin rings.

"Good." Diane chopped a rib of celery into half-moons. "We'll get the salad ready and leave it in the fridge until the potatoes are done."

In the living room, Diane pointed to a spreading brown stain on the wall and the carpet in one corner. "That's from a leak in the roof," she said. "When snow builds up on the top, it slowly melts and runs down the inside of that wall."

"There has to be something you can do about your landlord," I said.

"Believe me, I've got some ideas. Unfortunately, none of them are legal. This guy seems to have the whole town in his hip pocket. I don't know if he bribes people or blackmails them. When the septic tank backed up in the yard, I called the health department. The so-called inspector said he came out and couldn't find anything wrong. I could go on, but you don't want to hear any more of my stories, Jamaica. It's too depressing."

"I'm sorry you're having such a hard time with the guy. I'm lucky. The man who owns my place lives up in Denver and I never see him. I fix things myself, but there's not much that goes wrong. And rent out there is cheap because no one wants to live so far from town."

Mountain, who had been lying on the carpet in front of the door since he'd finished his supper, suddenly rose to his feet and sniffed the air.

I sniffed, too. "Do you smell gas?" I said, and I yanked open the front door, letting the wolf out in front of me. "Where's the propane tank?" I called behind me as I ran out in search of the main gas valve.

While the house aired out, I talked Diane into coming out to see the luminarias along the adobe walls, roofs, and roadsides in Taos. We rode together in my Jeep, with Mountain in his customary place, filling up the cargo area created by folding down the backseat so that there was a large flat surface on which he could lie. This was the way he and I always traveled, and the wolf liked to lie as close to the front as possible, usually with his chin on the back of the passenger seat, or even on my shoulder, as I drove.

Along the edges of Lower Ranchitos Road for several miles, locals had lovingly placed *farolitos* every few yards on both sides of the road. These paper bags with sand in the bottom and a lit candle nestled in the center were there to light the way for the centuries-old neighborhood Christmas processions known as Las Posadas. Along the adobe walls and the rooftops of homes, more of these small paper bags, also known as luminarias, created a charming line of golden light outlining the contours of the earthen architecture.

At a humble neighborhood church, we saw a procession coming out the doors, a man escorting a woman, both of them wearing shawls over their heads, and a group behind them dressed as shepherds and wise men. "Look!" I said. "It's La Posada!"

We pulled over to watch as the cortege passed, singing in Spanish as they walked down the road, their breath making gossamer wisps of white as they rejoiced.

"What is this?" Diane asked.

"It's an ancient Hispanic tradition. For nine days preceding Christmas, members of the community play the roles of Mary, Joseph, the shepherds, and the wise men from the Christmas story. They travel from house to house as if they were seeking room at the inn. One home in the village will be designated as the host for the night, and will give shelter to the wanderers. There are special hymns and readings, and even delicious holiday treats associated with it. This custom came over from Spain in the 1500s, and all the little mountain villages here still celebrate La Posada in its authentic form."

"Wow," Diane said. "I never knew that."

It began to snow as we drove on, and a layer of white soon cloaked every surface. I felt my heart lightening a little from a long day of turmoil. "Look at that," I said. "The luminarias on that rooftop and adobe wall make such a soft light on the snow."

"It really is magical."

I looked at Diane with disbelief.

"What?" she said. "I can like the way it looks here, can't I? I like lots of things about Taos. I love the mountains, the art. They have great coffee. I just can't advance in my job, that's all. And I have a jackass for a landlord. Tomorrow, I'm going to have to do something about him. I'll file a complaint in the local court, I guess."

In the plaza in Taos, we stopped to buy enchiladas from a street vendor who had stayed after dark to capitalize on the after-mass crowd pouring out of the Catholic Church nearby. Farolitos were lit throughout the small central square in a pattern of concentric circles. Buildings surrounding the plaza boasted strings of electric luminarias along the rooflines. While Mountain sat and watched the passersby, Diane and I perched on a park bench, the snow falling around us and building up on our hats and the shoulders of our coats, as we ate the enchiladas from paper cartons and sipped cups of steaming Mexican hot chocolate.

"I have to admit," Diane said, waving her spoon in the air for emphasis, "all this is pretty enchanting. But it could be so good for my career if I got transferred to someplace where my talents would be noticed. I talked to the Silver Bullet about that just briefly today."

"So the Silver Bullet's name is Agent Sterling. What's his first name?"

"I don't know. I don't think anyone knows."

I laughed. "I looked at the card he gave me the other morning after he questioned me. It just said: 'Agent Sterling, FBI.' That was it. And then it listed his contact information."

Diane laughed, too. "The Mystery Man. I'll see what I can find out."

I picked up the cup of hot chocolate that I'd set on the bench beside me. I felt the warmth of the liquid through the cup and thought of Tom Leaves His Robe with his coat that wouldn't close. "On the way into town this afternoon, I gave a ride to a guy who used to go to that boarding school. Seems like everyone I've talked to at Tanoah Pueblo lately has a tale to tell about it. And the stories are all so sad."

Diane was quiet.

"How is the murder investigation going?"

"I don't have much to report," she said. "There aren't any forensic specialists this side of Albuquerque, and we don't have state-of-the-art labs and technology here. People watch those television shows, and then they think we have endless resources and personnel to put on every crime we come across, but that's not the case. We haven't been able to pinpoint the exact date of death. Without knowing when Cassie Morgan died, there is no way to establish who might or might not have had an opportunity or an alibi. So we have to go on motive."

"You have a motive?"

"A revenge motive involving a former boarding school resident seems likely. Especially with the nature of the crime. We've begun interviewing some of the former residents at the school, looking for a suspect."

I thought of Sica Gallegos, her legs crippled from the beating she had received from Cassie Morgan. And I thought of the broken spirit of Tom Leaves His Robe, who had sought Morgan's support when he was being abused, only to suffer worse for having done so. I suddenly felt sick to my stomach, and I turned my face up and let the cold snow fall on my cheeks and my chin.

"How are you coming with your mountain lion?" Diane asked.

I shook my head. "No sign of her so far. Or the cubs." I felt a wave of sadness move through me. A gust of wind rippled through the plaza, and all at once the farolitos in their carefully made circles flickered and their flames died, the brown paper bags wet with snow collapsing with the force of the gale onto the candles and snuffing out their light.

18

The Church

The next morning, I drove to the pueblo before sunup, as Momma Anna had requested. Tanoah Pueblo was observing old ways for the week of the Solstice through the Epiphany on the sixth of January, and members of the tribe were discouraged from driving during these times. So Momma Anna had requested that I bring my Jeep to help transport the bultos, the large carved and painted figures of the Holy Family, to their home for the holidays with Sica Blue Cloud Gallegos and her family. It was of no apparent concern to her that a motorized vehicle would be used for this chore, so long as a member of the tribe did not drive it.

When she got in the passenger seat, Momma Anna pulled her blanket from her head and turned to look at Mountain, who wagged his tail ecstatically to see her. "You maybe move that wolf one side," she said to me. "He take up the whole back now."

"As long as we put the bultos in the very back, Mountain will stay up close to the front, and it won't bother him. I put things back there all the time."

My medicine teacher turned to pat the wolf and gave him a little smile. "You ride with Joseph," she told him. "You maybe get be a saint, too," she chuckled. "Saint wolf."

I laughed out loud at this idea.

At the old mission church inside the perimeter wall of the historic part of Tanoah Pueblo, I parked my Jeep in front of the gates to the churchyard, which also had its own low adobe wall around it. Momma Anna pulled her blanket over her head as she was getting out of the Jeep, and—because I had learned from past experience to do so—I pulled a blanket over my shoulders and my long blonde locks as well, leaving my hat in the driver's seat of the car. Inside the door of the small, dark church, Momma Anna stopped to touch the holy water with the tips of her fingers and press them to her forehead, where she made the sign of the Christian cross. I looked around me at the narrow nave with its dark cottonwood pews, the garishly painted images of the stations of the cross on the wall, a carved image of the Virgin Mary in a large nicho behind the altar. In a long box of sand, candles were burning already, indicating that members of the Tanoah tribe had come to pray even before morning mass.

A small figure hurried to us down the center aisle. She was dressed in a black habit with a short black veil. "Mrs. Santana," she said. "It is so good to see you! Good morning, good morning, and God bless you."

Momma Anna turned and opened a palm to include me in the conversation. "This my daughter, Jamaica," she said.

The sister smiled and reached out a stubby palm. "Good morning. How do you do? I'm Sister Florinda Maez. I oversee things here at Nuestra Señora de la Purísima Concepción."

I took her hand and smiled in return. "Jamaica Wild. Forgive me, my Spanish is limited. Our Lady of the Immaculate Conception?"

She nodded, still smiling. "Very good. That is the official name for this Catholic mission here at Tanoah Pueblo. I divide my time between here and San Lorenzo de Picurís, at Tanoah's sister pueblo."

"It's good to meet you," I said. "There's no priest here, then?"

"No. There is a priest part-time at Taos Pueblo, where they have a larger congregation. He consecrates the sacrament for us and hears confession once a month, and of course performs marriages and other ceremonies. But we have a strong lay community here who help to perform the other duties of the church."

Momma Anna had moved away from our conversation immediately after the introductions, and she was kneeling at the altar. She rose now and turned to Sister Florinda. "We take Holy Family to their good place."

"Yes," Sister Florinda said. "They are all ready out here in the vestibule. The wise men, the shepherds, Joseph, and of course, Our Lady."

"But isn't that Mary in the nicho behind the altar?" I asked, pointing at the large bulto.

Momma Anna scowled at me for the question, but Sister Florinda responded kindly. "Our church is named for Nuestra Señora. She is our patron saint. We cannot leave this church unprotected by Her grace and light, and so a *santero* from Chimayó has carved a second bulto for ceremonies such as this, when Her presence is required beyond the church's physical walls."

In the small, dark entry, Momma Anna pointed at a large carving and grunted, "You take."

I started toward the bulto.

"You come back," Momma Anna said, "bring those blanket I bring. And wrap him in blanket, make sure he is safe."

As I picked up the carving, I turned to the nun. "Did this church have anything to do with the San Pedro de Arbués Indian School?"

Both women bristled when I said this. Sister Florinda put a hand on my shoulder, turning me toward the entrance. "That was a long time ago, my dear," she said, as she pushed open the door.

I brought back the stack of thin blankets when I returned from the Jeep so Momma Anna could wrap the rest of the statues before I took them out. "So this church was involved with the school?" I said.

Florinda Maez gave me a look of resignation. "Yes, this church was involved with the school. The whole diocese supported it, along with the Bureau of Indian Affairs."

"Do you know what role this particular church may have played?" I pressed.

Momma Anna shoved another bulto into my arms. "Take," she ordered.

When I returned for the next statue, Sister Florinda had disappeared, presumably back into the dark recesses of the nave. Momma Anna was tenderly wrapping several small figures of shepherds and their sheep into one large blanket. I peered in toward the altar and was surprised when the sister approached me from behind. "Why do you ask so many questions about the Indian school?" she said.

"I don't know," I admitted. "It has made its way into my life, and I'm trying to discover its meaning."

"May I give you a little advice, from a poor sister of the cloth?" she said.

"Sure," I answered, not buying her false humility. I knew a lecture was forthcoming.

"I advise you to leave well enough alone and stay out of the business of the church and the Indians. There is still much healing to be done, but it must be done by the parties involved, and you cannot change that. God knows what He is doing, Miss Wild."

As I was loading the last figure into my Jeep, I remembered the gift from Tecolote. I reached under the folded-down seat, where I had placed the Howdy Doody doll on the floor so Mountain could not smash or chew on it. I helped Momma Anna into the passenger seat, and then hurried back into the church with the gift.

"Sister?" I called as I came back in the door.

The nun turned and came back up the aisle from the altar. "Yes? What is it?"

"An old curandera from Agua Azuela named Esperanza told me to bring this to you."

Sister Florinda Maez looked down at the proffered package with alarm. "What is that?"

"It's a doll, I think."

"Is this a joke?"

"A joke? No, why? Esperanza asked me to give this to you."

The sister reached with two hands and sternly straightened the sides of her veil. "I don't know anyone of that description. I'm afraid I cannot accept the gift. We take vows of poverty, you know, and that is no doubt of some value. Please return it with my apologies."

"But—"

"And now, if you will please leave, I have to prepare for morning mass." She pressed her hand against my shoulder once more, turning me toward the door, and walked behind me, still pushing lightly against my back until I was through the entry doors.

"I don't understand," I said.

But Sister Florinda Maez did not answer. Instead, she closed the chapel doors right in front of me, without uttering another word.

When Momma Anna and I arrived at the Gallegos home, the sun was up and the day was already proving to be warmer than its predecessor. Snow had melted and the packed dirt plaza of Tanoah Pueblo had turned to mud. "Rather than both of us tracking dirt into Sica's house," I said, "why don't you go on inside, and I'll carry the bultos to the door and hand them in to you?"

My medicine teacher nodded, approving this plan. She took the first bundle and headed toward Sica's doorway while I grabbed another, larger statue and then lowered the hatch. "You stay," I said to Mountain. "This won't take long. Stay."

I approached the Gallegos home right behind Momma Anna, who had plodded slowly around the mud puddles. We got to Sica's door just as Rule Abeyta was hurrying out of it with something in his hands. He and Anna almost collided, and Rule looked up at us with a start. He dropped a small carved figure, then hurriedly picked it up and tucked it under his blanket. He nodded respectfully to Momma Anna. "I told this old auntie we needed to move the *monito,*" he said. "This looks bad for Sica." Rule Abeyta walked briskly past us and on toward the small río that ran through the center of Tanoah Pueblo.

I turned to Momma Anna and tried to think how to ask what the "monito" was, but I knew better than to phrase it as a question. Before I could find a way to pose the query, Eloy Gallegos spoke from the doorway, "Hurry up, you two. Get inside. It's cold out there, and Auntie Sica wants us to close the door."

◂ 19 ▸

Over the Edge

I took Mountain with me and again rode the Coldfire/BLM land boundary in my Jeep to check on the traps that Charlie Dorn and I had set on the previous day. I prayed we would catch the cougar family so we could ensure the mother would live. Without her to hunt for them, the cubs would die. The day was warming nicely, but a strong wind was stirring out of the southwest as the sun rose higher in the sky and the cool air dissipated. When I got to the lookout I'd used previously, I scoped the traps once more with field glasses and found them still empty, the meat lures intact. I hoped the warmth of the day would permit the smell of the meat to spread and perhaps entice the cats to the cages.

Again, I scanned the horizon with my field glasses. On an impulse, I decided to drive my Jeep toward Pueblo Pena as far as the terrain would permit and then hike in the rest of the way. I knew from my chase after the ATV that there was a long finger of land I could take to the south for a half mile, and so I struck out driving in that direction.

We left the Jeep on the finger mesa and started hiking, the wolf and I both wearing our packs. Mountain was delighted to be out in open country after so much time spent confined in the Jeep. As we moved to the southwest, a series of fierce gusts whipped across the high desert, pushing against us. At first, I watched for sign of the cougars, even though I felt sure the cats would be in a cave on the other side of the little spring. Eventually, I admitted to myself that I wanted to see the cemetery that Lorena Coldfire had spoken of visiting each year on the Day of the Dead. There was something about the abandoned boarding school that still haunted me, even after Cassie Morgan's remains had been carried off to the morgue.

Outside the wall, behind the school, I saw a pair of tilted stones that might once have been grave markers. On further examination, I could see the outline of several small raised mounds of earth in a row, the telltale signs of graves. I stopped to give Mountain water from the tube of my CamelBak and then took a drink myself. I studied the ground and tried to discern the scope of the school cemetery. A section of downed barbwire in withered ricegrass hinted at a forgotten fence line. Using that as one perimeter, and the back wall of the schoolyard as another perpendicular one, I walked out from the adobe wall and searched for the farthest limits of the graveyard. These were not readily apparent, but the more I examined the area, the more the land revealed to me. I made out five distinct rows where the ground had been groomed in some way, probably by the digging of graves. I walked the length of the row that had been the least disturbed by the ravages of wind, the one next to the schoolyard wall. I counted twenty-three berms, some more obvious than others. Twenty-three!

Five rows of twenty-three, possibly even more, a design for twenty-five? Five rows! Over one hundred children had died at the San Pedro de Arbués Indian School!

Against a clump of cactus, a hint of something red fluttered in the wind. I went to examine it and found a petal from a fabric flower stuck in the spines of the cactus. This, no doubt, was left over from the loving vigil that Lorena Coldfire made on the Day of the Dead, when she came to bring food and offerings to these forgotten children.

I decided to look for the ancient stone staircase that Scout Coldfire had spoken about, with the two shrines on the ledge below. Mountain had found a shady spot next to the adobe wall and had parked himself out of the wind. I called to him, and he joined me, and we headed toward the canyon rim near Pueblo Pena.

Following Scout's directions, I located a series of large boulders at the lip of the canyon. These marked the meager path leading down, and—as instructed—I worked my way carefully around the big stones, on a packed-earth ledge not twelve inches wide that slanted at a precarious pitch. This short, steep trail led to a silty shelf under the cliff lip. Mountain followed me with an unaccustomed trepidation, carefully placing his paws almost in single file, unsure whether he wanted to proceed, but drawn by the code that said we always traveled together. We cautiously descended to the ledge. Above us, the lip of the canyon jutted out more than two feet, creating a concave bowl in the cliff face beneath it. I stepped carefully to the edge of the narrow terrace and looked down as a gust of raw wind sandblasted my skin.

Below, on the sheer side of the canyon wall, I found the pecked-out hand- and footholds leading down the stone face to the bottom, a nerve-wracking way down at best. I imagined the ancient ones who had made these, the daring and determination that were required to dangle off the face of a sheer cliff wall and chip away at it with stone tools. Above, these amazing people had built a stone city on the high rim of a canyon, a place from which they could see and be seen for miles around. And below, in this wide rent in the earth, lay the life-giving river. As I stood looking down into the canyon, I thought of when Momma Anna had told me about the hole in the top of everything, how the People came up through the hole in the Indigo Falls, how the Creator breathed life into a baby through the hole in the top of her head, how the spirits traveled in and out of all things material through the hole in the top. And I saw this canyon as perhaps the ancients did, as a hole or crack in the land from which the Earth's spirit came forth. Perhaps the spirits of the ancient ones still traveled up and down this primitive stone stairway, up and down the hand- and footholds from the source to the place where they could see all the way to the horizon.

As I returned to the present from my glimpse into the past, Mountain stood watching me, unsure what we were going to do next. It was obvious to him that we'd reached the end of the trail. "Hang on, buddy," I said. "I want to look at these." I pointed at two short stacks of stones a few feet apart under the narrow rock overhang. These were certainly the two little shrines that Coldfire spoke of. I knelt in the dust and looked closely at the cairns. Bits of leather thong and withered feathers peeked between the stones, the remnants of offerings of beauty and honor. One tiny turquoise bead nestled in a recess of one of the stacked stones. I remembered Sica's story of the two little Apache boys and felt certain that these cairns marked their secretly made graves. Who had been coming here and leaving offerings?

Mountain came to see what was drawing my attention and then suddenly stopped, eyeing the ground in front of him. A slender snake seemed to be sunning in the dirt at the edge of the shelf, but the reptile didn't move.

"Hold on, Mountain," I said, rising to my feet. "You stay." I approached slowly, only to find that it was not a snake at all, but rather a piece of nylon rope. I picked it up and shook off the dust. It was new-looking, knotted and burned at each end to prevent fraying, a strand perhaps three feet in length, at best.

As I held up my find to examine it, a sprinkling of grit and gravel pattered on my hat brim. Then more, a frantic tap dance of tiny bits of sand and granules, a storm of mineral debris. I looked up just as an avalanche of rock and red soil rushed toward me. Pebbles, sand, and sediment bombarded my neck and back. A large rock struck the top of my head, producing a shooting pain down my spine, then another—a jarring smack on my shoulder, and another—a whack on the hip. And more like that, lambasting my back, hammering at the tops of my buttocks, my arms, my legs. Shards of the cliff edge pounded down on me, and then basketball-sized boulders began to fall. I threw myself under the slim stone protrusion, and hard into Mountain, who was now cowering against the cliff wall. The backs of my legs took a beating as showers of shale and chunks of rock and sandstone pummeled the parts of my body exposed beyond the overhang. One great stone the size of a beach ball struck the shelf next to my heel after it shredded the back of my jeans and stripped the skin from my calf.

When the slide subsided, I stood frozen in place by fear and pain, still stunned from the blow to my head. Mountain, trapped between my body and the indent in the cliff wall, had escaped harm, but he, too, seemed to be in shock, as he didn't try to escape the confinement of my body's weight pressing on him. My shoulder, back, and legs felt as if someone had skinned them and salted the wounds. My head throbbed from the blow it had taken before I'd ducked under the rim. Even my jaw hurt, as if the impact of the rock against my skull had compressed everything from the crown down. As I pulled myself off him, Mountain stepped warily over the rubble of the slide. I looked down at the back of my right leg and saw the source of the unbearable stinging that struggled to compete with the pain in my head. A rash of long, red streaks and shredded flesh speckled with grit covered the surface of the leg. The heel of my boot leather had been sliced away, exposing a circle of green sock that had somehow managed to remain intact over the back of my foot.

Mountain led as we struggled our way back to the top, where the boulders I had carefully stepped around no longer graced the rim. While the wind buffeted my body, I examined the place where the stones had once stood. I saw scrapes in the sandstone where someone had levered the big rocks and deliberately started the slide.

I stood up and looked around. My attacker could easily be hiding behind the ruin wall a hundred yards away, waiting to ambush me again. I felt vulnerable standing on high ground in the open, and I called Mountain to me and made my way to the north, away from the ruin, and then back to my Jeep as fast as my bruised body could go.

20

Wild Life

Diane helped me to clean my wounds and sat on the floor to apply antibiotic ointment to the backs of my legs with a cotton swab. "You didn't see anyone? You didn't hear anything?" she said.

"The wind was coming right at me. Whoever it was used that to their advantage."

"But you can see forever out there."

"I didn't see anyone. They must not have gotten close until I was down on that ledge. Ouch! Be careful."

"Sorry. This is twice you've been out on that mesa since you discovered the body, and both times . . ."

"Yeah. Somebody's either following me or hanging around out there, and they don't like it when I get close."

"But why? I mean, why hang around and risk getting caught?"

I held up a finger. "Wait until you see what I've got." I started to walk away.

"Hey, where are you going? I'm not done yet. You've still got a—"

"I'll be right back. I have something in my pack I need to show you." Wearing only my panties and bra and a virulent red rash of scrapes and bruises, I limped out of the bathroom and then came back holding the length of nylon rope with a pair of tweezers. "Look what Mountain found on that little terrace under the canyon rim."

Diane's mouth gaped open as she got to her feet. "Nylon rope?"

"The real deal," I said. "Look at this brown stuff embedded in the middle, too. It looks like it could be dried blood. I'm sorry I didn't have an evidence bag or anything. I zipped it into its own pocket in my backpack and have tried not to touch it."

She took the rope carefully by one knotted end and held it up to the light. "Here," she said, picking up a pair of soft sweatpants off the bathroom counter. "Put these on. I'm going to call the Silver Bullet. This rates some overtime."

While Diane took the nylon rope to her office—where a courier with an evidence bag had been dispatched to wait, bag the item, and then drive it to the lab in Albuquerque—Mountain and I spent a miserable hour unable to relax and rest.

I began to feel the beating I'd taken in the avalanche as soon as I slowed down. There was no way to be comfortable with my backside skinned and stinging. I tried lying on my belly on the couch, but my shoulder and neck ached unbearably, and I couldn't do anything to distract myself while lying prone. I was too wary to sleep, my mind whirling over the events of the past few days trying to discover new evidence that would make sense of my situation.

Worse still, my normally isolated and monastic lifestyle made me ill-suited to be at ease when I heard people moving outside, the noise of sirens—and even the crash of a car accident at a nearby intersection, which caused both me and the wolf to jump with fright. At my cabin, the sound of a car engine meant an imminent visitor. The din of traffic here at Diane's house was constant, and Mountain sprang to his feet dozens of times, expecting to greet—or challenge—someone at the door. Even the sound of children shrieking with laughter as they rode past on bicycles grated on both our nerves.

By the time Diane returned from her office, Mountain had taken to pacing back and forth across the living room looking out one window and then another, and I had figured out a way to roost on the rim of the couch and was cleaning my handgun on a towel spread across the coffee table.

"I thought you were going to get some rest," she said.

"Where's the Silver Bullet?"

"He's working a lead. He'll be over later. Let's see if our salad we made last night is still any good." She headed for the kitchen.

"So what are you going to do about the landlord and the oven?"

"I found out about a tenants' rights agency in Santa Fe and called them. It turns out I do have rights as a tenant. But I have to take my landlord to court and get the judge to enforce the law."

A siren sounded nearby and Mountain erupted into a throaty howl. Diane came to the door of the kitchen and watched him, amused. I began to howl along with the wolf, to show my sympathy for his misery—and mine. Diane joined in, and for almost five minutes, we yipped and howled like a regular pack.

About ten minutes after that, a police car pulled up in front of the house, and an officer came to the door. Diane answered, Mountain came to peer around her, and I looked over her shoulder. I recognized the patrolman from a recent incident involving a youth from Tanoah Pueblo.

"We've got a complaint of disturbing the peace," the uniform said.

"What?" Diane bristled.

"How ya doing?" I reached through the opening between Diane and the door frame and extended my hand. "Jamaica Wild, BLM. We had a chance to work together just a few weeks ago when a young man from Tanoah Pueblo—"

"Oh, yeah." He smiled. "I remember you. Thanks for helping us out on that."

"No problem, Officer. And we're sorry we got a little carried away there with our group howl, but we'll keep it down from now on."

"That's a big dog," he said, eyeing Mountain with curiosity.

"I'll keep him quiet," I said. "He's just not used to being in town."

Diane looked at me, then at the patrolman. "I'd like to know who made the complaint."

The policeman started to turn back toward his car. "Just a neighbor, ma'am. If you'll promise to keep it down, that'll be the end of it."

That night, I went to bed early and tried to sleep, but with the highway through town less than a half mile away, the sound of the traffic kept me on alert. I tried lying on my stomach, then on my side, but I couldn't get comfortable. My legs, my shoulder, even my neck hurt. As I stared at the four walls of the small bedroom, I began to feel confined. My cabin, with its one big room, seemed expansive by comparison. I grabbed my sidearm and clipped the holster onto the sweatpants Diane had loaned me, wrapped myself in a blanket, and snuck down the hallway with Mountain on his lead. Beneath the door to Diane's room, I could see a wedge of yellow light, and I heard her muffled voice through the door—she must have been talking on the phone. I took Mountain out the front door with me in hopes of finding a quiet place to sit and watch the stars. But tall power poles topped with mercury vapor lights on either side of the yard created too much light pollution, and the stars were invisible. I wasn't sure I could sit for long anyway, with the stinging scrapes on my backside.

I unlocked my Jeep and put the blanket in the driver's seat. I reached beneath the folded-down seat in the back for a jacket I kept there. On top was the box with the Howdy Doody doll, and I pulled it out and set it in the passenger seat, then groped around the back-seat floor until I felt the soft fleece of the jacket. I tugged on the sleeve to pull the garment out, then put it on and zipped it up against the cold. Mountain and I walked down the street past a few run-down adobes to the end of the road, where a new-looking sign stood at the edge of a wide dirt lot. It read:

BACA LAND DEVELOPMENT COMPANY

As I walked around the sign, Mountain hiked a hind leg and marked it. I nodded my approval. "Some people have more money than brains," I said out loud to the wolf. "There's not enough water here to develop this place any more." My companion paid me no heed as we crossed the field, headed in the direction of the Taos Armory. I knew there was a stretch of open sage flat behind the armory, and it was the closest patch of natural ground I could think of.

Once we were out on the flats, I could see the stars. Not as well as at my place, but at least they were there. I inhaled cold air and smelled the pungent scent of the sage. I blew out my breath with relief. Mountain scampered along in the scrub, and the two of us struck out across the big, open stretch of land. I took long strides, and I felt the scrapes on my backside stinging as I stretched the skin. Two coyotes came near to playfully taunt Mountain and attempt to lead him on a chase through the sagebrush. The wolf darted after them, and they began a game of hide-and-seek. But Mountain would only go a dozen yards or so, and then he would return to me, making sure he kept tabs on where I was.

A hundred yards into the brush, the crack of gunshot sounded and one of the coyotes yelped and flipped into the air, landing on the dirt with a thud. I drew my gun and ducked. Mountain slithered to my side and trembled. I shouted, "Federal agent! Cease fire!"

A man's voice shouted back from the darkness, "There's no law against killing a coyote!"

"I am an armed federal agent. You will cease fire now or be considered armed and dangerous."

There was silence for nearly a minute, as I looked around for an escape route. And then the voice called back: "Coyotes killed my dog, and I'm going to kill every one of them I see."

I took Mountain by the collar and moved to better cover behind some piñon and juniper, staying low as we moved along a line of vegetation until we were a safe distance away. Then, Mountain and I made our way back to Diane's house. I couldn't believe that someone had chanced to be hunting for coyotes in the same field where Mountain and I had walked that night; the whole idea troubled me. But I was at least grateful that the wolf wasn't shot instead of the coyote.

As I was about to open the front door of Diane's house, I glanced in the window and saw the Silver Bullet standing in the living room. I was feeling cold and stressed, and I paused for a moment thinking of polite ways to bypass him and go straight to bed. I suddenly remembered the blanket I'd pulled off of the guest bed and then left in the car, and went back to the Jeep to get it, still keeping Mountain close on his lead. When I got back to the door, I saw the Silver Bullet through the window again, this time with his back to me. He was reaching in front of him, and I looked more closely. Diane was standing with her back to him with her hands high on the wall and her legs spread apart. Agent Sterling was pretending to frisk Diane, thoroughly searching her torso for an imaginary weapon.

"Come on, Mountain," I said, as I headed for the Jeep with the blanket in one hand and the wolf's leash in the other. I got in the back of the car with Mountain, moving gingerly as I curled up on my side under the blanket, spooning him, my chest pressed into his back. We would have to keep each other warm and wait until the two lovers inside were through with their tryst. But the Howdy Doody doll in the passenger seat seemed to be looking at me and I was too disturbed to sleep. I could have gotten out and shoved it under the seat again, where I couldn't see it. But it was cold outside, and I was sore and tired and it hurt to move. Besides, I much preferred to face whatever trouble there was, rather than have it lurking somewhere unseen.

◂ 21 ▸

Four-Legged Trouble

I woke in the morning feeling painfully sore and stiff. It took me several tries to get out of the bed in Diane's guest room, and when I finally got myself upright, I felt as if my back had fused in a bent-over position. I had to work hard to get my hips and legs to flex and move properly. I grunted and groaned as I pulled on the sweats my hostess had loaned me, gasped as I bent over to tie my boots, then forced myself to walk to the kitchen to start the coffeemaker. I took Mountain outside on his long lead to do his morning business. The frost from overnight coated the duff around Diane's house, and I felt the cold seep into my aching joints. Once I was up and moving around, I wanted a shower, but the idea of taking off my boots, undressing, and then dressing again dissuaded me. I settled for the plan of washing my face at the sink, but as I reached my arms up to brush my long hair and tie it back in a ponytail, I realized that nothing was going to be easy for a while; I was too bruised and beat up.

Diane and I drank coffee and ate bowls of cereal in the kitchen. "The Silver Bullet was here last night," she said. "You were asleep so we didn't bother you. But he said the power company is checking out clean so far. Nobody with anything more than a traffic violation."

"I don't know how whoever it was got my number, then. The guy called right after I phoned the power company."

"Who knows? We're still checking everybody, but Agent Sterling doesn't think that's where the perp is. Maybe someone at the BLM gave out your number."

I thought for a minute about that. "Roy says he didn't."

"Someone else there, maybe?"

"I guess it's possible. It's posted on a list on the bulletin board in the back."

"Maybe someone called asking for you and a clerk or something gave them the number."

"Maybe. I mean, everyone knew I didn't carry the darn thing, but . . . I think I'll go home, then."

Diane looked at me with wide eyes. "No, you ought to stay here. Or go stay with Kerry. Whoever this is knows too much about you."

"Kerry lives in housing at the ranger station. He can't have a wolf there. Now that you've checked out the power company, I need to get my electricity back on. I need to clean the rotten food out of my fridge."

"I don't think you ought to."

"Kerry's back from training in Albuquerque today. I'll ask him to stay with me."

Diane studied me a moment. "Okay, if you'll have him stay. At least there's some safety in numbers."

• • •

I used Diane's phone, rather than the Screech Owl, to call the service number at the power company. When a real live man answered, I was delighted. He seemed sincere. "We sent someone out to see about the power yesterday but they couldn't find your house. You have to put a sign at the end of your road that has your name and meter number on it and then we'll send someone out again."

I thought for a moment. "How about if I just put the words 'Power Company' with my meter number on it, so they will know they're at the right place?"

"That would probably do."

"Can you send someone back out today?"

"Oh, no. He's out of range now. You know, radios, cell phones, they don't work out there. We'll have to send him back to do your house next time out. But we're going to take care of you once we find you, don't you worry."

As I was putting Mountain in the back of my Jeep, preparing to leave for home, the same officer from the police department who had come about the howling noise pulled up in front of Diane's house. I walked over to greet him. "We're not making any noise here today, Officer," I said, smiling.

He got out of his car with a piece of paper in his hand. "We're helping out the sheriff's department with some service of papers today."

Diane came out on the front porch to see what was going on.

"I'm sorry to be the one to tell you, ma'am," the policeman said. "Your landlord has filed a notice to evict."

The weather had changed and it was a relatively warm day with plenty of sunshine. Back at my cabin, I hiked with Mountain to La Petaca for water. It took five trips to fill my two big black shower bags with buckets of water from the icy stream. I propped the bags at an angle against an outcropping of moss rock to warm in the sun. Next, I used my water buckets to carry smooth river stones from La Petaca to make a floor for a shower among the pines. I planned to enjoy this treat later in the day, once the water in the bags had absorbed some solar heat.

While I was wiping down the inside of the refrigerator, Mountain began begging to go for a walk, and this after our many trips back and forth to the stream. He paced back and forth to the door. "Hang on, bud," I said. "I have some chores to do. I can't walk you any more right now."

But the wolf pawed at the door, scratching at the wood.

"Mountain, no!" I said.

He pulled at his leash and toppled the coatrack, knocking over the broom that stood in the corner behind the door.

"Darn it, Mountain!" I yelled. "I'm busy right now. You already had some time romping in the woods when I was getting water."

But the wolf would not give up. He bolted across the room and then back to the door, as if to say how urgently he needed to go outside.

I looked at him with skepticism. "Are you telling me you have to go?" I asked. "I don't believe you. You were outside half the morning." But just to be sure, I put the wolf outside—fastened to his airplane wire and carabiner restraint—while I went back in the house to do my chores.

I finished cleaning the fridge, emptied the trash—including the mess of things that Mountain had destroyed when I had left him alone the other morning—and I cleaned the ashes out of the woodstove. Just as I headed outside for wood to lay a new fire, Mountain lunged on his line and snapped the carabiner, breaking loose. He raced toward the woods like a bullet, where a pair of coyotes were chasing after a young deer. The hunt immediately led into the forest.

I ran after Mountain, screaming: "Mountain, no! Mountain! Mountain, no, come here!" My legs stung and ached at the same time, the bruises and scrapes from the avalanche still painfully sore. It was no use. I couldn't keep up.

I stopped in a patch of pines where a mottling of shade and sunlight fell on my face, and I winced with pain as my scraped skin stung. I remembered my rancher neighbor's warning, and my spirit sank. I turned and walked back to the cabin, stepping gingerly on the right leg, feeling a pressure in my chest, as if tiny strands of silver barbwire were tightening around my heart.

In the shed out back, I found a length of heavy iron chain that the landlord had left on the property. Using a pair of channel locks, I worked to secure it to the solid stainless steel eyebolt that I had sunk six inches into the foundation of my cabin.

Nearly an hour later, Mountain returned, tired and happy, his tail wagging with the excitement of his adventure. I received him with a hug and I cried as I held him next to my chest. I took hold of his collar. "Oh, Mountain," I wailed, my nose running, my chest heaving as I sobbed. I hooked the wolf to the heavy chain, blubbering as I did so. "I can't trust you to run free anymore, buddy," I bawled. "You don't stay with me anymore when I let you run free. You don't come to me when I call you."

The wolf sat watching me, confused at my emotions. He was obviously happy to see me and had no understanding of the significance of this moment in his short life—this moment when I chose to take away his freedom, to constantly confine him in order to save his life.

◂ 22 ▸

Kerry's Places

When Kerry pulled down my long drive in his Forest Service truck, I experienced a bizarre mix of emotions. I was overjoyed to see him, and had missed him while he'd been away at his training. It broke my heart to watch Mountain rise and strain at his heavy chain when he recognized Kerry's truck. And I dreaded telling my lover about the events of the past few days.

Kerry got out of the truck, smiled, and opened his arms to me. I ran to him and he grabbed me and lifted me off my feet with a big hug. I cried out as I slid down the front of him and his hands rubbed across my bruised back. Kerry pulled his head back and looked at me. "What's up? Are you hurt?"

"A lot has happened. I'll tell you about it." I reached with my lips and gave him a kiss, inhaling the scent of his skin and the slight hint of soap.

"What's Mountain doing on that big chain?" He put his arm around me and we walked toward the wolf.

Mountain lunged against the thick iron links, raising up on his back legs, then dropping to all fours and racing back and forth at the limits of his restraint.

Kerry dropped into a squat and patted the wolf, rubbing his haunches and stroking his back. "What have you done now, Mountain?"

"He runs off," I said. "He runs away, he disappears, and he doesn't come back for hours. The man on the next place over said he was going to shoot him if he saw him on his land. He thinks Mountain killed his steer."

"That's just nonsense. Mountain didn't kill that beef."

"I know, but the rancher said he would shoot him if he saw him running loose. And I can't trust Mountain anymore—he runs off every chance he gets now. He doesn't come back when I call, he just bolts away after anything that interests him, and I can't keep up."

Kerry shook his head as he scratched Mountain's ears. "You've done it this time, bud," he said. "You've gone too far."

We sat outside in the sunshine with Mountain and I gave Kerry a rundown of all that had happened in the past several days. He frowned as I talked, shaking his head back and forth. "I'm staying with you tonight," he said. "I don't want you to be alone out here. We'll figure this out as we go along, but I don't want you to be alone." He jumped up and offered me a hand. "Come on," he said. "Let's go for a ride."

With Mountain in the backseat of the crew cab, and Kerry and I in the front, we set off in the green truck for an outing. Kerry drove west from my place, toward the forest lands he patrolled. He reached a hand across the front of the cab and squeezed mine. "I'm going to take you to some of my places," he said, smiling.

Deep in the section of Carson National Forest that was managed by the Tres Piedras Ranger District, an area flourished almost undiscovered, protected as a watershed, off-limits to all vehicles except those driven by the rangers who infrequently patrolled it. We unlocked a series of gates and closed them behind us as we drove up a two-lane dirt track and wound around the side of a mountain. The rumbling of the truck's engine and the occasional call of a raven were the only sounds that broke the morning stillness, the rhythm of the truck's tires as they navigated the dips and rises in the road reminiscent of a small seafaring craft easing over swells. Mountain fell asleep in the back, and I watched out the window as we went. Along the upslope side of the road, determined mounds of snow huddled blue-white under the shade of tall ponderosa pines, while the morning sun gilded the grasses, warming the air and surrounding us with saffron-colored light. At the last gate, I got out and used a key Kerry had handed me to unlock a padlock and chain, then swung back the long welded triangle of iron pipe that hung across the path. The *tot-a-tt-tt-tot* of a woodpecker echoed through the air. Two deer eyed me from a stretch of sunlit grass twenty yards away, then returned to grazing.

High at the top, the road circled a small, raised crown of granite, large enough to pitch a tent and make a dry camp on the summit's highest point. In a swale in this outcropping, a ring of stones had been set for a campfire. As the truck slowed, Mountain woke and peered over the back of my seat and out the passenger-side window. Kerry parked the truck at the end of the track. We got out and walked to the eastern edge of the point, where we gazed across the sunlit thirty-mile-wide Taos Valley at the voluptuous blue Sangre de Cristo Mountains in the distance, crowned with their snow-white tops.

"Don't you think it would be all right to let him run loose here?" Kerry asked, watching Mountain strain against the long lead and bridle as he nosed along the ground, pulling me from rock to tree.

"I don't know. I don't think he would get too far from me here because he doesn't know where he is. But at home, that's another story. At some point, though, I have to get him used to this. It's his life now. It's *our* life now." I bit my lip. My chest felt as if we'd parked the truck on it.

"I hate it that you have to do this. And it's especially sad that you have to keep him chained up when you live out on a big stretch of land like you do."

"What else can I do? The neighbor said he would shoot him. Mountain ran off for hours the other night. He could have run all the way to the highway in that amount of time and gotten hit by a car. I—"

"Shhhhh," Kerry said, moving close to me and tipping his head to one side to look into my face. He brushed a strand of hair back from my eyes. "It's all right, babe. We just have to do the best we can." He knelt down and patted his thigh. "Come here, Mountain," he said.

The wolf looked up from sniffing a clump of grass and then trotted over to Kerry.

"You stay here with us," Kerry said, reaching to unsnap the bridle. "If you run off, that's it, okay?"

Mountain heard the snap of the plastic keeper and shook off the nylon webbing. He bolted back to the clump of grass, delighted to have his freedom back.

"But—"

"It's okay," Kerry said. "It's like you said, he'll stay close to us here because he doesn't know where he is. At your place, he's probably just trying to expand his territory. Maybe the coyotes are trying to move in on him, and he's out marking his boundaries. He's growing up. That's what the big boys do in the wolf world."

I shook my head and blew out a breath. "I can't have him running off, Kerry. And that rancher warned me."

Kerry took my hand and started walking. "I bet he'll stay right with us here. I think it's at home that he's having a turf war with those coyotes. Come here." He led me to the round rise of elephant-back granite.

I looked down at the blackened circle of stones and the stack of small limbs next to it. Someone had gathered these sticks from the forest floor and left them in place, ready for the next fire. I could smell the carbon residue on the rocks. "Who uses this campfire ring, if this area is off-limits?" I asked.

"I do."

I grinned. "You come up here by yourself and build a campfire?"

"Sometimes. I think that campfire ring has been here since the first ranger worked this district. They may even have climbed up here to spot forest fires back then. If I look out that way"—he pointed—"I can almost see your place."

I imagined my boyfriend sitting here under the stars with only a flickering fire to keep him company, and it made me think of my days riding range. I had spent a thousand nights like that, and those times were some of my happiest memories.

"Come on, I have more to show you," Kerry said, heading back to the truck. "Come on, Mountain!" he called, slapping his thigh again.

The wolf looked up, and bounded toward us with delight, eager for the next adventure.

• • •

For our first leg of this journey, we had wound up the exterior of a tall peak at the eastern limit of the ranger district. But in the interior, surrounded by four mountains, lay a wild, unspoiled valley. Here was the protected watershed that the Forest Service had deemed off-limits to hunters, to motorized vehicles and bicycles, and even to horses and mules. That left only hike-in backpackers and fishermen, who also had to get there on foot. Not many did. The result was a pristine place flush with fish and game and almost completely devoid of the dominance of man.

Kerry drove us back in along a low ledge that bordered a rushing stream. At a bend in its course, vertical walls of sheer granite rose behind it, and the banks were lined with granite boulders as big as my house. We got out and climbed in among the rocks along white-capped waters and roaring rapids as the ground rose upward, the deluge of water thundering in our ears. More than once, Kerry took my hand to help me climb, and the scrapes on the backs of my legs stung as my skin stretched over flexed muscle. After a time we reached an impasse, where the riverbank and the cliff face met. Mountain, who had been working his way carefully over the rocks just ahead of us, looked at me for direction. Kerry pointed across the surging headwaters to a waterfall, streaming silver-white down the sheer wall of granite, the water foaming into a halo of glistening spray at the bottom. A luminous rainbow shimmered in the air.

We hiked back along the river, downstream. The banks widened, and a grove of aspen congregated on one side, the bare, gray-white limbs like upturned arms supplicating for spring. Kerry pointed out a series of caves in the rock shelf along one side, and the impressions in the ground made by a mother bear and two cubs when they slept and fished along the river during the late autumn. I was delighted to be invited into Kerry's private world, and—as always—I was enchanted by his obvious love and affection for the land.

He stopped walking, boots on a rock on the bank. "Come here," he said, holding out a hand.

I looked at him, his handsome face framed by a Forest Service hat. He was grinning at me, one side of his mouth just the slightest bit higher than the other, a feature I found immensely attractive. His eyes fixed on mine, and I felt a spark of sexual energy arc between us. I stepped forward and took his hand.

"Close your eyes," he said. "Let me lead you."

I did as I was told, placing one foot cautiously in front of the other as he led me along, coaching me to watch out for a branch here and a depression in the ground there.

"Stop for a second here, don't open your eyes," he said, tenderly grasping my shoulder with one hand. "Now turn just slightly to the left."

I followed his directions.

"Okay, lean forward . . . just a few inches. There, that's far enough. Now, what do you smell?"

I inhaled deeply. "Pine sap. And something else."

"Take another deep breath," he said.

I drew in air, filling my lungs. "It's sweet," I said. "Sweet and a little nutty, all at the same time."

"To me, it smells like vanilla. Open your eyes."

Inches in front of my face stood an old-growth ponderosa pine, easily three feet in diameter. I pressed my nose right to the bark and inhaled again, and this time I swooned as the smell of vanilla filled my nostrils. "I never knew these trees smelled like vanilla," I said, looking at my lover with delight.

"All ponderosas do," he said, "to some degree. But this old tree here is probably the oldest, and the best-smelling one here."

I smiled and shook my head, amazed at this new discovery. "I love that you taught me that," I said. And I also loved that he went around sniffing trees to learn about them.

"I love the way you smell, too," he said, "especially when I come by your cabin at night and climb into bed with you. You always smell warm and sweet."

◂ 23 ▸

This Land Is Your Land

On the way back from our outing, Kerry and I decided to go to visit Tecolote. "I'll bet you money she's waiting for us when we get there," I said. "She always is."

"How do you figure she does that? I mean, we didn't know we were going there until a minute ago. How could she be expecting us?"

"I don't know, but she always is. It never fails."

"Maybe she has a lookout down in the village."

I giggled at this. "And what? He sends a carrier pigeon? She doesn't have a phone!"

He laughed, too. "A raven, maybe. A trained messenger raven."

"An owl would be more like it," I said, and we both laughed.

Sure enough, Esperanza de Tecolote was standing on the *portal* looking expectantly in our direction as we came around the bend on the goat path that led to her place. The bruja held a large hand-woven basket by the handle, and before we had even finished our greetings, she handed it to Kerry and asked him to gather kindling for her. Kerry took Mountain up the slope with him while Esperanza and I went inside to make tea. "We will fix a little something for those boys," she said, wiping off the table with the corner of her apron. I noticed a pot of beans with *epazote* bubbling in a pot over her fire.

Tecolote picked three dried chiles off a *ristra* hanging from a viga in her ceiling. She set a round, cast-iron griddle right into the coals on one side of her cook fire and tossed the chiles onto the top of it, picking them up with her fingers and turning them as they heated. The skins softened as they warmed, and the rich smell of the roasting peppers filled the casita. Esperanza put the hot chiles into a bowl and covered them with boiling water from the cast-iron kettle that always hung from a hook over her hearth. She blanketed the bowl with a big piece of sackcloth that looked to be the same material from which her dress was made.

Next, the bruja made *masa,* adding a little water from the kettle to a mix of ground corn, lime, and a walnut-sized lump of goat butter. When she'd gotten the dough to the right consistency, she set the bowl on the table in front of me. "You make the tortillas, Mirasol," she said, "and I will cook them."

I got up to wash my hands in a pan of warm water near the fire that Tecolote also used to wash dishes, then rolled balls of masa out onto a stoneware plate and pressed them with the back of a cast-iron skillet until they were round and flat. Each time I finished one, Tecolote plucked it up and threw it on the griddle, never using any kind of utensil, picking up the tortillas with her bare fingers to turn them in the hot pan. Each one was then placed between layers of a sackcloth which had been folded over many times to make enough pockets to keep a dozen tortillas warm and separated so they would not stick together.

"You are having a nice day with that boy of yours," Esperanza said as we worked.

"Yes. I am having a very nice day with Kerry. And with Mountain. You know, Kerry loves the land so much. Today, when he showed me some of his favorite places, I realized that his love for the earth is as deep as mine."

"You are like *los indios* in that way, Mirasol."

I smiled. "I am like the Indians in a lot of ways, I think."

"*Sí,* but you know there is something about this place over here. The peoples are very different, one from the other. When the Spanish came here, you know, *los indios* already lived here. They were happy here, and they believed that they belonged to this land. On the other hand, *los conquistadores,* they wanted to conquer this place, they believed that the land belonged to them. Maybe it has changed a little now, but that was the difference then, you see, and that is what has caused all the trouble for hundreds and hundreds of years.

"But you," she said as she crushed the softened chiles against the side of the bowl with a wooden spoon, their dark red flesh dissolving into the hot water, "you do not believe that the land belongs to you. You believe that you belong to the land." She poured the chile paste into the beans and stirred the mixture.

I gave a small smile. Tecolote knew me well, better than I would have thought.

"Those boys are coming in now," she said.

Seconds later, I heard Kerry's boots on the wood planks of the *portal*, and Mountain ran in the door, waving his tail with excitement.

Tecolote fished a bone from the beans and set it in a tin pie plate to cool. She cooed to Mountain about it, speaking to him in Spanish, and the wolf sat at attention, fixed on her every word, a long strand of drool dripping from a corner of his mouth. When the bone had stopped steaming, she held it up above the wolf's head, pointed to her eyes with two fingers, and held his gaze. Tecolote waved the two fingers and said an incantation over the bone: "This gives you the strength to run, but you must not run until it is time."

As she handed the bone to the wolf, I muttered, "My thoughts, exactly."

Esperanza hobbled to the hearth and used a large gourd ladle to scoop the beans into bowls. *"Un grito a tiempo saca un cimarrón del monte."*

"What?" I asked.

She put a bowl of beans in front of me. "It is an old saying over here."

"But what does it mean?"

She turned back to the hearth. "A shout in time, it gets the stray animal out of the woods."

I gave a soft snort. "Not always."

Kerry winked at me and grinned. He grabbed a large round log from the firewood on the porch and brought it in to use as a stool, since there were only two chairs.

We ate the beans from pottery bowls and rolled the tortillas and dipped them into the soupy chile sauce that surrounded the legumes. It was a delicious, simple meal.

"I want to ask you about a Spanish word I heard," I said to Esperanza. "Can you tell me what a 'monito' is?"

The old bruja held her big spoon in her fist like a small child might. She stopped midpoint between bowl and mouth, and sauce dripped from the spoon as she hesitated long enough to answer my question. "Monito—it is a little doll." She shoved the spoonful of beans into her mouth and began macerating them with a delighted smile.

I remembered the box that had been riding shotgun in my Jeep. "Oh, that reminds me," I said. "I tried to deliver the doll in the box that you gave me to Sister Florinda at the pueblo, but she would not accept it. She asked me if it was a joke."

Tecolote shrugged. She made a loud slurping noise as she sipped the chile sauce from her spoon.

"I'll bring it back to you," I said. "I don't have it with me today because it's in my Jeep and we came in Kerry's truck. But I'll bring it next time I come."

The old bruja stopped eating and thought for a moment, her spoon poised in midair. Then, she held it up and waved it to give emphasis to what she said next: "Instead, Mirasol, I think you should find a child who would like a doll for La Navidad."

Kerry reached for another tortilla from the sackcloth bundle. "This is delicious," he said. "We've been out in the fresh air all day, and I didn't realize I was so hungry until now. Thank you for the meal."

"*De nada,*" the old bruja said, grinning. "It will give you *la fuerza* for the afternoon."

"*La fuerza?*" he said. "What's that?"

"Strength," I said. "Right?"

"*Sí.* You will be glad for a little extra energy today," Esperanza said, giving a mostly toothless smile.

As we left Tecolote's cottage, we stepped off the *portal* into brilliant sunlight and a relatively warm, beautiful New Mexico winter afternoon. We started down the goat path, waving our good-byes.

"Mirasol," she called to me, waving me back.

I came back up the path.

"It is better that we do not speak about this in *la casita*. You do not have a monito in your possession, do you?"

"No."

"Good, that is very good. I did not see it around you, but I wanted to be sure. Many times, over here, when the people are saying 'monito,' they are speaking of a witch doll."

◂ 24 ▸

The Shower

Back at my cabin, I hooked Mountain to his chain, and I choked back tears as I did so, trying hard not to show weakness.

Kerry tried to console me. "Maybe he'll learn something from this. Maybe he'll learn that if he runs off, he's going to be restrained."

I looked at the wolf, who dropped to the ground and refused to meet my eyes. "I think he is learning to long for his freedom even more. And to hate me for depriving him of it." I had been trying to control it, but the worry and sadness welled up in me, and I began to sob. I knelt on the ground and lifted Mountain's muzzle, but he looked away and struggled to free his chin from my grip.

Kerry and I built a campfire near my makeshift shower at the edge of the woods. I brought a large pot and a grate to place over the fire for heating water to add to the sun-warmed water in the shower bags. I put Mountain on his long lead and bridle and we took him with us to La Petaca to get buckets full of water for the big cauldron. The wolf scampered along exploring in the woods, wandering in and out among the low limbs and brush so that I had to repeatedly disentangle him.

"What did the power company say about why you don't have electricity?" Kerry asked as we returned to the stream for our second round of water.

"They never made it out here. I called several times, but the only time I ever got a real person on the phone was this morning, and he told me they had sent a guy out yesterday but he couldn't tell which place was mine. I'm supposed to place a big sign up at the end of my drive where it meets the road."

"And the FBI didn't find any connection between your call to the power company and the guy who phoned you about the elk?"

"Apparently their sheets are all clean as a whistle at the power company. They just can't deliver electricity."

"But it does seem odd. You don't know of anyone else who has that cell phone number, anyone who might have given it to anyone else?"

"It's posted on a list on a bulletin board at the BLM. I never paid any attention to that list before, but it's possible someone might have given it out, if asked."

He shook his head. "I don't get it. Whoever it was knows who you are, they know where you work, and they know what you do. I'm worried about that."

"Yeah," I said, stopping to work the lead out from around one of Mountain's front legs, which had gotten lassoed in it. "Me, too."

While the water heated, Kerry helped me make a sign for the power company and secure it with a bungee cord to the fencepost at the corner by my drive. Later, when the cauldron had come to a boil, we added steaming water to top off the sun-warmed reservoirs in the black shower bags. We raised them up—one in each of two tall ponderosa pines—via a rope over a tree limb used as a come-along. With Mountain secured by his heavy chain to a nearby tree, we undressed in the pink-gold glow of the last of the day's sunshine and stepped onto the river stones I had placed on the ground for a shower floor and into the sheltering arms of the pine branches. We opened the valve on one of the bags and I felt the top of my head tingle, sending a telegraphic message of comfort down my spine. The luxurious sensation of warmth fanned across my back and shoulders, soothing the scrapes and bruises, radiating a delicious sense of heat over my arms and chest which spread to my lower torso and then my legs as the water flowed over my skin.

I turned my face up into the spray and felt the rain of wet warmth on my cheeks. I smelled the sharp, spicy sap of the pines, the ancient musk exuding from the moist stones, the earthy scent of damp grass and ground, and the incense of Kerry's skin, redolent with clean sweat, maleness, and his own aromatic signature. As our hands found one another's shoulders, a flood of red light unfurled from the orb of fire on the horizon, rippling along the contours of the land, burnishing everything with the beautiful crimson blush of the surrendering sun.

Kerry drew me to him, holding me against his chest. Our skin seemed somehow more naked for being wet. "I could stay like this forever," he said. "This is so perfect, this moment. Right now."

"Except for Mountain," I said into his shoulder.

He pulled back slightly. "What did you say?"

"Except for Mountain. This is perfect for us. But he's over there on a chain. He's not free."

Kerry raised his hand and held the back of my head as he looked into my eyes. His skin glowed bronze with sunset light and the tiny streams of water on his chest glimmered. "We'll make it up to him, babe. He's safe. That's what matters. Now, come here." His hand gently traced a trickle of water along my spine all the way to the round curve of my bottom.

◂ 25 ▸

Solstice

It was cold and dark when we set out for Tanoah Pueblo the next morning, Kerry in his truck, and Mountain in my Jeep with me. We had been invited to come prepare for the solstice rituals and then participate in the festivities. At the pueblo, Kerry took Mountain along when he and a few of the men went to gather up wood from the foothills of Sacred Mountain. Here in the pueblo, there was to be no using machinery, digging, chopping of wood, or excessive moving about during this time of "staying still" or Quiet Time, as it was more commonly known. Kerry, a non-Indian and thus immune from these restrictions, would bring the previously stacked, cut, and dried wood back from the store-piles in the foothills by the truckload, and under the direction of the men from the pueblo—and with their help—pile it in great mounds, dotting the large dirt plaza in the center of the walled village of the pueblo. This firewood would be used for the solstice ceremonies, and to build huge bonfires on Christmas Eve for the procession.

Momma Anna had instructed me to meet her outside the church after the first morning mass, but I was early. I stood outside the low adobe churchyard wall, wrapped in a blanket my medicine teacher had given me. I waited in the cold, listening to the sound of water flowing under the ice that nearly covered the small río that ran through the center of the village. Big tissue-paper flakes of snow began to float down from the dark sky.

I heard a hinge creak, and a Tanoah man emerged from a nearby doorway, wrapped in a blanket. He stepped out onto the hard-packed earth in front of his home, holding one hand high to offer cedar to the coming sunrise. As his soft moccasins marched in place, he closed his eyes and gestured with the offering to the seven directions—first to the east and the rising sun, then to the south, the west, the north, the earth below, the sky above, and to the "Within," holding his pinch of cedar to his heart. As he completed this ritual by sprinkling the cedar tips over the ground, he opened his eyes and saw me. He walked in my direction, but stopped a few yards away from me. We studied one another for a moment, and I recognized Sevenguns just as he discerned that it was me. "It is cold," he said. "You want some coffee?"

"That sounds good," I answered, emphatically. Once again, the morning had reminded me of how painfully stiff and sore I still felt from the beating I'd taken in the avalanche two days ago. The cold seemed to exacerbate the experience. "I think I have a while to wait before the early mass is over."

"You could go on in there," he said, pointing at the church. "Might get some Jesus."

"No, that's okay." I grinned. "I was told to wait outside, so that's what I'll do."

"You come to my house." He waved an arm for me to follow him. "I leave the door open, you are just like outside. Only I got coffee and a good fire over there."

Sevenguns spooned instant coffee into two mugs, then poured boiling water from a blue-speckled, enamelware coffeepot into them. "A man and a woman from the FBI come here," he said, handing me one of the mugs. "They ask me, ask all the old ones here did we go to that school."

I stared into my coffee, trying hard to be patient as I waited to see if more details would be forthcoming—and trying even harder not to ask any questions.

"They ask one thing, then another thing, then they leave me and do not come back. They can already see that I am too old and feeble to be the one who kill that woman out there."

"I'm sure they ruled you out for other reasons. You don't seem that old or feeble to me."

Sevenguns smiled. "You the one talk good, now." He got up and added some sugar to his coffee and stirred it in. He scooped another spoon of sugar and held it up with a questioning expression.

"No, thanks. This is good like it is."

"Those FBI, they talk Rule Abeyta three time. Also Sica Blue Cloud, go her house two time. She is lot more feeble than me, but still they go there and go back a next time."

I looked out the door at the falling snow, then back at Sevenguns. "I have been hearing a lot of stories about the school lately. You told me about being hungry there, and hunting and fishing for the staff. Others have told me about their experiences, too. I would like to know more about the kinds of things that happened at San Pedro de Arbués Indian School."

"That one get herself killed, now everybody want to know about that place. Another day, nobody want to know about it."

Again, I waited quietly, glancing between my coffee and the churchyard outside the door.

"You want me to talk about that time, the most sad time my life. You can see I have lot of more thing to be happy about, we can talk about them." He looked directly at me. "I wonder why you want to know those sad story."

I raised my eyes to meet his. "I don't know. I feel like I was drawn right into the story of that place myself, when I had to take refuge there to survive that storm."

He drank the last of his coffee and set the mug down. "It is the same for the children who grew up there. They are forced to be there, so they take refuge in that place so they can survive. Whatever kind of refuge they can find. Those thing that happen there leave us a lot of trouble and pain, even today. Some pain never get heal or feel much better, but we learn how to bring balance when we seek at least that same much joy."

Just then, the church bell rang, a loud, booming peal that pierced the darkness. The doors to the church opened, and I saw a square of light stretch across the churchyard like a shadow in reverse.

I turned to Sevenguns. "It's time for me to go," I said, handing him my mug. "Thank you so much for the coffee."

"Did you catch you a big cat?" he asked, taking the cup.

"Not yet."

As I stood at the gate to the churchyard wall, I watched Sister Florinda Maez and a small, dark-haired boy in a lace collar and black robe emerge from the chapel and stand beside the door in reception. A dozen or so people came out and bid the sister good-bye. Sica Blue

Cloud was the last parishioner to come out of the church, limping as she did so, leaning on her nephew Eloy's arm. They stopped to shake the sister's hand and to exchange the compliments of the day. Eloy glanced out into the churchyard as the two women continued to talk, then noticed me, wrapped in my blanket. He leaned his head forward as if he could not make me out, then came down the short path toward the gate. Seeing me, he chuckled a little as he said, "Jamaica? I thought that was you. What are you doing here?"

"I'm waiting on Momma Anna. Why?"

He flagged a hand. "Oh, of course you are. Of course you are. I apologize. I was just surprised to see you on this dark, cold winter morning."

By this time, Sica had hobbled up to her nephew. She smiled. "Oh, Jamaica, I am so happy I see you. The Holy Family, they are now at my house, stay with me. You must come visit them."

"Yes, I'll have to bring an offering—"

"But one of our important guest," she frowned, "they are not there."

I started to speak, but before I could say a word, Sister Florinda Maez hurried toward us with a hand in the air, her long black tunic and scapular billowing behind her, dusting a path in the snow. "Miss Wild," she said, "Mrs. Santana is waiting inside the sanctuary. She asked me to tell you that she would like a moment with you."

When I stepped into the tiny chapel, the flickering flames of candles created firefly silhouettes on the whitewashed adobe walls. Only a few gas lamps hung from the vigas in the ceiling, and the corners were black, in deep shadow. I was aware of the stark contrast between light and darkness in the sanctuary, a place where the most sacred spiritual elements of two very vivid and varying cultures had fused into a host of mythic and iconic hybrids. Momma Anna stood before a bulto at the back of the nave, just a few feet from the entrance. She appeared to be speaking to it as she might a living man. I approached slowly, my blanket over my head as was the custom. My mentor looked up and nodded at me. "This my daughter," she said to the bulto. She held her open palm in the direction of the statue and said to me, "This San Quarai. Patron saint, Tanoah Pueblo."

"How do you do?"

Momma Anna frowned at me. "He *do* just fine. Him not patron saint if not do fine. You listen, not talk." She pointed at me to enforce this last, then walked away toward the doorway of the church, leaving me in the presence of the bulto.

I looked at San Quarai, who was carved and polished from a thick cedar log, with three distinct waves of color graining through the wood: blond, red, and gray. He was close to three feet tall. His body was bent, curving according to the naturally beautiful shape of the cedar limb from which he was made, making him appear to be leaning to one side in a dancelike pose of rapture. He wore a hooded cloak and held his hands up high in front of him as if to welcome the sun or the moon. He had a broad, smiling face, a small, pointy beard, a thick, protruding brow, and he looked like a Spaniard.

I listened for any message San Quarai might have for me, but all I could hear was the hissing of a nearby candle with a greasy wick. Just in case, I nodded my head slightly to the bulto to show my respect, and then I went to join my medicine teacher.

At the entry, Sister Florinda had dismissed her choirboy and was folding his robe and collar over her arm. Momma Anna was intently watching the rooftops of the main structure of the pueblo. The village priests had climbed from level to level on aspen-pole ladders up to the highest place along the back wall. They were wrapped in white blankets and stood stark against the dark western horizon. The brief snowfall was over. The world was silent, hushed by the newly fallen white blanket.

"The cacique is about to mark the solstice," the sister said.

As if on cue, one of the priests began to call a singsong chant. Residents of the small, central part of the village opened their doors and came out of their houses onto the snow-covered, packed-earth plaza. They turned to the east and watched the light from behind the shadowy mountains begin to appear over snow-capped peaks.

I had seen a similar observance of the sunrise take place in the summer at the solstice. Of the two, the winter practice was more significant at this pueblo. The cacique, or town chief, created the calendar for ceremonies for the entire year based on the winter solstice. The medicine societies then took the cue from that calendar as to when they could perform important rituals and dances. The rhythms of the tribe were set by this day, the moment of sunrise, and the careful calculations done by the cacique and the leaders of the medicine societies, the tribal priests.

"We go now," Momma Anna said. She started down the path to the gate in the churchyard wall.

"I'll be right there," I called after her. I turned to Sister Florinda. "Was the priest here for mass this morning?"

"No. He was at Taos Pueblo conducting the morning mass there."

"So, do you give communion when the priest is not here?"

"Yes." Sister Florinda smiled. "The priest consecrates the Eucharist, and I then deliver it to the parishioners."

"Can you hear confession also, with some predispensation from the priest?"

"No, not technically speaking, although sometimes one of the Tanoah will unburden himself to me and perhaps I can offer some counsel. But I cannot give absolution. And confession is not complete without contrition and absolution."

Momma Anna stood at the churchyard gate waiting for me. "Come," she barked, waving her hand for me to come.

"I better go, Sister," I said. "Just one more thing: did you, by chance, take communion to Cassie Morgan sometimes? Was she involved with this church, maybe through her work at the Indian school?"

For an instant, Sister Florinda seemed to melt inside her habit, her shoulders softening from their square, upright placement, her face drooping, revealing a slight hint of suffering. But then she recovered, speaking in a clipped voice, "I am sure that you are aware that I cannot answer that."

"Okay, I understand. I was just wondering. Thank you for answering my other questions. I was curious about how all this worked, you being here without a priest."

"You are full of questions, Miss Wild. We have not uttered two statements between us, it has all been questions. Did you ever hear that curiosity killed the cat?"

Momma Anna and I hurried to the home of her mother, Grandma Bird Woman Lujan, an elder whose age was reputed to be nearing the century mark. No one was sure about either the year or the day of her birthday, because at the time she was born, birth certificates were not issued for Indian babies on the reservation. She still lived in the old part of the pueblo and was cared for by her two daughters, Momma Anna and her sister, from day to day. The men in the family—old and young—offered help by providing firewood and hunting for meat for their beloved matriarch.

When we arrived at Grandma Bird's house, we went in through the turquoise-washed door and found Grandma sitting on a bench by the fire in the dark. She had risen alone this morning and dressed herself. She was wrapped in a colorful wool blanket, and her long silver hair was gathered into one loose braid down her back. I went to greet her, taking her slender brown hand tenderly as I made a slight bow. "You take me," she said.

I helped her stand up.

She pointed at a folded blanket on the nearby bed. "Take," she said.

I picked up the blanket, and Grandma Bird took hold of my arm and clenched it tightly for support. Momma Anna made for the door and held it open. I helped Grandma Bird out the door without knowing where we were going. Anna led us back the way we had come, to the center of the plaza, walking slowly and quietly in front of the thick brown adobe walls of the homes facing onto the square. On we went, past the churchyard and right up to the snow-covered banks of the río that spilled down the slopes of Sacred Mountain and gave the village of Tanoah Pueblo life. All the members of the tribe who had come out to observe the sunrise were now standing in the snow at the river's edge, some of them on each bank. They were clustered in family groups, clutching babies and the hands of small children, quieting adolescents; and many had helped elders to the water's edge just as Momma Anna and I had. Even as we approached, more Tanoah came from their houses toward the river from both sides of the pueblo—individuals, couples, and whole families.

Grandma Bird had shuffled slowly along beside me, holding on to me for support as we came across the plaza. But when we got to the riverbank, she suddenly let go of my arm. She slipped the blanket off of her shoulders and handed it to me. Then, to my surprise, she slipped off her dress, under which she wore nothing. Her body was tiny, brown, and shriveled. Her spine was slightly bent, but there was a lean, sinewy strength to her that seemed to defy age. Her small breasts had shriveled to almost nothing, and her belly made the shape of an empty spoon. Grandma Bird grabbed my arm again and kicked off her moccasinlike boots, then let go and walked right through the snow and into the río at a place where fast-flowing, frigid water surfaced between large floes of ice. Up and down the riverbank, the elders went in first, wherever there was a break in the frozen canopy.

Next, Momma Anna followed suit, heaping her blanket in my arms on top of Grandma Bird's spare blanket and the one she'd been wearing, creating a mound that I had to stretch my neck to look around because I could not see over it. My medicine teacher pulled her dress over her head, then wriggled out of the leggings and undershirt she wore beneath, and into the water she went.

All along the banks of the río, the other Tanoah men and women of her age did the same. They splashed the water over their bodies without complaint, wetting all of their exposed skin with the freezing fluid. And down the line it went, through the generations. Family members took turns holding one another's things as they ritually bathed in the life-giving water that moved through the center of their world. Adults came out and adolescents went in. Then the young children, some holding the hands of their toddler siblings. Finally, parents dipped naked, crying babies into the icy water.

First to go in, Grandma Bird Woman had also been first to come out and up the banks in the snow. She grabbed at the heap of things I was holding, pulling Anna's blanket off the top and throwing it over my head, finally getting to the spare, folded blanket at the bottom that she'd had me bring. When I uncovered my face, I saw the old woman wrapping this toga-style around her chest, shivering as she tucked one corner of the blanket in at the top to hold it in place. She bent over and pulled on her moccasins, then raised up and grabbed the blanket she'd worn for a wrap, which she threw around her shoulders. She took her braid in her two hands and squeezed the water out.

By this time, Anna was dressing. No one had spoken a word, not to me, nor to one another. The sound of toddlers shrieking and babies crying at the shock of the cold water had been the only human sounds. One by one, the Tanoah emerged from their icy baths and wrapped or dressed on the banks.

Grandma Bird faced the east, the sun struggling to rise over the mountains while a mass of thick clouds tried to push it down. Grandma closed her eyes and began to move her lips almost silently in prayer, her voice only a breath, a mere whisper. I watched as the others did the same, up and down the banks of the río. The sun did climb, but it slipped behind the deck of clouds, and so it offered little light. Grandma Bird muttered something aloud in Tiwa, then grabbed my arm and turned back toward her house as if to say, *Let's go.*

After we had gotten her back home, we lit the gas lanterns hanging from the ceiling, stoked the fire, and made sure that Grandma had coffee and some thick slices of pueblo bread with butter and homemade chokecherry jam for breakfast. I made ready to leave, pulling on my coat and hat, and said my good-byes to Bird Woman. Momma Anna stepped out the kitchen door with me. She pulled her blanket over her head. "Last time," Momma Anna said.

"I'm sorry?"

"That what my mother say at river. Last time. She is ready now go join my father, join her ancestor, all the one who travel beyond the ridge."

"I don't know. She still looks pretty spry to me. I wouldn't be surprised if she was still around next year for the old blue bath in the river."

"Not next year. Not next time. Last time."

Once again, Momma Anna and I were entering the cultural gap between my world and hers that concerned the matter of time. I was beginning to understand that the Tanoah did not see time as linear, but rather as a journey in which the self was always at the center, therefore always in the "now." There was no other time. However, since there was both memory and anticipation, Momma Anna often referred to any time outside of the immediate—whether past or future—as "next other time." The Tanoah sense of self was as a moving element in a moving universe. Like a hoop dancer stepping and twirling at the middle of a host of spinning hoops, the Tanoah were always ritually dancing at the core of life, and the events of their own journey, and of their ancestors', were always circling around them, never static. In other words, everything was always in motion, including the self, and especially the now. Therefore, for Momma Anna, there was no moving into the future or into the past, as she always took the now with her wherever she went.

I was quiet a moment. "I miss Grandma Bird already," I said, meaning it.

"Me, too," Momma Anna said. She started to go back in the kitchen door, but she turned and looked back at me. "This time, you think *Indun*."

◂ 26 ▸

Top of the List

I started my workday on Monday morning at the BLM with a phone call from Diane. "You all right?" she asked.

"Yeah, I'm good."

"Kerry stay at your place with you over the weekend?"

"Yes."

"I wanted to make sure you were okay. Hey, that rope you found—they're working on it at the lab in Albuquerque. We'll keep our fingers crossed for some DNA evidence."

"Yeah, good. Listen," I said. "I've been thinking. If you can't tie the phone call about the elk to someone at the power company, all I've got to go on is that ATV chase I got involved in several days back. I'm going out to talk to the shepherd who shot the cougar again. I'm going to ask him if he has seen or heard anyone riding ATVs in the area where he grazes his sheep."

"We're way ahead of you. Remember, you described it as a larger-sized all-terrain vehicle? That's a UTV. Only two people at Tanoah Pueblo own UTVs, or at least that's all that we know of now. And one of them has a strong motive and has moved to the top of a short list of suspects."

"You have a *list* of suspects?"

"We do. Remember, I told you the Silver Bullet works fast and smart. And it gets better—we think we might have the date of death now, because of the housekeeper's schedule and the number of bottles of wine in the kitchen. Cassie Morgan ordered a case of wine delivered every two weeks, and she was in the habit of drinking a bottle a day, except on Sundays, according to her cleaning lady."

"It sounds like you're making good progress. But the stakes are still high for me until we figure it out. So I'm still going to go talk to that shepherd. I need to check on my traps anyway, so I have to go right by him. I'll let you know what I find out. When I come back, I'll return the sweatpants I borrowed. Want me to drop them by your house?"

"That will be fine, just throw them in the front door. It doesn't lock, as you know. I'm on the way to the courthouse to file a complaint against the landlord to dispute that eviction notice. They have to hear my complaint within seventy-two hours, so I'd like for you to stand ready to appear as a witness."

"You can count on me," I said.

"Likewise."

As I was walking down the hallway to leave the BLM, Roy called me into his office. He held up a bunch of papers. "You're scheduled to go to BLM ranger training this spring. Have you given any thought to what you're going to do with that wolf when you go?"

I had been dealing with this by avoidance so far, but here it was confronting me in the person of my boss. "I don't know. Maybe Kerry could come stay at my place with Mountain."

"Kerry? I don't think he's going to be here. I heard he has applied for a public lands job posting in Washington State. Looks pretty good for him, too—I think he's the best-qualified applicant and has the most seniority."

"My Kerry? A job out of state?"

"Yeah. Forest supervisor. He didn't tell you about it?"

"It must have slipped his mind."

The Boss looked down. "Uh-oh. Looks like I just stirred something up," he muttered.

"Could we talk about this another time?" I was barely able to contain the mixture of distress and anger that was welling up within me.

"Sure. Go on. You can get back to me later on that wolf-care thing."

I left the BLM upset and confused. Not only was I conflicted and concerned about leaving Mountain with anyone else, but I was stunned that Kerry had not mentioned applying for a job out of state. My chest felt crowded, and I blew out a big breath to make room for all the feelings clamoring to be recognized.

◂ 27 ▸

Counting Sheep

When a winter day is warm and pleasant—like Saturday had been—the residents of northern New Mexico know to bring in more firewood for the weather that will follow. And—true to form—Sunday had been a cold and cloudy solstice with snow falling off and on throughout the day. This morning, too, had started cold but still when I came to work in the dark. Now, as the sun struggled to climb higher in the sky, it grew weak from the effort, and the winter wind charged triumphantly across the high mesas, pulling a train of frigid air and slamming it into the slopes of the Sangre de Cristos.

I found Daniel Kuwany huddled against the red-dirt wall of an arroyo, squatting on a square of soiled carpet. The wind made it impossible for him to have a fire, so he had pulled several blankets around him, creating a woolen cocoon. His flock conjoined in a narrow—a dark face occasionally popping up here and there out of the one great wall of wool that stretched from one side of the draw to the other.

As before, I kept Mountain on a lead hooked to my belt with a carabiner. As we approached, the shepherd stood and looked warily at the wolf. “Don’t get up,” I yelled over the wind, signaling with my hand for him to duck back down out of the icy blast.

Kuwany squatted once more, and rearranged his blankets. One started to slide off his back, and he tried repeatedly to tug it back over him, but his attempts only unfurled more layers. I reached out a hand and grabbed a corner of the wool and pulled it across his neck and shoulders where he could clasp it from the other side. “Thank you,” he muttered, shifting his eyes from me to Mountain and back again.

I gingerly lowered myself into a crouch beside him, my legs and back still sore. I was thankful for the windbreak offered by the slope of the draw. “I wanted to ask you a couple of questions.”

He turned his head slightly, still shrouded by the blankets. “I never did see your cougar. I told you it was a ghost.”

I nodded and observed a minute of deliberate quiet. He had not seemed to mind that I had mentioned questions. I decided to try one. “Any more attacks on your sheep?”

“Nope.”

I smelled alcohol. Kuwany had been drinking, probably had a bottle tucked under his pile of blankets, thinking the booze would keep him warm. “It’s pretty cold out here. That wind is gruesome.”

“Unh.”

“Anyone ever come out here on an ATV? You know the four-wheelers with the *ying-yang*-sounding engines?”

“I know what it is.”

I remained silent.

"One guy got one of them big ones. He carries firewood in the back, got a big cargo box on it."

"Do you know who it is?"

"He comes through here a few times lately. It always scares my sheep and they scatter. Makes a lot of work for me."

"Someone from the pueblo?"

"Uh-huh."

"I'd like to know his name."

Kuwany turned to face me. He squinted one eye, and the corner of his mouth rose on that side, contorting his face into a skeptical expression.

I held his gaze and did not flinch.

"You know Rule Abeyta?"

I nodded my head, but didn't speak.

"He got one of them big ones. He comes all the time through here, even when I told him not to mess with my sheep. He doesn't give me any firewood for the trouble, neither, and I could use it. Nothing but sagebrush out here to burn."

I simply nodded again, as if I were commiserating with him. After a minute or so, I started to get up.

Kuwany held up a hand. "Do you know a wolf like that can bring the fog?" He puckered his lips and pushed his chin toward Mountain, who had curled up in a donut next to me and tucked his nose underneath his tail. The shepherd went on: "When a lone wolf howls, it will sometime bring the fog in at night. That kind of fog, made by wolves howling, people get lost in that, sometime they stay lost forever."

◂ 28 ▸

Trapped

I drove back far enough toward town to see a couple signal bars on the Screech Owl's network indicator. I planned to let Charlie Dorn know I was headed out to check on the cougar traps, but before I could pull over and dial, the thing sounded off with its customary shrill shriek. I looked at the screen before answering. The call was from the BLM.

"Well, what do you know?" Roy said. "She answered her phone. Will wonders never cease?"

"Very funny. What's up?"

"You got a call here at the office from Lorena Coldfire," Roy said. "Under the circumstances, I figured I better not give out your cell phone number, so we took the message. They got a lion in one of those traps."

"The she-lion? Or one of the cubs?"

"Sounds like they got your mama cat."

Since I was close by, I took Mountain to the pueblo and left him with Momma Anna. When I got to the Coldfire Ranch, Lorena was parked in the place where I had previously pulled up to check the traps from a distance. "The cubs are nowhere to be seen," she said as I got out of the Jeep. She had her binoculars trained on the trap containing the mother mountain lion. "I drove back to the house to call you the moment I saw her. Scout and Charlie Dorn are waiting on a crew to come with the trailer. They'll be along shortly."

Charlie and I approached the cage on foot to assess the condition of the cougar. Weak with hunger and the gunshot wound, the tawny tiger sat upright in the cage, her injured thigh revealing the meat and sinew of her muscle where she had licked the hair and skin from around the black, oozing hole where the bullet had entered her body. Her eyes fixed on Charlie and me, and the dark tip of her long, muscular tail flicked up and down in the cage in a pendulumlike rhythm that tapped out the tempo of her mood—a panicked but calculating meter. Her broad face tracked us like a sunflower does the sun, turning slowly, her large, amber eyes trained on me, her broad, rose-colored nose emitting pulsing vapor clouds as her breath steamed in the cold.

"She's mighty thin," Charlie said softly as we drew near.

The cat stood and angled her backside away from us, to the extent that she could move in the cage. Her chest quivered rapidly, the tips of the whitish fur on the prow of her breast fluttering.

"She's undefeated," I whispered.

"What did you say?"

"Look at her, Charlie. She's starving, she has been shot, and she's letting us know she hasn't been whipped."

We paused a few yards from the cage. I could smell the cougar's musk, see the rough patches in her sandy coat, the gleaming tips of whiskers that were—even now—probing for sensory input, helping the cat to compute every detail about us.

She stood on huge, tight-fisted feet, ready to defend the only remnant that remained of her freedom—the choice to remain wild, even in a cage. This was the sacred cat revered in ancient Pueblo myth for helping to defend the People against raiding tribes, the one who taught the People to hunt in a previous world—but who was so vicious and violent that she had to be sent through the smoke hole of the kiva into the next world, where she lived high in the mountains and fiercely protected the towering blue peaks of the realm. The Tanoah knew the puma as a wild thing that would never be tame, as an elusive spirit that was both majestic and terrifying.

As I studied the beast before me, a blast of icy wind whipped my hair from under my hat and out in a fluttering tail behind me. The cougar's head made a quick movement to watch this flapping yellow flag, and I remembered Sevenguns's advice about using something that moved to trap the animal. As the cat's eyes darted quickly back and forth, watching the flittering wisps of my mane, I felt the same sinking sensation in my spirit that I had felt when I fastened Mountain to the heavy chain. Somehow this was wrong. I had used my small but clever mind to figure a way to capture this cat in the name of saving her and her babies. But now that I saw her in the cage, I knew I could never truly capture her, nor could I save her, for she was both doomed and indomitable. Her experience of life, and of death, was far greater than mine. I wanted to dash to the cage and free her, to shout at her to run for her life and never come close to anything that walked on two legs again, to take her babies farther and higher into the blue world above and to never test her powers against anything so devious as a human being. If only there were another world, a smoke hole through which she could jump into the wild, sacred freedom in which she belonged.

Instead, I knew there was hardly a place anymore where she and her babies could hide, where her life did not intersect with the danger and temptation of what we called civilization. We pushed ever farther into the wild every day with our sprawl and technology; we invaded the wilderness for recreation in exploding numbers; we trapped, hunted, and reviled the wild things that belonged to the beauty we wanted to claim for our own; we sought ever more ways to experience what she had, even as we dominated and feared and destroyed it. If we managed to save her today, we still robbed her of the nobility of a natural life. And death.

I squeezed my eyelids shut, unable to bear the sight of what I—what we—had done.

Charlie nudged my arm. "Well, will you look at that," he almost whispered.

I opened my eyes. The puma looked right at me. Her expression was suddenly calm, even passive. She was lying down on one side, her tail still flipping, but slowly now—back and forth, back and forth—as if she felt safe.

An hour later, we watched as Charlie's crews loaded the lion in her cage onto the trailer. "We'll have to feed the babies," he said. "They'll probably eat about anything right now. Jackrabbit, deer, whatever we can get for them."

"Do you think we'll capture them, too?"

"I doubt there's a chance. We'll just have to put out some food and try to hurry and bring their mama back. If she survives, and if she's a good mother, she'll find them again. And they're young enough, they will stay close by wherever she left them. We just have to hope we get the meat close to where they are so they don't starve."

"How do we know where they are? Do you think they're somewhere near here?"

"I'll tell you straight, it's a crapshoot. We never have much success with saving cubs, no matter how we try to do it. We'll put out food in a scatter pattern around this spring and watch for sign. That's about all we can do. Finding this place to set the traps, that was a good call on your part. If you want to improve the odds for those cubs now, though, I'd say you should pray."

◂ 29 ▸

The Slam

Before going back to the pueblo to get Mountain, I stopped by Diane's house to return the sweatpants I had borrowed. When I pulled up in front of the house, I felt a strange, alerting sensation. The back of my neck tingled, and my temples felt cold. I thought of the cougar with her long whiskers probing the air. I looked to both sides of the Jeep, then checked the rearview mirror. Nothing.

I reached across the passenger seat and picked up the boxed Howdy Doody doll to retrieve the pants from beneath it, then set the doll back in place. I grasped the door handle and hesitated. Diane's street was more quiet now, at one in the afternoon, than it had been in the middle of the night when I had tried to sleep while staying here.

I stepped up on the front porch, still experiencing a disquieting, red-flag feeling that I couldn't quite sort out. The front door was slightly ajar, and I looked around once more before pushing it open just enough to drop the sweatpants on the floor to one side of the entry. I recalled Diane's complaint about the door needing to be slammed so it would stay closed, so I gave it a hard tug to make sure it shut.

When the door met the jamb, a blast hit my head like a concussion bomb, and with it, light and force exploded—a shock wave slammed my torso so hard it hurled my stunned body backward as if I weighed nothing. I remember flying through the air, across the *portal* and into the dirt yard, where I skidded and twisted and rolled across the ground.

I landed on one side, my face and neck pressed into the frozen ground, my body in a near-fetal position, my head rumbling with a cannonade of sonic aftershocks. I spent a moment struggling to orient myself between up and down, then rolled onto my hands and knees. One hand collapsed and a shooting pain forced me to lean onto the other arm. My back hurt, my vision swam. Still kneeling, I put one foot down and felt the ground twirl beneath me. Using my one good hand to support my body's weight, I put the other foot down—both knees deeply bent. I pushed the ground away and brought my hands to my bent knees. I nearly fell forward but caught myself by pushing one foot ahead of me, then did the same with the other, until I made it the few yards to my Jeep. I could barely hear when I used the Screech Owl to summon the fire department. The dispatcher reminded me several times that it was not necessary for me to yell, however my senses informed me only that I was moving my lips, not that I was successfully making sound. My head felt like someone had pounded a bale of cotton into it through each ear. I sat in the driver's seat of my Jeep, the door hanging open, and waited for help to arrive. I leaned back against the headrest and suddenly felt like I might pass out, so

I forced myself to sit upright. I blinked my eyes and felt rough grit on my eyeballs. I turned my head to the side and saw Howdy Doody smiling at me. "What are you laughing at?" I asked. But I didn't hear my own voice—instead, the pealing thunder of artillery sounded over and over again in my head.

I barely heard the wail of the sirens through this thick, pulsing fog. I started to get out of the Jeep when I saw the red truck approaching, its lights flashing blue-white-red, but I put one boot on the pavement and thought how hard it would be to stand up. I decided to wait.

While firefighters unfurled hoses, a paramedic tended to me through the open door of my Jeep. I began to regain my hearing as he tested my pupils with a flashlight, then determined that I was awake, alert, and oriented, and checked my neck for trauma. More than anything, I felt like my insides had been turned upside down and shaken and now my brain wasn't right side up: everything worked, but with great difficulty. The medic diagnosed me with lacerations and contusions on the side of my neck and chin where I'd skidded across the ground, and a sprained left wrist, which he packed with a cold pouch and then wrapped with an Ace bandage. He warned of the more dangerous possibility of a closed head injury. I declined a ride in the ambulance for further tests.

Diane arrived as firefighters finished putting out the flames. A third of the house was blown open and charred. The worst was the kitchen. While the paramedic applied ointment to the rashy scrapes on my neck, I watched Diane pacing furiously back and forth on the road in front of her home. With the first aid finished, I rose gingerly from the seat and stood upright, holding the roof of the Jeep for a few moments before I went to comfort my friend. My balance was still a little off-kilter. I walked slowly toward Diane as she flipped her cell phone closed. She tried to keep her composure, but tears filled her eyes. "I can't handle it anymore!" she said.

I put my arms around her, noticing sharp pain in both shoulders as I raised my arms, the tenderness in my sprained wrist. I hugged Diane and she hugged me back, patting a particularly tender spot along the back of my ribs.

"If I saw that bastard landlord of mine right now, I'd probably kill him," she said.

"Me, too."

"I'm taking the sonofabitch to court, and if he pays off the judge and I can't win, then I'm going to find a way to settle the score."

I paused a moment to note the ringing in my ears. "I'll help either way. It's not just you. I could have been killed; either one of us could have. That's got to be criminal negligence or something. Let's get him, however we have to do it."

Diane pulled back and looked at me. "That's big talk from you," she said. "You sounded like me just then. Not even angry. Just determined."

I swallowed. My mouth was dry, my throat raw. "You know, it's been a long week." I started counting off the events on my fingers. "I've been thrown by a horse, slammed into a gate so I got splintered and bruised. Gone without sleep and endured incredible cold, never mind the body I found and the big cat that nearly ate it. I've been whipped by the wind, and pelted with snow. Then someone called me out to witness a despicable act of cruelty and took a shot at me.

"The electricity at my house has been off, I've had to squat outside to go to the bathroom and fetch all my water from an icy stream. The wolf has run off and acted out and nearly gotten himself shot. And then someone started an avalanche and beat the hell out of my whole back side. Now, I've damn near been blown to bits." I was out of fingers. "It's hard to stay pleasant and even-tempered through all that."

Diane gave me a sober stare, as if she were analyzing all I'd just said. Her lips bent slightly upward into that wry, cynical grin she so often gave in a dark moment, when humor was a sort of coping mechanism that made her grisly line of work bearable. Then she suddenly burst into laughter. "Okay. You win," she said. "Your week has definitely been worse than mine."

I tried not to, but I laughed, too.

We must have looked like a pair of maniacs to the nearby firefighter and the crew from the propane company that had been called to the scene.

"So now you need a place to stay," I said to my friend. "I don't know if the power is back on yet, but you're welcome to come crash at my cabin until you can figure something else out."

Before Diane could answer, Agent Sterling pulled up in a black SUV. He stepped from the vehicle and started toward us. "Thanks. But I think I'll just get a motel room," Diane said. "I need to stay in town."

30

Monito

When I got to Momma Anna's house to pick up Mountain, no one was home. I drove to the old part of the pueblo, parked in the corral, and went over the wall by the cemetery, planning to head for Grandma Bird's, where I hoped I might find my mentor. But when I knocked on the door, no one was home. I proceeded toward the church, but it, too, was closed up. From the center plaza, I glimpsed Sica Blue Cloud across the río, hobbling along the front of the main structure on the other side of the pueblo. I hurried across the footbridge to the Winter side, hoping to catch up with Sica and ask if she had seen Momma Anna and Mountain.

But before I reached her, the old auntie went through a door into one of the lower-level dwellings. I stopped in my tracks, wondering what I should do. I was incredibly exhausted; my whole body ached. I just wanted to fetch Mountain and go home. After a few moments' hesitation, I knocked at the door I'd seen Sica Blue Cloud go through. I heard muffled voices, the shuffle of footsteps, and then Rule Abeyta opened the door. He didn't speak at first, his furrowed face looking down at me with that same pained expression I had seen on the day I had met him in the governor's office.

"I'm sorry to disturb you, to arrive uninvited. I wonder if I could speak to Sica Blue Cloud for just a moment? I saw her go in here."

Rule Abeyta gave me a wary look. "What happened to you?"

"I got . . . I fell. I slid." I reached my good hand to my neck and felt a smarting report from the inflamed flesh.

From inside the room, I heard Sica's husky voice. "Let her come," she said.

In the one-room dwelling, a fire crackled in the kiva fireplace in the corner. A bed and small table filled one half of the room, and in the other, Sica sat at a table with a cane resting against her straight, outstretched leg. I approached her without speaking, nodded as I gave the slightest bow, and took her offered hand.

"She is a good girl," Sica proclaimed to Rule. "This one know a lot of old way."

Rule did not speak, but made himself busy preparing coffee.

"I was looking for Anna Santana," I said. "She has my wolf, and I am ready to take him home. It's been a long day."

Sica did not offer a response to that, nor did she offer me a seat. Since I had not been invited to sit, and it was also not appropriate for me to press for information, I waited for what would come next, pretending to be interested in the artwork that Rule Abeyta displayed in his home. I knew when the coffee was ready, there would be some conversation. Until then, I had no choice but to forbear. As I perused a faded print by one of Tanoah Pueblo's better-known artists, a carved cottonwood figure on the mantel above the kiva fireplace caught my eye. Even though I had only seen it previously for an instant, I recognized it as the same small statue that Rule had dropped and then hid under his blanket when we'd brought the Holy Family to Sica's house. I moved toward it, examining the figure closely. The carving depicted a nun holding her rosary up above her head with one hand in such a way that she appeared to be hanging herself. The figure's head was tipped at an unnatural angle, swollen-looking and stained blue and black, and there were yellow lightning bolts painted on her cheeks. She seemed to be wearing some kind of fibrous bracelets around her ankles. I gasped aloud, remembering Cassie Morgan's desecrated body. "What is this?" I asked. I turned and looked from Sica to Rule, not caring that I had just violated the no-questions custom. "Is this what you called the 'monito'?"

Sica spoke. "This the important guest I tell you. This the monito."

"This looks like a nun," I said.

Sica nodded again. "Yes. This nun hang herself with her own religion."

"But I don't understand."

Rule brought two cups of coffee to the table. He offered me a seat, then handed me a cup, but he remained standing. "The monito is a living presence. It is a reminder to all the children who suffered at the Indian boarding school to be compassionate, even to those who captured us and tortured us."

Sica spoke again. "Those one who do that, they are sin doing that. They killing themself with those evil deed. All children who suffer from that, they not need hold bad feeling in they heart." She thumped her chest emphatically.

Rule went to the mantel and picked up the carved figure. "The monito shows us the pain and the shame of those who were cruel so that we do not need to hold any revenge. As you can see, the monito tells us that evil is taking its own revenge on itself. The figure is of a nun, who might represent goodness to some. But the monito is the reminder that evil takes its own toll."

"I can certainly see why you said it looks bad to have it around at the present time," I said. "Someone could easily misinterpret its meaning."

"Yes." He gestured for me to drink my coffee.

Using my good hand, I took a sip. "I presume you know about the death at the old Indian school?"

Abeyta looked right into my eyes. "I heard the old matron was killed, if that's what you mean."

I held his gaze, but he did not flinch or look away. "Do you know how she died?"

"They said she was shot, I think."

I nodded. I was not going to challenge this bit of misinformation since the crime was still under investigation. "I understand you gather wood in one of those all-terrain vehicles," I said.

"My brother and I do. We got it for Christmas, just got it a couple weeks ago."

"Do you go out by the old school on that thing?"

Abeyta put the monito back on the mantel. He turned his back to me as he did so. "You won't catch me out there."

After we had drunk our coffee, I rose to leave. "Thank you for the coffee. I have to go find Anna," I said, "and my wolf."

Sica struggled to her feet as well. "I go now, too. My nephew Eloy coming for supper. I make rabbit stew today, bake bread."

When we stepped out the door of Rule's abode, the three of us saw Anna Santana walking by the río with Mountain, encouraging him to get into the river to drink. He waded into the icy water and lapped at the surface; then he became rambunctious. He began to romp and splash and gallop in circles. Rule took Sica's arm to help her along, and the three of us walked over to watch the wolf play.

I greeted my medicine teacher with a nod.

She looked at me, studying my neck and the Ace bandage on my wrist. "You bang up. What you do?"

"I . . . I fell," I said.

My medicine teacher appraised me with a concerned look. "You take care," she said. "Get rest. Maybe you take next other day off."

"Yeah, maybe I will," I said. As sore and worn out as I felt, several days off sounded like a better idea.

"That wolf all happy now," Momma Anna said. At this, Mountain noticed me, and bounded toward us, plowing up short and shaking himself vigorously, spraying water on everyone.

"Eeeee!" Sica said, pulling her blanket over her face to block the spray.

"Mountain, stop!" I said, but the wolf gamboled over to me and rubbed his wet coat against my legs, overjoyed to see me. The muscles around my knees were tight and tender, and now my jeans were wet and cold. I pushed the wolf away, but he smiled at me and raced in a hoop around us, ecstatic with joy. "I'm sorry to be in such a hurry, but I've got to go," I said. "Thank you for keeping Mountain. I need to take him and head home now. I still have to stop by the market and pick up some candles, and hopefully I can get home before dark."

Momma Anna looked at me out of one eye. "You keeping old way this holy time?"

"What? Oh, you mean the candles. No, my electricity is off. It has been for days. I've been unable to get someone from the power company to come out to make whatever repair is needed on the line."

Rule spoke up. "My brother Oriando works for the power company as a lineman. I know if I ask him that he will help."

I wasn't quite sure that I trusted Rule Abeyta enough to want his help, but before I could reply, he pulled out a cell phone and punched in a number. He turned away, talking in Tiwa.

"*Tst-tst.* You got bad hurt, that neck," Momma Anna said.

"I do." I nodded. "I got hurt everything. I'm really tired. I need to get home before I drop. I've had a bad day."

My medicine teacher studied me in silence.

Sica did not speak either. She was waving enthusiastically at someone across the río on the far side of the plaza. I followed her gaze. A man was walking toward us, his face indistinguishable in the shadow cast by the massive and venerable four-story adobe structure that was the hallmark of Tanoah Pueblo.

"There Eloy!" Sica called as her nephew crossed the little footbridge and came to join us on the riverbank.

Before we could exchange greetings, Rule Abeyta stepped toward me and held out the cell phone. "My brother said he will help. Tell him where you live."

I hesitated.

Abeyta pushed the phone toward me. "Go on. Talk to him. He said he will get you going before he clocks out today."

In a matter of minutes, I had made arrangements for Oriando Abeyta to meet me in an hour at the intersection of the Forest Service road and the highway a few miles from my cabin so that I could lead him to my place. And in only a few minutes more, Mountain and I were in my Jeep heading west, the wolf snoring in the back while I daydreamed in Technicolor about the soothing comfort of a long, hot shower and going early to bed.

◂ 31 ▸

The Smell of Vanilla

I got to the intersection where I had agreed to meet Oriando Abeyta and pulled off on the side of the gravel road. I was more than fifteen minutes early. It was bitterly cold outside, and yet I dared not sit in the Jeep and wait. I felt so beaten down by all the physical trauma I had suffered over the past week that I feared that if I allowed myself to sit idle for more than a few minutes, I would pass out right there beside the road and not come to for days. I forced myself to get out of the car. My body had stiffened and I had to work to straighten up and stand erect. I opened the hatch and—with some effort due to the sprained wrist—I finally managed to put Mountain on his lead.

We walked down the roadside about fifty yards in the softening frost-light of dusk. Mountain sniffed the white grassy clumps alongside a tall growth of pines. He marked tree and scrub, straining at the lead, galloping from one tree to another. As we ambled along, my shoulders felt stiff and sore, especially with the wolf tugging at the long leash. I rotated my neck and heard a loud snap as my neck vertebrae realigned. An unexpected onslaught of olfactory information bombarded me and I realized that my sense of smell—which had vanished without my realizing it—had suddenly returned full force for the first time since the explosion at Diane's house. I drew in a deep breath and reveled in the rich array of aromas. I smelled moisture in the air, and I looked up into the twilight sky to see a low deck of clouds promising snow. I closed my eyes to isolate and identify more scents: pine needles, dry winter grass, gravel dust, wet wolf. I raised my eyelids and looked around for more ways to exercise this newly reclaimed faculty. A few yards into the woods, I saw a large, old-growth ponderosa. I stepped inside the tree line, aiming to sniff the bark of the big pine to see if it smelled like vanilla. The wolf was delighted that we'd left the road, and he bounded past me, pulling at his long lead and brushing hard against my leg, where still-tender bruises sang with pain.

The roar of an engine cut through the air, rapidly growing louder and closer. I turned and peered through the trees, looking back down the road toward the sound of the approaching machine. I watched as a big truck veered off the highway at high velocity, its front end armored with a welded steel deer guard. Like an enraged animal, the monstrous machine sped forward and crashed full-on into the back of my Jeep, sending it hurtling down the road a hundred yards as if it were a cracked cue ball. Before I could react, the truck geared up and rammed the Jeep again, creating a deafening slam of pile-driving metal and shattering glass. At this, Mountain lunged and bolted deeper into the woods. His leash whipped and tightened and I moved to grip the end with both hands, but instantly let go of it for fear my sprained wrist would snap. As the wolf fled into the forest trailing a red ribbon of nylon webbing, I stood stunned, insensible, my mouth hanging open, my brain unable to engage. The Attila truck fast-backed to the highway, swerved around, and roared out of sight, leaving a cloud of petroleum fumes.

"Mountain!" I shouted into the darkening woods. "Mountain, come back!"

It took a few minutes of calling and then waiting before I heard the sound of twigs snapping in the direction the wolf had fled. I began to talk softly to Mountain, even though I could not yet see him. "It's okay now, buddy. It's okay. Come on. It will be all right."

After minutes of my reassuring monologue, the wolf finally crept toward me, dragging his leash, his ears down with fear. Two small branches were entangled in the leash and I stooped to unravel the mess. A bolt of pain in my back radiated out to both hips and through my legs. I realized as I compromised with a bent-over half squat that I was so sore that I felt about the same as I might have if I had just stayed in my Jeep.

I coaxed Mountain carefully between the trees, and he balked, but came along, staying close to me. We walked down the road to the car and studied the damage. Most of the glass was gone. The Jeep's body was crumpled in the back and all along the driver's side, and it looked like the frame was bent. I tried the rear hatch, but it was smashed in and wouldn't budge. I led Mountain around to the passenger door and pulled on the handle. It opened with a loud metallic squawk. I folded the seat down and loaded the wolf in, and he climbed eagerly into the safe and familiar cargo area in the back. I crawled over the gearshift in the center console and threaded one leg and then the other down beneath the steering wheel, crying out as I bent and bumped various body parts, finally easing carefully into the seat behind the wheel. I checked the Screech Owl but there was no cell phone service available there. I had left the key in the ignition, and I grasped it and closed my eyes for a moment and silently prayed. I sat up tall, took a big breath and blew it out, and then I turned the key.

The motor started right up! I drove away with the wheel pulling hard to the right, and—sprained wrist notwithstanding—I steered that Jeep like a ship in strong current and headed back to Taos and the BLM.

◂ 32 ▸

Remote Chance

It was dark by the time I got to the BLM, and everyone had gone home. I called Diane first.

"Rule Abeyta was at the top of our suspect list," she said. "I'm having him and his brother Oriando picked up immediately."

"But why are they out to get me?" I said. "They must know we would have brought them in by now if I had them on Cassie Morgan's murder."

"You must have gotten too close to something or someone, and they figure you'll put it together eventually. That's what I would guess. Anyway, we'll know soon enough, because we're bringing them in and I'm going to make sure they talk."

"I still don't get it," I said. "It just doesn't quite square up somehow."

"You're making it too complicated. The Silver Bullet says that's what trips up most investigators. He says almost all murders are fairly simple. And this one is obviously all about revenge. If I can wrap this case up with no loose ends, the Silver Bullet has assured me a transfer. I'm going to get these guys."

I made two more phone calls:

"What? Dammit to hell!" Roy growled into the phone. "I'll be right there."

"No, don't. I know you've got family visiting this week for the holidays. I'm all right, I'm leaving now anyway. I wouldn't even be here by the time you could get to the office."

"You're sure you're all right? You don't need to go to the ER or anything?"

"I'm fine, Roy, really."

The next call was to Kerry, who said four words: "I'm on my way." He hung up before I could reply.

I grabbed the keys to an old, four-door Chevy Blazer that was used by the river rangers at the BLM during the summer. I went out to the parking lot and began transferring all the things from my wrecked car to the Blazer as Mountain paced back and forth, not permitting more than a foot of space to open between us. After I'd secured my rifle on the floor behind the driver's seat, I folded down the bench seat in the back to create the same large, flat cargo area for transporting the wolf that he was accustomed to in my regular work vehicle. I lifted the hatch, then stretched Mountain's thick fleece blanket, still wet from his earlier river romp, across the flat, carpeted back area. "Come on, buddy," I said, patting the blanket.

The wolf stood at the rear of the strange new automobile and sniffed at the carpet, but he didn't move.

I patted the blanket again, careful to use my good hand, as the other had swollen up like a pink pork roast above the Ace bandage, which now strained painfully tight across the palm, between the thumb and fingers, and around the wrist. “Come on, Mountain, get in,” I said, losing my patience.

Mountain sat down and lowered his head. This was not an unusual gesture for the wolf. A new vehicle, an unfamiliar object, or a strange surface often made him cautious at best, and sometimes even frightened him into wild, erratic behavior. I climbed into the back of the Chevy and drew my stiff legs up and folded them in front of me. “See?” I said to the wolf. “I’m in here. It’s okay. Now, come on.” I patted the fleece again.

Mountain raised his head and sniffed the carpeting once more. Then, without any further hesitation, he jumped into the cargo area with me and sat upright, his head pressed down and forward against the top of the car. He gave me a pleading look and whimpered. He dropped to his belly and put his chin on my leg and whimpered again, then began panting in spite of the deepening chill of oncoming night. He was clearly afraid and anxious. With each breath out, he made a soft, high-pitched whine.

I began to stroke his head, the tufted fur around his ears, the long mane at his neck, and I felt like I might cry, too. Every part of me ached; I was tired. Even sitting in the back of the vehicle in the cold hurt my back, my legs. My wrist throbbed.

Mountain nuzzled into my lap. I began to sing quietly under my breath, a little lullaby I had made up when he first came to me as a tiny pup—a song about how we were family. As I sang, the wolf’s breathing slowed and he stopped panting, his head pressed into the crook of my knee, against my thigh. I stroked his face, and he closed his eyes.

I opened my heart
And in you came
You gave me wild,
I gave you tame.
No more lonely,
You and me.
No more lonely,
We are family.

While I was singing that last verse of the lullaby, a vehicle pulled into the fenced compound behind the BLM and lights swept across us. I felt a wave of panic and moved to get up and out, reaching for my sidearm as soon as I was on my feet. Mountain scrambled upright, too, and sat up in the back looking out.

Kerry pulled right in behind the Blazer and jumped out of the door of his Forest Service truck. He strode two long steps and reached to embrace me, then checked himself and slowly and softly gave me a gentle hug. He looked down at me tenderly and stroked the side of my cheek with one hand. "I'm taking you someplace safe," he said. "We'll go to a motel or something. I'm not leaving you."

It was those last four words that tripped the lever on the gate in my mind that had been holding the last vestiges of my composure in place. I snorted. "You're not leaving me? You're not leaving me?" I pulled away and shoved him hard in the chest. "Don't lie to me and tell me you're not leaving me! What about your new job in Washington?"

By the stark light of the security flood on the back wall of the BLM I read the astonishment in Kerry's face. "I was going to tell you about it if . . . when I got the job."

I started shaking my head up and down as if this all made sense to me. "I see," I said, my voice too loud for normal conversation. "I see. You were going to tell me—when? While you were packing your things?"

Mountain jumped down out of the Chevy and began pacing in a tight pattern, back and forth, repeatedly putting his body in the charged, narrow gap between Kerry and me, trying to distract us.

Kerry reached down to pet the wolf. "It was only a remote chance that I would even get the job—"

"A remote chance that looks all sewn up, according to Roy."

"I didn't want to worry you unnecessarily."

"You didn't want to face me and tell me the truth. You lied to me. You were going to leave and not tell me!" By now, I was shouting, and Mountain was panting hard and panicked, pressing his haunches against my legs. "People who lie about leaving and then sneak off . . . that just . . . hurts!" I sobbed.

Kerry moved to take me by the shoulders but I reached again with both hands and shoved him hard in the chest, a burning pain shooting up my arm from the swollen wrist. I grabbed Mountain's collar and shouted, "Mountain, get in," as I dragged him in the direction of the Blazer's back end. The wolf jumped up into the cargo area, and I reached up for the hatch.

Kerry grabbed it before I could and lowered it carefully down until the latch snapped. "Let's talk about this," he said. "I wanted to talk to you about this and—"

"Go on and leave!" I shouted, moving toward the driver's door. "Go on and leave me alone!"

As I drove out of the parking lot, I looked in the rearview mirror through stinging tears. Kerry stood stock-still and watched me drive away, his face as stoic as stone.

◂ 33 ▸

What Trees Dream

Driving down my long dirt-and-gravel road, I headed half-aware for the beacon of yellow light from the porch lamp. It wasn't until I had turned the Blazer face out and started to open the car door that I realized that a lit porch lamp meant that the electricity was back on. I was so overjoyed, I could hardly wait to get in the house. I gave Mountain a quick romp on his long lead to make sure he had done his business and then got both of my guns out of the car and went inside. When I flipped the switch inside the door, the hardwood floor and log walls flooded with light from the three high-powered bulbs that hung from the center of the ceiling fan in the one main room. "Oh!" I gasped, as if I had suddenly had a ponderous weight removed from my shoulders. "Oh, light! Electricity! Power!"

I fed Mountain first, then built a fire in the woodstove. It was cold in the cabin, but I got a good blaze going and stacked up some logs to keep it fed. Then, I used a few of the gallon jugs of water I had bought to prime the pump that supplied water to the house from my underground cistern. I wanted to leap for joy when I heard the sound of fluid trickling into the toilet tank. *Indoor plumbing!*

I opened the taps in the bathroom and kitchen sinks to bleed air from the pipes, and when they began to flow water, I turned them off to conserve the precious liquid. I lit the pilot light in the bottom of the water heater, and relished the thought of a hot shower—indoors. I hung towels on the back of the rocking chair to warm by the woodstove, which now had a good fire going inside, so I closed its cast-iron doors and dampered the air down for maximum radiant heat. I heard the hum of the refrigerator and vowed to go to town for groceries tomorrow. I had to move the shoe box on my nightstand to get to the digital clock. As I set the box on the outside edge, I made a mental note to get out the leather burning tool and my mother's poem and make the bookmark for Diane in the morning. I checked my watch, set the clock, and I noted the time and planned to allow an hour for the water heater to bring its tank up to temperature.

But I did not make it to the shower. I sat on the side of my bed to remove my boots, reached down to untie one, and felt a volcanic flow of hot pain flood from my lumbar joints outward to my hips and then upward along my spine. I couldn't bear to bend over even a second more. I straightened, sitting up, and then I drifted to one side, falling onto the soft down comforter. I stayed like that a minute or two, then drew my knees into a fetal bend, not even caring that I was still wearing my boots when I lifted my feet up onto my bed.

While I lay sleeping in the delicious cloud of down, I became aware of a rhythmic murmuring noise, like the gentle snore of babies. I opened my eyes and listened, and then I rose and moved toward the sound. I walked out to the grove of pines behind my cabin, where I stood barefoot, a green blanket wrapped around my naked body.

The trees began to sing softly. Holding on to the earth with their long, delicate root-fingers, they stretched upward toward the stars, reaching and breathing, reaching and breathing and humming the notes of a winter song, from which I felt a cold cloak of air encircle me. I realized that the trees were asleep and dreaming—animated, restless, conjuring with the night a creative vision of the morrow. Through their dreams, the substance of life force flowed fluidly between the already created world of earth where they stood and the infinite possibilities in the stars, in the air, where the spirit of longing brought things not yet created into being. The endless cycle of life's love for itself moved through their reverie. I closed my eyes and felt my blanket slip away as I entered the dreams of the trees.

Where my naked soles touched the earth I sensed the power in the heart-womb of the world, the center of the universe, and it moved upward through me and out the tendrils of my hair, which floated above my head like the needles on the high branches of the pines. The day was deconstructing into the night, the carbon of the earth decomposing into the outbreathing sighs of the standing people, the trees. All that was being released was material for the nonmaterial, stardust for the sacred birth of the new world that would emerge out of the nothingness the trees and I were making. The two worlds—the substance and the spirit—met in the dreampoint where everything became nothing and nothing became everything. Here was the timeless beginning and ending, the primordial feminine womb-void that birthed the world, the medicine power at the always moving dream center that could only be found where it did not exist.

In an instant, I stopped holding on to who I was, what I was and had been, and I blissfully ceased to be. Stardust!

◂ 34 ▸

All That Mattered

I have been hung over and I have been beaten down, and the way I felt when I woke up the next morning was more of both than anyone sober deserves to endure. My tongue felt like a rancid mattress that someone had shoved in my mouth. I had drooled all over my pillow, my hair was matted and stuck to one ear, and one arm and hand had gone numb. My ankles and feet had swollen up in my boots, and I ached all over—especially my head. My breath was foul and my bladder begged to be emptied. I forced myself to a sitting position and started to get up when my boot knocked into the empty shoe box on the floor beside my bed.

I looked down with horror at the litter that covered the lambskin on the floor where Mountain slept. The wolf was rapturously snoring at one end of this, lying on his back with his hind legs spread apart, his front paws curled under on either side of his big, upturned chest, the expression on his sleeping face indicating he had reached wolf-nirvana. But across the rest of the rug sprawled the chewed-up remnants of my most valuable treasures. Multicolored bits of the pages that once had contained my mother's poems were strewn like confetti across the long-haired mat. And beneath my boot was a wisp of shiny, colored paper. I stooped and picked it up. It was a thin strip torn from the center of the photo of my mother, the tip of it punctured with tiny piercings from the wolf's sharp front teeth. The only likeness of my mother I had ever had was now in shreds.

"Oh, no!" I cried, and the wolf rolled onto his side and raised his head to look at me. "Mountain, what is this?" I yelled, picking up a handful of his paperwork spit-wads. "What did you do?"

I grabbed hold of the lambskin and yanked on it hard, bowling the wolf off the edge of it and out onto the hardwood floor. Mountain scrambled to his feet and dove toward the front door, his head down and low, his ears pointing backward and listening as I came right behind him in a fury. As he bolted past the wrought-iron coatrack, he caught the leg of it and tipped it over, the top of it knocking him on the back end and then bouncing onto the toe of my boot. I screamed with pain as the heavy iron bar struck the top of my foot, and Mountain came full about in the corner by the door, his back paws slipping on the hardwood and pedaling hard for a purchase. As he pushed away from the door, the broom that had been propped in the corner came down, too, causing him to volt to one side and make for the table, where he hoped to take shelter beneath. I grabbed the broom handle before it, too, fell on me, and limped the two steps to the table, yelling, "What did you do to my mother's things? They were all I had that mattered!" I raised up the broom and struck Mountain hard across his back end, and he yelped with both pain and alarm. He cowered on the floor, and from beneath his quivering body, a puddle of urine spread across the dark wood planks.

"Oh, no," I said, realizing what I had done. "Oh, God, no." I dropped to my knees and Mountain flinched and tried to make himself smaller, in terror of another onslaught of anger. "Oh, Mountain," I said, reaching out a trembling hand to touch him. "Mountain, I'm so sorry!" I remembered Sica's story of being beaten with a broom, and I felt like evil incarnate. I looked down at my beloved wolf-companion, who was now fearful of my touch and traumatized by my outburst of rage. I stroked Mountain's back and he flinched again, so I held my hand in place for a moment, gently touching his trembling haunch. I eased into a seated position, careful not to alarm him with any sudden moves. I continued to pet him as I shook my head in disbelief, unable to fathom the insanity that had come over me. And unable to forgive myself for what I had done to my best friend, a creature whom I had sworn to protect from harm.

I took Mountain to Tecolote's house, and the wolf and I climbed the slope against an icy gale. Esperanza opened her door and looked out just as we approached the casita, but she was wise enough not to wait out on the *portal* in the arctic air. Once inside, seated at the plank table near the comforting fire, I asked the old bruja for help. While the wolf lay on the floor at our feet in her warm little dwelling, Esperanza rubbed a thick salve on my sprained wrist and listened to my story of the dream experience with the trees, and then of my striking the wolf with a broom.

When I finished, the old woman was quiet.

"Tell me what to do, Esperanza," I said.

"What to do? It seems you are doing too much already! Maybe you should try *not* to do."

I pressed my lips together. "Maybe so," I muttered.

"You must leave Montaña here with me for a little time, only a few hours, or maybe a day. I will keep him safe for you during that time, and I will give him a *cura* so that he can forgive you."

"Can you give me a *cura* so that *I* can forgive me?"

She gave a sad, toothless half smile. "That one is beyond my humble powers."

The salve on my hand had begun to create an intense heat and I wanted desperately to rub it off. "You told me to listen to the trees and watch the sky. I was dreaming with the trees last night. The sky was—"

"*¡Ya chole!* Stop talking, Mirasol!" The bruja held up her finger. "You lose the power that has been given to you when you talk about it all the time."

"But I don't have any power. I don't know what the dream means."

"You will not find its meaning outside of you. There is no need to speak of it."

"But—"

"Wait!" she said. "I know you want to rub it, but you must leave it alone. Even though you do not understand it, the medicine is working. You do not need to understand everything for it to work for you."

I hesitated. "Are we talking about my wrist now?"

"I can tell you this, Mirasol: you are traveling the path of the heart. You must get your heart straightened out! It is the first thing you must do."

On the way into Taos, I stopped alongside the road and phoned Charlie Dorn.

"You're sure you want to do this?" he asked.

"I'm sure."

"It will have to be after Christmas. Probably going to take a couple of guys to do it right."

"Just tell me when, and I'll arrange to be there."

"You'll need a good three feet of digging wire all around the inside, and probably at least a nine-foot-high fence for the enclosure. Wolves are escape artists."

"I know. Let's make it as big as we can. And we'll need a sturdy gate with a good latch. Mountain can chew through almost anything, and he's really smart."

"Your mama cat made it through surgery all right," Charlie said. "They got the bullet out, packed it with antibiotics, and they're watching her, but it looks like she'll survive."

"And the cubs? Any news?"

"We scattered some meat. No one has seen them, so we don't know anything. With the holidays coming, I gave the Coldfires your cell phone number in case they can't get hold of me. They'll call one of us if they spot them."

"Thanks for the update, Charlie."

"Listen, I'm sorry you're going to have to confine Mountain. We were all surprised he was acting like a pet for so long, following you around more or less like a dog."

"He's no dog," I said.

"No, I know that—now especially. I guess his instincts finally won out."

"Yeah, they won all right. Big prize. Life without parole."

35

Injustice

I met Diane at the courthouse. "How are you doing?" she asked.

"I'm better. My wrist, it was really swollen last night, but it's quite a bit better now."

"Good. Listen, Oriando Abeyta had an airtight alibi for the time when your car was smashed. We had to cut him loose."

"An airtight alibi? What was it?"

"He and another lineman from the power company were installing two new transformers, replacing the one that blew at the junction a quarter mile down the road from you and the one that feeds your house."

"But Oriando was supposed to meet me—"

"They got out there early, drove down a couple nearby roads, and saw the sign at the end of your drive. So, instead of meeting you as agreed, they just started working on restoring your power. According to their written report, they also removed limbs that had blown down onto the line, probably during that windstorm that trapped you out on the mesa last week. There's no way they could have been anyplace else. One guy was in the truck running the lift and the other was in the cherry picker. They ran two digital tests on the new transformers a half hour apart. The power company had a computerized readout with the times on it."

"What about Rule Abeyta?" I asked.

"We retained him in custody because of evidence we found at his home. We got a search warrant last night. He had this effigy of a nun that was marked and painted to look the same way that Cassie Morgan's body had been desecrated."

"That's the monito," I said.

"What's that?"

"It's . . . never mind. I hope that's not all the evidence you had."

"No. He had some papers where he had written out the abuses that Cassie Morgan and others had heaped upon him as a child. And beside each thing on the list that Morgan had done, he wrote that he hated Cassie Morgan and wished her dead."

"That's still not hard evidence, is it?"

"Not hard enough. But if we have the murder weapon—and I think that rope you found might be it—then, we have him good. We're just waiting for the DNA evidence to come back from the lab in Albuquerque to lock that down. In the meantime, we're running down his story about where he was on the day that Cassie Morgan died. He better be able to account for every minute of it."

"But then who smashed my Jeep? You think that was Rule? Does he have a truck like the one that did it? Did you question him about me?"

A clerk stepped out of the courtroom and announced the next

hearing on the docket. Diane stood and gestured for me to come with her. "Come on. Let's go get my landlord."

Once we were seated in the front of the courtroom, I saw Eloy Gallegos come in behind another man. He gave me a nervous smile when he saw me, and went promptly to the table on the opposite side at the front. "He's your landlord?" I said.

"Yeah, that's him."

The judge, a Hispanic woman in her fifties, suggested that each side should present its case in its entirety, and that afterward—should it be necessary—there would be an opportunity for cross-examination of any witnesses.

Diane presented her own case. She had kept meticulous notes of times and dates when she had called for requests for repairs, of the slow response from the landlord in having someone come out, and of the time she had taken off from work and the hours that she had spent at the house while the landlord's cousin, Benny, was supposedly making those repairs. She presented lengthy receipts for replacing all her groceries which froze or spoiled due to the refrigerator not working, showing three repeat purchases within a matter of a week of nearly every item, from commonly long-lasting condiments such as mayonnaise and hot sauce to staples such as eggs and milk. She had prepared a list of the four different complaints in particular with respect to the oven not working. She showed photos of the house after the explosion and fire, and a list of her losses from the claim she had filed with her renter's insurance, along with the deductible she would be assessed out of pocket. She called me as a witness concerning the incident when the oven pilot light went out, and of course for the explosion. She even produced the medical report from the paramedic who had treated me on scene.

Gallegos's attorney called a service technician from the local natural gas company—a company which was not in any way involved—since the landowner leased a propane tank for the property. The serviceman nervously responded to the counselor's leading with grunts, nods, and one-word replies in such a manner that the explosion was made to look like an isolated incident caused by a leak in the external propane line, probably due to the series of recent hard freezes in the Taos area—thereby shifting any responsibility for the blast that might have befallen the landowner onto the propane company, which wasn't there to defend itself.

The lawyer then presented papers that indicated that every repair Diane had requested had been made, flourishing them in a bunch as if they were proof positive that she had recklessly harangued the landlord into mounds of unneeded expense. Next the attorney produced a notarized statement from someone who had claimed to be a witness to a conversation two months before in which Gallegos had informed Diane of a raise in the price of the monthly rent. Then the counselor exhibited receipts wherein Diane had underpaid that amount by several hundred dollars a month. The attorney claimed that Eloy Gallegos had only let the tenant remain there in spite of the discrepancy in the rent payment because he was such a compassionate man.

While the attorney was performing this circus, Gallegos sat quietly in his seat, his face completely without expression, looking straight ahead and never glancing in our direction. Diane was seething, fidgeting in her seat, and—more than once—whispering under her breath to me, "That's a lie."

After the two sides had each presented its case, the judge was quiet for a moment, writing on a legal pad. Without offering the opportunity for any further discussion or the previously mentioned chance to cross-examine, she said, "I think it is obvious, from the body of evidence we have here, that there is a misunderstanding between the parties about the price of the rent and the desired condition of the rental property. I am going to dismiss the complaint brought by Miss Langstrom. I will not award any compensation to the landlord for the loss of rent for which he is undoubtedly due, because there was no request on his part that I do so. It is unfortunate that both Mr. Gallegos and Miss Langstrom suffered losses because of the incident with the propane leak, which seems to be due to an act of God, and I do not find any cause for a finding of negligence. Costs for this proceeding will be assessed to Miss Langstrom." At that, she smacked her gavel on the bench, and the clerk instructed us all to rise.

Diane rose and cocked her head slightly to one side, one eye narrowed, her expression on the verge of a sinister smile. Her eyebrows toggled up and down at me, and she bit on her lip and did not speak. I watched the judge leave the bench and go through a door into her chambers. I turned back to console my friend, but when I saw her expression, I thought better of it. With her eyes, Diane was drilling a hole through Eloy Gallegos's skull.

Gallegos and his attorney were shaking hands and smiling when the door to the judge's chamber opened again, and the woman who had presided over the sham of a hearing came through the door minus her black robe and dressed as a civilian. Diane and I watched with amazement as the judge threw her arms around Eloy and hugged him. "You look just like your mother," she exclaimed, holding him at arm's length and then embracing him again. "You don't know how much I miss her. We were just like sisters when we were young."

"Come on," Diane said as she headed for the door. She walked so fast I had to hurry to keep up.

"What's our plan?" I said. "Can we appeal this in district court?"

Diane just kept walking and didn't speak. Outside the courthouse, she pulled up short on the steps to one side of the doors and said, "Wait here. Stand over to the side here where you can't be seen through the glass."

There was a steady stream of foot traffic coming and going from the parking lot up and down the steps and through the glass doors. We stood in the cold for a minute before Eloy Gallegos came to the doors and peered through. "Watch this," Diane whispered.

Gallegos opened one of the doors tentatively and looked out at the crowded parking lot. A man and a woman leaving the building passed through the door as Eloy held it open, and he looked annoyed at them as they did so. Another man coming into the building from the parking lot started for the open door, and Eloy narrowed the opening, causing the man to stop short and then pull open the other door to enter. Gallegos looked from one end of the lot to the other. Satisfied by what he saw—or didn't see—he came through the door.

Diane shouted from the side, startling Gallegos, and drawing the attention of everyone in the area. "Eloy Gallegos, we know what kind of a landlord you are, but what kind of a soldier are you? Why aren't you doing your job? Isn't your unit deployed? Why are you still here, Sergeant Gallegos?"

Eloy froze in midstep.

"*Sergeant* Gallegos?" I said, my mouth hanging open.

"Yes," Diane said, her voice still loud enough for everyone in the vicinity to hear. "He's in the National Guard." She swept her hand outward to encompass the crowd of onlookers in the parking lot and on the courthouse steps. "Why don't you tell everyone why you're not overseas with your unit in Iraq?"

Gallegos's eyes bulged with alarm, but he stood unmoving, like a trapped rabbit.

"Now I know where I had seen you before," I said to the man.

Eloy's eyes met mine, and then he sprang into action, darting down the few steps and out to his car.

Nina Enriquez, the clerk who had helped me identify the Coldfire property, had come out of the courthouse on her way to lunch when this scene began, and she had paused on the sidelines to watch. As Gallegos rushed away, she came over and held up her hand as if she were about to whisper to Diane and me, but she spoke in a normal tone of voice so that others could hear. "He has some kind of foot fungus. It got him out of going overseas to fight. But it sure hasn't kept him from fighting with everyone around here who gets in the way of him making money on all his property." She winked and then went on toward the parking lot.

Diane turned to me. "If he wants to fight, I'll fight."

"Hold on, I think I might have some ammunition for you," I told my friend. I raced to catch up with the clerk, calling as I went, "Nina? Could I talk to you a moment?"

As I was headed back through town from the courthouse, I saw Tom Leaves His Robe sitting on the side of the road in the cold. I pulled over, but he didn't recognize me in the Blazer. I would have leaned over to open the passenger door, but I was too sore. Instead, I waited, and Tom got up to look into the car. When he saw that it was me, he smiled.

"Want a ride someplace?" I asked.

"Okay," he said.

I picked up the boxed Howdy Doody doll that had been lying on the floor of the passenger's side and started to set it in the back, where Mountain's bed was. Tom leaned in and said, "Wait. Is that Howdy Doody?"

I held the box up to show him. "Yes, it is. It's kind of an antique, I think."

He leaned in even farther, still standing outside the car, and he smiled, his face like that of a child. "Howdy Doody," he said. "That's Howdy Doody." He seemed transfixed by the doll, and he stood unmoving, bent over in what had to be an uncomfortable position.

"Do you want to get in?" I said. "You can look at it while we ride."

Leaves His Robe worked his way into the passenger seat, and once again, I helped him fasten the seat belt. He closed the door, and then stared out the windshield. I held the box with the Howdy Doody doll in front of him, and he took it without looking at it and placed it on his lap. He gazed out the windshield again.

I put the car in gear and said, "Where are you headed?"

He turned his head and looked at me blankly. "I am not headed no place."

"Well"—I made a little noise in my throat—"where would you like me to take you?"

He continued to stare at me without expression. "Do you have a TV?"

I shifted back into park. "No, Tom. I don't have a TV. Why do you ask?"

"I like TV."

"Are you okay, Tom? Do you want me to take you to the hospital?"

"No."

"How about the church? Or to your sponsor's house?"

"Did you ever watch Howdy Doody?"

I shook my head. "No, I . . . that was before my time, I think."

"On Saturday afternoon, if we did not have no trouble that week, they let us watch TV sometimes. We watched Howdy Doody."

"You mean at the school?"

"Yes."

I was quiet a minute, wondering what to do. I didn't know Tom Leaves His Robe well enough to know what his norm was, but even so, I thought he seemed confused today, perhaps depressed. He didn't appear drunk, or smell like he usually did when he was drinking. I was concerned. "I tell you what. I'm going to take you out to the pueblo. We'll go see if we can find your sponsor." I put the Blazer back in drive and started down the Paseo del Pueblo, the main drag in Taos.

"All the boys like to play Wild West. Cowboys and Indians."

I smiled at the thought of little Indian boys playing cowboys and Indians, imagining that the scenarios might have played out a little differently than when white boys did.

"We all wanted to be cowboys," he said. "Nobody wanted to be Indians."

I made an involuntary grunt as the sadness of this thought hit me. It hurt my heart to hear what he said. I shook my head.

"I want to get out here," he said, as we stopped for the light at the plaza. He opened the door, then turned and handed me the boxed Howdy Doody doll. "Do I owe you money?"

"No, Tom, you don't owe me money. Do you need some money?" I reached into the pocket of my jeans and pulled out a five. "Here. Get a hot meal."

He took the money, and I helped him unfasten the seat belt. He got out of the car just as the light was turning green. "Thank you for the ride," he said, and he stumbled away.

◂ 36 ▸

Package Proposal

Even though I had told Tecolote I would leave Mountain there for the day, I decided to go and pick up the wolf over my lunch hour and bring him to the BLM and Forest Service holiday gathering scheduled for that afternoon. I was sure that everyone would be disappointed if he didn't come to the party, and a few people would bring little gifts for Mountain. And besides, I wanted to make up for my unspeakable behavior that morning.

When I was leaving the bruja's house with the wolf, Esperanza handed me a cloth bag with several items inside. "I put a little *carne de cabra* in there for Montaña."

"Good. He loves goat. Or did you mean antelope?" I had heard the locals use the term *la cabra* interchangeably to mean either one.

"*Sí,* some goat meat. And I made a little soup for you, to help you. And there is a *cajeta* of *mermelada de manzana,* you know, the sauce from those apples we get down there by the river. I cooked up many of those apples before the winter. You can put it on some hot bread, Mirasol. Together, this will help you to get your strength back."

On the way back to Taos, I talked to the wolf while he lay in the back of the Blazer. "I'm sorry, buddy," I said. "I'm going to make it up to you. I know you get bored when I don't take you out and run with you, and you take your frustration out on the things around you. I'm so sorry I hit you, Mountain."

He held his head upright and looked out the windows, ignoring my attempts to make up to him.

I kept talking. "I'm going to have Charlie Dorn's guys come out and build you an enclosure. We'll make it as big as we can so you'll have a place where you can be outside, where you can smell things and feel the wind, where you can run around a little bit when I can't go running with you."

Mountain gazed out the window as if he were fascinated with the side of the road whizzing past.

"I hate putting you on a chain. I can't stand it. This way you can be outside more and get exercise, be stimulated. But I'll never leave you out there when I'm not home. I want you to be safe, and I just couldn't trust that you'd be safe if I'm not there. So it's just so you can play outside when I'm at home, okay? I'll still always try to take you with me, and if I can't, I'll leave you in the house, where you'll be safe. And I'll never leave you for very long, I promise."

Finally, Mountain put his chin on the back of the passenger seat. I glanced over at him and he was looking at me. There was hurt in his eyes. Mistrust. I could feel it.

My lip started to quiver. "We'll get through this, buddy," I said.

• • •

When Mountain and I arrived, the party at the BLM was already in full swing. All the employees from the Forest Service office next door had come over to join in this combined agency event. The mood was festive, the conversation was loud and boisterous, and Christmas music played from a little boom box. Several tables boasted a gourmet spread of potluck delicacies. The gang welcomed Mountain and slipped him treats from the tables over my protestations—meatballs, an occasional cold cut or bit of cheese.

The Boss came over with a beverage in his hand and offered it to me. "Ginger ale, right? That's your favorite?"

"Yes, thank you."

"I wish I would have been here last night when—"

"It's all right."

"I saw your Jeep."

Here it came: Roy maintained that I could conjure trouble out of thin air, and that whatever vehicle I drove was cursed with certain doom. Unfortunately, events had proved this out. In the past several years, I had managed to demolish several Jeeps and get myself into deadly danger more than a few times.

"Are you all right?"

I eyed him cautiously. "Yes. I wasn't in the car when—"

"Good," he said, and he winked and raised his own glass. "Merry Christmas."

"You're not going to chew me out about the Jeep?"

"Not today."

"Wow. Well, in that case, I have a present for you." I went to the little artificial Christmas tree that had been set up on a card table in the lobby and pulled out the package I had placed beneath it earlier, when I had come in. I brought it back and handed it to Roy.

He smiled. "What's this?"

"Open it."

The Boss ripped open the newspaper I had tied around his gift. He held up the braided horsehair hatband with its silver conch and horsetail end. "Did you make this?" he asked. "Must have taken you hours."

I smiled.

Roy whipped off his cowboy hat and removed the simple leather band, replacing it with the new one I had made. "You got the color just right," he said. "Thanks a lot." He shoved the hat back over his head and looked down at me. "How do I look?"

"Good." I smiled. "That suits you."

"Wait. I got something for you, too." He headed across to the Christmas tree and picked up a sack from the floor beside the table. He came back and held the open paper grocery bag in front of me. Inside were several dozen small, colorfully wrapped packages. "Get yourself one," he said. "Let's see what you get."

I reached in and picked up one of the little parcels.

"Open it."

I did as I was told. It was a small, orange plastic pocketknife, no longer than my pinky. "Thanks," I said, thinking this would end up in the kitchen drawer along with most of the other little gadgets Roy had given me over the years.

"That one there's a special little tool," Roy said. "Open it up."

I pulled the blade, folding it out from the handle. It had a hook at the end and was curved, unlike a regular pocket knife.

"It's a seat belt cutter." The Boss beamed. "If your car gets submerged in water, or if you're in some kind of wreck where you can't get to the seat belt latch, that will get you out. You put that little elastic thing over your gearshift knob, or on your key chain, whatever works so you have it handy when you're in the car."

"That's neat," I said, trying not to laugh. I couldn't imagine a way that my car could become submerged in water in the high desert of northern New Mexico, unless I drove it off the Rio Grande Bridge, and even then, I was pretty sure the eight-hundred-foot fall would kill me before I had to worry about getting out of my seat belt. "Thanks again." I smiled.

"You got a good one. I'm glad you like it. I'll just pass these other goodies out to the gang." Roy proceeded to walk the sack around the room as if he were Santa Claus, inviting everyone present to take one of the little packages. I enjoyed watching as each gift was opened. There were tiny compasses and bear bells, hiker's whistles and bottle openers, compact ice scrapers and miniature thermometers that hooked on the zipper of a coat and affirmed that it was cold enough outside to need the garment. As they opened their packages, the recipients feigned surprise that the Boss had given them yet another little tool, as he did every year. And Roy was having the time of his life, explaining the versatility of each little item, often demonstrating its use. It was such fun to see him so happy.

I noticed Mountain nibbling at a piece of cheese from a plate on the corner of the food table. I dashed over and grabbed his collar, remembering to be gentle even though he deserved some discipline. "All right, buddy," I said, leading him toward the door. "You can't be trusted, and besides, you've had enough. I'm putting you in the car to sleep it off."

I was headed back inside when I saw Kerry pull into the parking lot in front. He tapped his horn and waved at me. I waited outside, unsure of how to greet him after what had transpired between us the night before. He got out of the truck and walked toward me, and I felt the undeniable pleasure of seeing his familiar silhouette. His body was long and lean, and he always looked ruggedly attractive to me in his boots and jeans, his ranger hat, even his just-worn-enough-to-be-tough-looking coat. "Wait," he said as he approached. "Just let me say one thing. Just one thing."

I waited.

"I'm sorry." He came close.

"That's the one thing?"

He reached a hand to touch my arm, then decided better. "I am sorry. I'm sorry that you found out about the job before I had a chance to tell you. I was going to tell you."

"Yeah. Okay." I turned to go in.

Kerry put his hand gently around my arm. His eyes looked into mine. "I wanted to ask you to go with me if I got the job, so I was waiting to hear because I wanted to make it a package proposal."

"A what?"

"I wanted to ask you to come with me. If I get the job, I want to take you with me. I was just waiting to hear for sure before I asked. But now that you know . . ."

I was stunned. As I stood on the sidewalk in front of the doors to the BLM, my lover looking into my eyes, I took a journey. I imagined waking up in the same bed with Kerry every day, the two of us hiking with Mountain, sharing meals, sitting by the fire, watching sunsets . . .

"I don't want to leave you. I don't ever want to leave you," Kerry said, bringing me back to the moment where the two of us stood in the cold afternoon air outside the place where I had worked for seven—nearly eight—years.

"I don't want you to leave either," I said.

Kerry embraced me and looked into my eyes for so long that I started to swoon. Then he brushed my forehead with his lips and kissed my eyelids, and I felt myself melt into the warmth of his chest.

As his lips touched mine, I felt a nudge against my thigh. I looked down. Mountain was sitting beside me, wagging his tail. "How did you get out of the car?" I said.

A few minutes later, Kerry and I had examined the Chevy and found the rear hatch and the other doors locked, except for one rear passenger door, which was standing open. Kerry flipped the handle on the door several times. "All I can think is that he must have stepped on the handle just right and it opened the door. Ninety-nine times out of a hundred, you couldn't do that when it was locked. The mechanism is just worn on this old door."

I reached in and hooked the elastic band of Roy's little seat belt cutter over the gearshift knob. "Great," I said. "The wolf can now open the car door."

"No, I don't think so, not every time." He flipped the handle again several times. "Look, it had to be a fluke, because most of the time, it doesn't trip the lock. He just got lucky. I've pushed down on it at least forty or fifty times and it's only given once."

Back inside at the party, I smiled and made small talk in one corner of the room while I watched Kerry moving smoothly through the crowd, shaking hands and slapping backs with the men, giving the women hugs and smiles. Friends hurried to bring him offerings of food to taste. Someone got him a drink. Roy hastened over with his sack of gifts.

With Mountain snoozing on the floor beside me, his belly full of rich food, I sipped my ginger ale and flirted with the idea of commitment. But even as I watched my bang-up boyfriend with delight, complications began to cloud my mental picture. I was scheduled to begin BLM ranger training in the spring, and I had not figured out how to balance this with my responsibility and desire to care for

Mountain. Even though I could envision a life with Kerry, I could not imagine that living or working anywhere else could be possible with a wolf in tow. Each time I tried, I saw us all back at my cabin: bringing in wood for the fire, making breakfast in my kitchen, Kerry and me snuggled in my big log bed with Mountain cuddled on his lambie beside it on the floor. All this felt wonderful as I pictured it, and I felt a narcotic flood of endorphins.

Kerry came across the room and kissed my forehead. He smiled down at me with a face I adored—that slightly crooked smile, those nearly fused eyebrows, the long lashes over his green-flecked brown eyes, the scars on his chin.

"What did you get from Roy's goodie bag?" I asked.

He held up a short silver plastic cylinder. "I bet I got the best one," he said.

"What is it?"

"A battery-operated nose hair trimmer," he said and winked. "Want me to try it out on you?" He reached one arm around my back to pull me close and playfully aimed the cylinder at my nose.

I pushed his arm away, laughing.

"So will you come with me to Washington?"

I stopped laughing, but held a big smile. It almost dashed my daydream, thinking of leaving this place I so loved. But in the next thought, I wondered if giving up my own path and following Kerry on his would be traveling the path of the heart that Tecolote had mentioned. "I'm thinking about it," I said.

Kerry grinned at me. "You're thinking about it, huh? I'll take that as encouragement."

I knew I had only been drinking ginger ale, but I felt drunk, giddy, and incredibly warm. *Maybe, somehow, this could work!*

As Kerry and I were imagining our romantic options, the Boss came up and touched my sleeve. "We just had a call from the rancher who took out a grazing permit for the BLM land near the Rio Pueblo. He says that some kids have gone in through that gate up at the road with their ATVs and they're scaring the cows. You mind running by there on your way home?"

◂ 37 ▸

Under the Cottonwoods

It was already dark. I was almost to the gate that led into the BLM land by the river when I saw a truck on the side of the road with its hood up. I pulled over on the shoulder behind the vehicle. I could see two men leaning over the front, their heads beneath the hood examining the engine. The pickup had California license plates. I thought to call it in for a plate check but remembered that everyone was having a good time at the party and I hated to interrupt their fun—this looked simple enough. I wrote the tag number on my hand before I got out to inquire if I could help. I had failed to transfer the flashlight from my Jeep to the Blazer, so I left my headlights on. I grabbed my automatic in its holster out of the glove box and clipped it to the back of my jeans. "You stay," I told Mountain as I closed the car door.

The two men looked up as I approached on the driver's side of the car. I held up my badge. "You guys need a tow truck?" I asked.

Before I had gotten abreast of the front quarter panel, the one nearest me lunged forward, seizing me by my extended arm. When I moved to push off his grip, he grabbed my other arm and yanked me forward, and I toppled toward the asphalt and crashed with a thud, my chest and knees hitting hard as I arched my head back to keep from banging my face. The other man had run up behind me and was now trying to grab my ankles as I lay facedown. I flailed my feet and kicked at him with my boots, and I felt one jab connect with what might have been his shin—he gave a loud grunt from the blow. Meanwhile, I was wriggling and squirming, and I worked myself up onto my knees, but the man who had grabbed me pressed my forearms hard into the grit and gravel and brought a foot up to step on my good hand, leaving me butt-up and vulnerable.

"Grab that holster, don't touch the gun," the one holding my arms said, and I felt the clip snap as it was pulled from the back of my belt, then heard a hard thud as my sidearm hit the blacktop and slid. "Grab her by the belt, pull her up."

They dragged me, kicking and thrashing, into the nearby field, the one man never relenting in his fierce grip as he held my forearms above my head—while the other fought to keep hold of my feet, grasping the cuffs of my jeans. I lashed out and freed one leg, but they wrung me like a rag, forcing my upper body in one direction, and the leg still in custody in the other, painfully twisting my arms in my shoulder sockets until the man at my feet had hold of both legs again. I cried out for help, I yelled and cursed at them. Neither man spoke, but they grunted and wheezed with the effort of wrestling my squirming weight. They threw me down onto frozen-hard ground under a stand of giant cottonwoods, the one man still painfully gripping my forearms with hands of steel. While he held me, I studied Steel Hands's face in the dark, determined to remember every detail

I could make out, but his face above me was in shadow. I saw wisps of coarse, dark hair escaping his stocking cap, a triangle tuft of beard left to grow in the cleft beneath his lower lip. The other man, heavier and much shorter—took a length of nylon rope from his coat pocket and looped it twice around my left wrist. They brought my two hands together as I struggled and screamed, and they tied them behind my back. When I saw Short Man move to grab my ankle, I rolled onto my side and drew up my leg and kicked, striking him square in the jaw. Suddenly, there were no hands holding me, but in a mere instant, I felt the blunt end of a boot drive into my back, and the air rushed out of my lungs as fountains of pain went off in my brain. A brick of a fist slammed into my abdomen, and another bashed into my right breast. I looked up at Steel Hands and tried to pull my knees up to protect my center, but Short Man moved to pin my feet to the ground while Steel drove his fist into my face, snapping my neck to one side and smashing the inside of my cheek between my teeth and partly into my nose. I felt blood fill my mouth and run from one nostril as another punch sledgehammered into my gut. My only thought was to buckle my body to try to protect myself from the next blow, but Short battened my boots to the ground—and whatever strength I had once possessed leaked out of me from a thousand weeping wounds.

Steel pushed me onto my back, my bound hands beneath me. "Get up here. Hold her down," he said.

Short scrambled across the ground from my feet to my head, and he knelt above me, breathing hard, pressing a hand on each shoulder, his weight causing my back to arch over my trapped hands. Steel, on all fours now, drew down close to my torso and hovered above me, his chin just inches from my chest, his breath fogging in the cold. He grabbed my shirt in his teeth and threw his head back and to one side, popping the buttons. Short laughed at this, and Steel—encouraged by his audience—pressed his cold face into my breasts and seized the elastic between the cups of my bra with a bite that scraped my skin. He pulled up, stretching the elastic away from my body, then let it snap hard against my chest. Both men chuckled at this, and Steel brought his face up beside mine while Short looked down from above. Steel blew on my cheek, his breath hot and moist and reeking of beer. He reached a hand behind my neck and seized a fistful of hair and jerked hard, twisting my head to one side, forcing me to look at him. He pistoned his tongue in and out like a snake and then he licked my face. Short spoke for the first time, in the elongated vowels of a hip-Hispano accent. "Come on, man! Quit fucking around. Let's do this, bro!"

Steel pushed himself back, raised up on his knees, and reached down and unzipped his jeans. I felt Steel's hands at my waist, fumbling with my belt. Then I felt the rip of my own zipper and I heard Short's breath quicken with excitement as he watched. And I caught the sound of something else in the distance, something that took me a second to recognize. As Steel grappled and tugged to work my jeans over my hips, I could hear Mountain pounding at the windows of the Blazer, yelping and shrieking. I wanted to go to him, to comfort him, to snuggle up to him and sing to him, but I couldn't move because Steel had climbed on top of me and was trying to spread my legs but my jeans were still bound up around my thighs.

I couldn't breathe, I felt sure a vein inside me had opened and I was drowning in my own blood, and I began to sink, to drift beneath the surface of my own being. I looked up through the cottonwood branches at the night sky, at the stars, and I recalled Tecolote telling me to listen to the trees, and I remembered the trees dreaming a new world. I wanted to go to that world. I saw light play on the limbs, yellow-gold light. It washed across the cottonwoods and then died away into the darkness. Suddenly, I heard a dull thud—and Short, who had been holding my shoulders, slumped to his side. In the next instant, Steel, who had raised up at this new development, was suddenly running away. I heard struggling, muffled cursing, and blows landing on flesh.

It occurred to me to get up but I felt an acute pain in my side. My jeans, which had saved me from an even worse fate, still prevented me from moving my legs apart. After the clash subsided, I heard fast footsteps retreating, a car engine revving to life and then speeding away. I listened to the staccato, high-pitched yip of my wolf-child and then I felt blackness start to well up around me.

Eloy Gallegos looked down at me from above. He wriggled out of his coat and threw it over me as he knelt on the ground at my side. "Are you okay?" He reached down and put a hand under my head, lifting it slightly off the ground. With his other hand, he tenderly brushed blood and hair away from my mouth and nose. "Don't worry," he said. "Those guys are gone."

He half pulled and half lifted me to my feet, and he tugged on the waist of my jeans to pull them up. We stumbled forward a few yards but I could not seem to stand. My knees collapsed before we could make it back to the road, and Eloy caught me, picked me up, and carried me the rest of the way to his car. "Oh, my God," he said. "What have they done to you? You're pretty bad off. I'm going to take you to the hospital." He propped me, standing, against the side of a black vehicle as he opened the door to the backseat. He eased me down into the car, holding me beneath the arms until he felt my weight release into the seat. "Lie down in here and I'll take you."

"No!" I said, seeing Mountain frantically pawing at the rear window of the Blazer parked in front of Eloy's car. The wolf yelped and looked through the glass at me with alarm. "No, I can't leave Mountain!"

"But you need help! You need medical attention. Your mouth is bleeding, you can't even walk! You need to go to the hospital."

I rolled myself to the edge of the seat and pulled myself up. "I'm not going anywhere without my wolf. I'm not leaving him."

"Okay," Gallegos said. "Okay, I'll call an ambulance, and we'll get them to come get you—and your wolf. Sit down. I'm gonna take care of it. We'll get you some help." He pulled a cell phone out of his pocket and punched three buttons. "Hello, we got an emergency here," he said, putting one hand on my shoulder to keep me from falling out of the car. "We need an ambulance. And send the police, too. A woman has been attacked."

When he hung up, he turned to me, pulled a handkerchief from his shirt pocket, and pressed it against my mouth. Even through the blood and the swelling, I caught a hint of a citrus cologne on the fabric. It smelled clean and comforting. "Don't worry," he said. "They're coming. Just hold on, they're coming."

"My gun," I said, half in and out of conscious thought. "My gun."

"Don't worry," Eloy said, retrieving the handkerchief from where it had fallen onto my chest and pressing it back to my bleeding mouth. "They'll find those guys who did this."

"Give me my gun," I said, and I pointed to the side of the road.

◂ 38 ▸

Fog Singer

I hate hospitals. My father spent the last few years of his life in and out of them, and finally died in one—unable to recover from a broken heart, the loss of an arm, and the disease of alcoholism. Since then, I'd had no faith in their ability to heal the sick or injured. And so, after I was poked and prodded and x-rayed in the emergency room, I checked out against medical advice with lacerations, abrasions, contusions, and cracked ribs.

According to the police, Eloy Gallegos had already given a statement that he had been driving out to his auntie's house at the pueblo when he saw the truck with its hood up, and the Blazer with its headlights still on, the wolf jumping in the back of the car in distress. He didn't see anyone else around, so he got out to investigate, and that was when he found the men assaulting and trying to rape me. He used an oversized metal flashlight to strike one man and then fought with the other, finally chasing the two of them off. He had declined treatment for his skinned knuckles.

The police had tried to take a statement from me as well, while I was in the emergency room, but Diane Langstrom arrived a few minutes into the process and told them the incident was part of an ongoing federal investigation. She dismissed the local cops. "Mountain's okay," she said. "Kerry's outside with him. They won't let the wolf come in."

Another reason to hate hospitals.

"Your landlord—" I started to say.

"I heard," Diane interrupted. "He's the big hero boy tonight. Well, I'm just thankful someone was there to help you, even if it had to be him."

Diane followed as Kerry drove me and Mountain home in the Blazer. I slept on the way, my head lolling between the back of the seat and the soothing cold glass of the window. When Kerry was leaving to go back to town with Diane to get his truck, I asked him to bring in the sack that Tecolote had given me, and to put Mountain—who'd been cooped up in the car all evening—out on his chain.

"I'll be right back," Kerry promised, propping my rifle beside the bed and putting my handgun, in its scarred leather holster, on the bedside table. "I'll get back as fast as I can."

Although Kerry and Diane had helped me undress and get into bed, as soon as they left, I painfully worked my way to the edge and pushed myself up to a sitting position. I got myself on my feet and shuffled to the bathroom, grunting and groaning like an old woman, holding my side, half-bent over and hurting with every breath. I stared into the mirror over the sink. Diane had carefully lined up the bottles of medication they had given me at the hospital: a prescription for pain, an anti-inflammatory, and an antibiotic. I swept my hand across them and knocked them into the trash can next to the sink, and as I did so, I said, "*Unh, unh, unh,*" as the women at the pueblo would have done.

I looked at my reflection in the mirror and saw a stranger there, a woman with a bulging red lip so swollen on one side that her nostril was partly occluded by it. The cheek on the same side ballooned as if it held half a day's rations—and the skin was already turning blue.

I ran cold water in the sink, and—not caring that my hair would get soaking wet—I bent over and put my whole face under the surface and watched the blonde wisps float like they did when I was dreaming with the trees. Only this time, the tendrils reached downward. I raised up and let my hair drain into the sink, then blotted my head gently with a towel, but it hurt so much I gave up and just let the water run down my skin inside my nightgown.

With great difficulty, I eased myself onto the toilet and sat for several minutes trying to relax my aching abdomen enough to pee. When I finally did, I felt a grabbing pain in my left kidney. I gasped and started breathing hard, rapidly in and out, like a woman in labor, and finally the flow stopped, and with it, the searing pain. When I got up to flush, I saw blood in the water in the bowl.

I picked up the gunnysack Tecolote had given me and went to the kitchen for a spoon. While I was there, I fished out the package of goat meat and put it in the fridge. I would give it to Mountain tomorrow. Back in my bed, I opened the bag. Inside, the big jar of soup had been wrapped with a piece of cloth and tied with string. I spooned the cold broth gently into the good side of my mouth and forced myself to suck it down. I did the same with the applesauce, not because I was hungry, but because I knew Tecolote had made this as medicine for me, and it would probably have more curative power than anything that came from a pharmacy.

After, I could hardly hold my eyelids open. I propped myself up against the headboard on my pillows with my rifle and handgun as my sleeping companions. As I turned out the light, Mountain set up a howl from his confinement on the strong chain, but I could not muster the energy to go out and bring him in. Besides, Kerry would be back soon. Just before I dropped off to sleep with the sonorous song of my beloved wolf in my ears, I looked out the window into the darkness and saw a cold, dense fog rolling in.

◂ 39 ▸

Double Entendre

When I woke, Kerry was sitting in one of the wooden kitchen chairs reading a book, his rifle on the table in front of him. I looked down and saw Mountain snoozing on his lambskin rug beside the bed. I put one hand to my face and felt gently around my mouth and cheek with my hand. My face was still swollen, but not as much as it had been last night.

I pulled myself up in the bed. Kerry turned to look. "Good morning," he said.

I tried to smile, but it hurt.

"Come with me to Santa Fe today," he said, helping me up and toward the bathroom.

"I can't," I said, my voice hoarse, my body stiff. "I have to go to the pueblo. I promised Momma Anna I would help deliver the Christmas baskets."

“You can’t do that, you’re hurt. They can get someone else to help with the baskets.”

I turned and looked at him. “I told Momma Anna I would do it. Those old women used up their gas money to buy candy and other things to put in those baskets. It’s the least I can do.”

“But you’re hurt. The doctor said you had cracked ribs.”

“I’m getting used to this,” I said, moving gingerly across the room. “I’ll bet this is the way a football pro feels on the morning after a game. If those guys can do it, so can I.”

Kerry shook his head. “I wish I could help. I would take the baskets around for you if I could. But I have to turn in some paperwork at the Santa Fe office for that job application.”

By that time we had reached the bathroom door. I stopped and faced him. “I’ll be all right. I’m just going to drive. Momma Anna and the aunties are taking the baskets in the houses.”

“At least you’ll be with other people,” he said, brushing a wisp of hair from my face and then turning to go back to his chair. “There’s safety in numbers.”

“Yeah, that’s what everyone seems to think, anyway.”

The women were gathered once again at Momma Anna’s house when I arrived. In the main room, the baskets that they had prepared the week before were lined up across the floor, their cloth coverings pulled back. The aunties, who had been baking and cooking for days, moved among them adding coffee cans full of posole, plastic containers of elk meat chili, loaves of fresh-baked pueblo bread, assortments of decorated cookies, and pocketlike prune pies to the array of goodies they had already packed into the baskets earlier.

Momma Anna came up to me as I stood just inside the door, watching the activity. "Eeeee! You got more hurt."

"Yeah, I got more hurt."

"This time, you look like somebody beat you." Her face was full of concern.

"That's right," I said. "Two men."

"What they do?" she said, anger rising in her voice.

"Just a couple of bad guys. They jumped me and beat me up."

Momma Anna reached a hand out and tenderly touched my cheek. "Eeeee! I go get you some snow," she said, and she turned and went toward the kitchen. I went to the kitchen table and sat down to watch the ladies as they finished their project. Momma Anna came through the back door with a pan full of snow. "It nice shady by fence, no wind there," she said. "Snow stay long time." She packed the white stuff into a dish towel, rolled it up, and handed it to me.

I pressed the cold pack to my face.

By this time several of the aunties had come to examine me and make exclamations of shock and worry. It seemed that each of them had a home remedy to recommend.

"My sister got a drunk for husband," Yohe said. "He beat her all time. She put that cactus jelly on her face. She say it best cure."

"Best cure that one," Momma Anna said, "big stick. Crack him over head, he don't come home drunk maybe."

When the goods had all been distributed, and the cloth covers tied once again over all the baskets, the women gathered in the kitchen. "Now we burn cedar," Momma Anna said, and she went to the woodstove for her little cast-iron skillet. From a micaceous pot that she had made with the figure of a small bear perched on the lid, she spooned out some cedar tips into the pan, struck a stick match on the rough cast-iron bottom, and then lit the cedar. It flared, then smoldered, glowing red.

The women formed up in a circle and as Momma Anna carried the smudge from one to another, they fanned it toward their faces, washing themselves in the smoke. When the time came for Yohe to bathe in the cleansing vapor, she began to pray aloud: "God, please bless our people, bless our old ones, bless our children, bless this white girl, she get all better, nobody beat her no more."

Anna Santana and I made five trips before we got all the baskets delivered. Mountain lay in the back of the Blazer, and we stuffed six or seven baskets in behind him each time, then ventured out on the ice-packed dirt roads around the pueblo. As we jostled over the rattleboards and ruts, the little plastic seat belt cutter clacked and clattered as it bounced against the gearshift knob. Finally, I was so annoyed by the noise that I slipped the short elastic leash off the shifter and stuck the small tool into the back pocket of my jeans. The brass wildlife identification tags hanging from Mountain's collar jingled, too, as the Chevy's suspension shuddered over the dips and drops in the narrow dirt lanes. Momma Anna turned to look at the wolf in the back. "Wolf sound like he got sleigh bell," she chuckled. "Jingle bell, jingle bell," she sang, pointing to Mountain with a smile.

We took the baskets to run-down adobes with sweet-smelling smoke twirling from the chimneys, to the small, thick-walled apartmentlike dwellings in the big adobe structures on the village plaza, and to stick-built HUD homes out on the flatter ground west of the village, where horses with shaggy winter coats stood and stamped in the snow, their breath fogging in the cold. At each place, I forced myself to get out of the car and help Anna get a basket out of the back; then she would scurry to the door, wrapped in her blanket, and spend a few minutes making the delivery while Mountain and I waited in the Blazer. By the time we had made the final round, my joints had loosened up from all the movement, and although I was still bruised and painfully sore, I found myself feeling a little better for having done some easy work. The swelling in my face had also gone down considerably after I had applied the cold compress my medicine teacher had made for me from the snow.

We delivered the last basket to Sica Blue Cloud Gallegos. I went with Momma Anna to her door. Sica greeted us with a smile and asked us in.

"We got work do," Anna said. "We got mud and snow on boot. Happy Christmas." She set the big basket on the floor just inside the door.

"Wait," the old auntie said, and she hobbled away for a moment, then returned. She held out a hand to me, her fingers closed over something in her palm.

"What's this?" I asked.

"Take it. You will see."

I opened my palm and the old woman dropped two small, shining black stones into my hand. "Obsidian?" I asked.

"Apache tear. For the deserter boy. You keep. Happy Christmas."

"Happy Christmas, Grandmother," I said.

As I followed Momma Anna out to the car, I saw Eloy Gallegos heading toward his auntie's house. "You go ahead," I said to my medicine teacher. "I'll just be a minute."

Gallegos approached me. "How are you today?" he said, smiling, giving a little nod. "I thought you would still be in the hospital."

"I need to tell you something. I'm grateful for what you did last night—"

"It was nothing." He shook his head as if to dismiss it.

"I wasn't finished."

Gallegos raised his chin and studied my face, but he didn't speak.

"I don't change sides. You need to know that. I think I've figured out what you've been up to, and as soon as I have the proof, you're going to pay." We stared at one another for a few moments, and then I dipped my chin ever so slightly and walked around the man and on to the car where Momma Anna and Mountain were waiting.

Back in the Blazer, I sat looking out the windshield, without starting the engine.

"You got angry heart," Momma Anna said.

I let out a big breath. "I do."

"Eloy?"

I nodded my head. "He seems like he's so good to Auntie Sica. But he's not what he seems. He's sick with greed. He's a monster as a landlord, lying, stealing, even endangering my friend's life with his greed—my life, too—causing people pain, and not caring that he does."

My medicine teacher was quiet for a moment. Then she spoke. "You got Apache tear. Hold up to light." She pointed a finger at my hand.

I held one of the stones between my fingertips against the window. With the light behind it, the black obsidian appeared almost clear, as translucent as a tear.

"You see that? That our sorrow, tear freeze like ice."

"I don't understand."

"This time, some sadness too big, our heart cannot heal. Some thing too evil, some thing too dark. We not understand, our mind cannot hold it all. We try, our spirit grow sick and weak."

"Like the Indian school?"

She nodded. "We have no way understand that. We have no way. We cannot. We need put that sadness someplace so our heart can live. Not enough power heal that, not this time. Maybe next other time."

"So, you . . . choose not to feel it."

"No! We all time feel it. We choose not carry it, not hold it. We ask Grandmother Earth, Father Sky hold it, that way we use heart for love, not for sadness."

I opened my palm and looked at the two stones.

"We all got them," Momma Anna said. "That one man live here, he keep the sheep. His father Tanoah, but his mother Apache. Those boy, his relative. He bring us those stone. They have legend, next other place about Apache tear, women cry for brave lost in battle. But we cry here for those boy, and for Tanoah children, too."

"The man who brought these to all of you here at the pueblo, is his name Daniel Kuwany?"

"That the one. He say he not forget his relative. Sometime he forget about sheep, though. He go off and leave them, go out there somewhere, wander off. He go for days, come back drunk. Take everybody long time, round up sheep."

As I drove Anna home, I said, "I keep running into stories about that abandoned Indian school. Everywhere I turn, I find another person who attended there, another sad story. And lately, I've had a lot of bad things happen to me that I don't understand—horrible things, abuses that came at me out of nowhere, like this beating. I'm just trying to get through but I'm confused and out of my element, and I don't understand what's happening. It makes me think of how the children must have felt when they went to that school."

"They children in story. This time, everybody all grown up."

"Sometimes I think that children who have suffered a lot never really grow up. They look like it, but part of them is still trapped in the past and can't move on, like those Apache tears."

"You grow up just fine."

"I know. But I can relate to all the stories because I knew a lot of pain and misery as a child, especially because I was abandoned by my mother."

"You always have good mother right there," Anna said.

"No. No, I didn't. My mother left when I was very small. I didn't really have a childhood. My father started drinking soon after that."

"Your mother all time there for you, maybe you just not see her."

By this time, we had arrived at the Santana home. I put the Blazer in park and looked at my medicine teacher. "No, Momma Anna, my mother was not there. She left. She left, and I was alone."

"You always have mother. You are beloved and cherish daughter to her." She opened the car door and began to get out.

I closed my eyes for a moment. I was too sore and tired to argue with this stubborn old woman. Maybe she was trying to reassure me that wherever my mother was, she would always love me, but I couldn't take any comfort in that.

"Come in," Anna said before closing the passenger door.

I followed her into the house, planning to say a quick good-bye and then leave. But Momma Anna gestured for me to follow her into the bedroom, a room I had never been in before. She showed me to a low altar that had been constructed from a plank of wood set on two large round aspen logs cut to the same height. Before it, she had folded a horse blanket, probably used for kneeling in prayer. On the altar was a framed photo of her father, Grandpa Nazario Lujan, who had passed away in November. In the picture, he was standing in front of a sunlit span of adobe with a white blanket draped over his shoulders, his long braids dangling in front of his chest, a cloth headband tied across his tall forehead. Anna had placed Grandpa Nazario's blanket, one of the drums he had made, a silver and turquoise cuff, his drum-making tools, and many of his favorite things on the altar and on the floor around it. Momma Anna handed me a box of wooden kitchen matches and pointed to the tall glass jar candle with an image of Our Lady of Guadalupe on it. As I was lighting the candle, she disappeared from the room.

I wasn't sure whether I was expected to kneel and pray at the altar, to remain and tend it, or to leave and follow my medicine teacher. I waited a moment and watched the flame flicker in the glass jar. Anna came back into the bedroom carrying a plate and a mug. She set them on the altar in front of the photo of Grandpa Nazario. She had fixed him a meal of some of the posole and elk-meat chili, a piece of pueblo bread, and a cup of coffee.

As I was leaving Momma Anna's house, she held the door for me. "You know that guy Tom Leaves His Robe?"

"Old Tom? Yeah, I gave him a ride the other day, and then I saw him briefly again yesterday."

"You maybe pray for him," she said. "They find him drunk behind that Wal-Mart. He almost froze to death again."

"Oh, no. Oh, no." I lowered my head into my hand. "He wasn't drinking when I saw him," I said. "And the other day, he said he'd been sober for seven months." Then I remembered Tom's urgency to meet with his sponsor to do his fifth step, and the roll of tear-stained yellow papers he had clutched in his hand. "I have to go, Momma Anna," I said. "I have to make a call."

It took three tries before I got through to Diane, and by the time I did, I was at the BLM. "Those papers you found in Rule Abeyta's home?

Were they yellow, all curled up and water-spotted, written on with blue ink?"

"How'd you know?"

"Those weren't things Rule wrote," I said. "Those were the fifth step that one of his AA sponsees had written out, a guy named Tom Leaves His Robe. I gave him a ride the other day, and he had those papers rolled up in his hand."

I heard Diane sigh on the other end of the line. "Damn. I can't believe I had this all wrong. All the clues are dead-ending: that license plate number you wrote on your hand traces to a car totaled in an accident and destroyed for salvage metal. The sister at the pueblo church has claimed that the statue of the hanging nun belongs to the church and is a harmless icon. A nun says this!"

"You talked to Sister Florinda?"

"Yeah, because there's a strange wrinkle there. Guess what our data guys found when going through Cassie Morgan's finances? She had a will, fully executed. She left her entire estate to that little church at Tanoah Pueblo, named Sister Florinda Maez as the executor."

I felt my eyes dilate. "Did the sister know about this?"

"She seemed surprised when I mentioned it. I haven't had time to run the whole thing down. Like I said, it's a little twist, but it's not giving me a buzz. Anyway, the lab report is back: the blood on the rope is Cassie Morgan's. But the DNA from the skin samples on the ends of the rope is not a match with Rule Abeyta's, so we are releasing him."

I was quiet.

"The Silver Bullet is upset with me because he says I arrested the wrong guy, even though he was with me every step of the investigation. I'm headed out to Tanoah Pueblo in a little bit. I'm going back over everything. We must have missed something."

"So we're back to square one."

"We are."

And I'm still a target, I thought.

"I'm having better luck with my personal sleuthing. I found out that the landlord's creepy cousin is named Benny Baca, and he's done some time in California. I ordered his sheet, and I'll know more when it comes across the wire. He's no appliance repairman. I can use this to discredit Eloy Gallegos in an appeal in district court."

"Wait a minute—Benny Baca? Have you looked at that sign in the big lot at the end of your street? It says 'Baca Land Development Company.' This supports what I suggested to you at the courthouse yesterday—that Gallegos wanted you off his land because he's either trying to put together a development deal of his own, or to sell to a developer. But he must need an easement."

"Good, that's good. I'll run the Baca Land Development Company and see what I get. Hey, guess what else I found out."

"What?"

"I know Agent Sterling's first name."

"Tell me."

"It's Sterling."

"So he goes by his first name?"

"No, that's both his first and his last name. He's Sterling Sterling."

◂ 40 ▸

Answering the Call

I sat at a desk in one of the cubicles at the BLM that afternoon, staring at the paperwork Roy had left for me. It was an application to the Natural Resource Police Training Center in Artesia, New Mexico, as a candidate for BLM ranger training in the spring program, which was a ninety-day residential assignment. Roy had already submitted my records, and this was more or less a formality.

Mountain had made the rounds of the few folks working there at the BLM office on Christmas Eve day and collected a minimal supply of rubs, scratches, and attention. Now he lay on the floor at my feet, snoozing contentedly. I worried over how to handle the issue of his care while I was gone to the training. The past summer, I'd deployed with an incident management team on a fourteen-day assignment to a wildfire, and entrusted Mountain to Momma Anna's care, but she had ended up bringing the wolf to the wildfire. And Tecolote couldn't manage the wolf for more than a few hours. Now that he was prone to running away and chasing coyotes, I didn't trust him with anyone but Kerry. And Kerry was going to Washington.

I filled out the first page with my personal information, then doodled on a notepad, unable to concentrate. I shoved the paperwork away. My side pained me terribly, as did my face. It still hurt to pee, although I'd stopped passing blood. I was not only worried and hurting, I felt edgy and confused. I didn't feel safe. I didn't know why the two men had attacked me, why any of the attacks in the past week had happened, or what it all had to do with the murder of Cassie Morgan. Until that case was solved and I was safe on the streets, I wouldn't be able to make any plans.

My joints had stiffened up while I had been sitting in the chair, so I forced myself to get up and move. Mountain fell in beside me as I pulled on my coat and walked down the unusually quiet hallway, through the empty lobby, and outside to the parking lot to get a breath of fresh air. A deepening cold was causing the afternoon to go gray and miserable. During the time I had been in the cubicle inside, most of the employees had left the BLM to begin their Christmas holidays. There were only a few cars parked in the lot. I went to the Blazer and took out the bag Tecolote had given me. In it, I had brought the *carne de cabra* from the refrigerator at home to give to the wolf for his dinner before going to the pueblo that night. Kerry was due to pick us up in fifteen minutes, so I thought I would go ahead and feed Mountain now.

Back inside, I filled Mountain's water bucket and then opened the packet of meat. There were five thick red slices of gamey-smelling flesh. I picked up one between my fingers and tossed it to the wolf. He raised up and snapped the meat between his jaws, then almost inhaled the whole piece without chewing. I made him wait for the next one, and this time I held it up and said, "Be nice, Mountain, be nice." A filament of drool stretched from his lip halfway to the floor. He came forward and took the slice gently, then chewed and swallowed it quickly. I set the paper with the three remaining slices on the floor and made the wolf wait—in terms of wolf behavior, this was an exercise that maintained my role as the alpha. I gave the release, and he gobbled the meat down in seconds. Protecting my sore ribs as I moved, I began working my way out of the chair to go wash my hands when the phone on the desk in the cubicle rang.

"Wild. Resource Protection," I said.

"I want to help you." The man's voice sounded muffled.

"Who is this?"

"I know you are in danger. I can help you."

"Who is this?"

"Come to Tanoah Pueblo tonight for the procession. I will meet you there. I can tell you who killed that woman."

I was quiet, trying to think what to do. Could I record this call somehow? Could we trace it?

"Are you there?"

"I'm here," I said. "Tell me now."

"Meet me tonight at the pueblo."

"I can't. If you have something to say, say it now."

"I will be wearing the mask of the deer. Look for the downy eagle feathers on the tips of the antlers."

"I won't be there, you'll have to talk to me now."

"I do this to help you. My standing among the tribe will be in jeopardy if anyone finds out I told. I do not know who is there with you, or who might be listening."

"I'm alone. No one is listening. You haven't even told me who you are."

"At five o'clock, I will be in my mask. You will not know who I am, but I will tell you who killed the woman. Until you know, you will not be safe."

I looked at my watch. It was four thirty. Kerry was overdue. "I can't get there in time."

There was no reply; the line was silent.

"Hello?"

I called Diane and recounted the call to her. "I'm out at the pueblo now," she said. "I'll be watching. I'll try to stay close to the footbridge that goes across the río. Don't come up to me—it might scare your guy off. I'll watch for you and try to keep eyes on you."

"I'll have to go in the back way to try to get there in time. The front entrance will be clogged with visitors coming to the procession from all around."

"Just be careful. Watch your back. And bring your cell phone—make sure you leave it powered on. If I see something I need to warn you about, I'll call you."

I left a note on the front door of the BLM office that read: *Meet me at the procession.* I loaded Mountain in the back of the Blazer and drove away muttering, "Damn it, Kerry, where are you?"

◂ 41 ▸

The Procession

Numerous events marked the eve of Christmas in the Taos Valley. One was the ongoing neighborhood reenactments of Las Posadas. Another was the spectacular ritual procession at Taos Pueblo, attended by hundreds of tourists and Taos town residents. And then there was the smaller, but more primal procession at Tanoah Pueblo—which drew few tourists, but rather mostly its own tribal members, some locals, and many rural villagers who traveled from the surrounding mountain communities where families had made the pilgrimage to the pueblo on Christmas Eve a tradition for generations.

I parked in the corral and came over the wall on the plank-wood steps near Grandma Bird's house, passed by the old cemetery, and went down a narrow alley between two massive adobe structures, entering the plaza at one corner, instead of through the main entrance gate by the church. Crowds of people packed the small square in the twilight, in spite of the merciless cold. Many wore traditional blankets, some were dressed in modern winter coats, and a few boastingly sported furs and fox-trimmed après-ski boots. Dozens of tall turrets, twelve feet high or more, had been framed from stacked piñon logs for the bonfires that would be lit as soon as the last of the day's light had left the sky.

The temperature had been dropping rapidly all afternoon and now hovered well below freezing. The waiting crowd queued up for spots nearest the soon-to-be-lit vertical pyres or visited the few resident vendors who sold refreshments out of their homes to buy cups of coffee and hot cider to warm their hands. The sky was clearing, and as the clouds broke, what little warmth had been trapped beneath them escaped upward to the stars.

I stood on a spot of high ground and scanned the crowd. Not far away, I saw Sevenguns waiting by the churchyard wall, wearing a chief-style woolen blanket. Under the hide-drying racks in front of the main pueblo building, a large group of Tanoah women stood gossiping, their blankets folded in half and fringed around the outer edges to make warm, beautiful shawls. In the near darkness, it was getting hard to make out details, and the individuals in the crowd began to look more and more like vague shapes in silhouette. I moved toward the center of the square. On the footbridge over the río, I spotted a tall, slender figure wearing dark jeans, a military-style jacket, and a black-billed cap. *Diane.*

I heard a burst of cheering come from one edge of the plaza and saw fiery yellow flames licking at the air, rising and surging like a wild beast searching for a way to escape its cage of crosshatched logs. The Tanoah tribe had signaled through the ancient and venerable medium of fire the passage of day into night. It was now officially sundown. I checked my watch: five o'clock.

Soon, twenty more towering piñon bonfires sparked to life, and the smoke and incense from the sap of the wood rose in great dark clouds, spreading across the plain of the atmosphere, blackening the air. The crowd grew animated, aroused from its former cold-dulled lethargy by the exciting emergence of light and fire, man's primeval friend and enemy. The people began to shift and move, to merge into one mass, emitting a cacophony of sound that took on one murmuring voice, and this herd—with an innate sense that something was about to happen—then coursed toward the gates at the churchyard wall. I made back for my post on the packed earth at one corner of the plaza, where I could see more of what went on.

The bell in the belfry pealed three times, then the earsplitting crack of gunshots heralded the beginning of the procession. At the front of the line, at the gates of the churchyard, six strong, stone-faced Tanoah warriors led with their hunting rifles aimed skyward, firing shots into the air, the shells ejecting around them, the deafening report of the gunfire parting the crowd and causing those close by to put fingers in their ears. Alongside them, a group of two torchbearers with flaming poles held high. Next, a contingent of Tanoah drummers, their long, log-and-hide drums laced onto leather straps hung from one shoulder across the torso. These men were ceremonially dressed, each wearing a burnoose or a colorful scarf tied across the forehead, a white blanket, white cotton or buckskin trousers, and soft-soled moccasinlike boots. Accompanying the drummers were helpers, who assisted with the weight of the drums for the elder drummers, or who simply walked in tandem and chanted and sang. And behind them, a group of children from the pueblo, each carrying a pair of rattles made from the shells of turtles mounted on handles. They danced as they rattled and sang in Tiwa.

The onlooking crowd had now parted into two camps, one on

each side of the procession. With each new contingent in the parade, another pair of warriors or torchbearers enforced the edges of the path so that there was sufficient room for the procession to pass through. The celebrants in the procession moved out from the ancient church at the east side of the plaza toward the south, the Summer side of the pueblo, while the spicy incense-laden smoke from the torches and bonfires created a curtain of black haze around them. The gunfire, the drumming, the chanting and singing—all created such a clamor that the skill of the mind to sort and separate sound seemed to vanish—and all this, together with the sights and the scents, melded into one magnificent sensory experience that spoke to something deeper than reason and understanding.

Pueblo elders came next, carrying the sacred santos and bultos from the church, and I saw Momma Anna among them carrying the bulto of San Quarai. Behind this, a group carried a litter bearing the Virgin Mary, and the women from the sidelines rushed in to kiss the hem of her white bridal gown, then disappeared back into the crowd of dark, indistinguishable shapes beyond the torchlight. Following the Virgin, a choir of women marched past singing *almas* in Spanish. And last: four Tanoah priests—each carrying a brilliant, blazing torch—led the sacred masked dancers, representing the spirits of the supernatural. These masked gods emerged through the smoke-laced darkness at the rear of the procession in their crocheted white leggings, their white woven kilts tied at the waist with long, colorful, fringed scarves, branches of cedar tucked in the waist and bound to their upper arms with cloth. Their naked upper bodies were painted white, their flesh rubbery in the relentless cold. Their eyes were open but unseeing, and they stepped off a silent rhythm, occasionally pausing in unison, holding one foot high. Each dancer in this prayer drama wore a unique mask. The Tanoah believed that the mask was the incorporate spirit of the supernatural it portrayed, and that when a dancer donned it, he became that spirit, and thus made the journey into that place of magic where he could commune with the gods. Through his dancing and chanting, his offerings and prayers, he was both the embodiment of the spirit and the summoner of its magic and power. Alongside the dancers, male protectors flanked, making a rapid, guttural trilling: "*Heh-heh-heh-heh-heh, heh-heh-heh-heh-heh.*"

As the dancers came past, I examined each one's mask. Two wore deer masks, but in the darkness and the smoke, I could not make out whether either mask had downy feathers on the antler tips. I tried to press forward, to get to the front of the sideline, but the edge collapsed when the crowds surged inward as the last dancer went by, everyone joining in the march to the four directions.

Amid the jostling of the crowd and the deafening noise and chaos, I felt a tug at the sleeve of my coat. An adolescent girl dressed as a corn maiden looked up at me, her one bare shoulder blue with cold. "Aren't you the lady who has the wolf?" she shouted, trying to be heard above the din.

This was a bad time to have someone inquire about Mountain. I nodded my head yes, and looked back at the procession, which had now passed me by.

The girl tugged my sleeve again. "Someone is t . . ." Her voice disappeared into the pop of more gunfire as the procession moved away.

"What?"

"Someone is bothering him in the back of a car down there." She pointed back down the narrow alley through which I had come. "I think they might be trying to hurt him."

◂ 42 ▸

Left Out

I raced up the narrow alley, the noise of the procession fading into the distance as I went. But the smoke from the bonfires was still thick and hung in clouds between the buildings and along the wall. I ran through a fog of blackness past the cemetery, and was halfway down the plank steps leading over the wall when I thought to call Diane. Just as I retrieved it from my pocket, the Screech Owl sounded off, startling me. I quickly punched the green button. "Yes?" I kept walking.

"Jamaica, this is Lorena Coldfire. I'm so sorry to bother you on Christmas Eve, but I thought you would want to know. Someone has taken one of the traps. And we think the cubs might have been in it, because we saw their little tracks nearby."

By now I had reached the edge of the corral. A mask hovered next to the Blazer, levitating in black space. It was an elegant molded-leather mask with the stylized white face of a deer, and a small set of antlers tipped with the white down of eagle feathers. A row of straight, green-painted sticks was set vertically above the forehead like a crown, and each of these twigs bore a tiny tuft of eagle down, too. Below the mask, the outline of a man's body began to emerge as I looked closer. He was not dressed as a dancer, but rather wore all black clothing, which nearly disappeared into the smoky night, so that the mask seemed to be floating, disembodied. I could hear Mountain in the back cargo area of the car, growling and threatening. The masked man held up a black-gloved hand and waved for me to come forward.

I reached with my free hand and unsnapped the guard on my holster. My fingers closed over the grip of my automatic. As I grew closer, I could see that the masked man held a pistol, its barrel pointed into the narrow opening made when I'd left the window partway down so Mountain would have fresh air.

I still held the cell phone up to my ear. "Lorena, I can't talk right now," I said. "I've got to see a man about a wolf." I punched the button to end the call.

"Throw it away from you." The voice did not come from the mask, but rather behind me and to my left. It was Steel Hands.

When I heard his voice, the imprinted memory of unbearable pain sent an electric shock through my brain stem, and I gave an involuntary jerk. At the same time, a hot flame seared through my gut, and I thought I might wet myself, or cry. But I did neither. I threw the cell phone on the ground, my right hand still on my weapon.

"Your gun next," Steel said. "Move slow. Leave it in the holster. Only use the tips of your fingers. Throw it to the side."

I made a pretense of having difficulty with this request. "I have a sprained wrist," I said, slowly easing my gun upward and out of the holster. I moved my head slightly to try to look around, but it was dark and smoky and I could not see much.

"Throw the gun or we shoot the wolf. Now."

I sent supersonic probes to the farthest galaxies of my mind, desperately seeking a better idea, but I could not think of a thing to do except to comply. I dropped the gun back into the cup, drew the holster up from my belt until I felt the clip snap, then tossed it to the side. I heard footsteps running toward me from behind and someone slammed into my back, throwing strong arms around me and trapping my elbows against my sides. Another set of hands pulled my hat off and shoved a dark cloth bag over my head. I tried to stay upright, but they pulled me to the ground and worked quickly to tie my wrists and ankles.

"Help!" I yelled. "Help! Someone help me! Help!" But the able-bodied of Tanoah Pueblo were all at the procession, and the sounds of the drumming and gunshots drifted muted through the smoky air. I knew my screams were in vain.

I heard Mountain snapping and snarling, barking and banging at the windows of the car.

One of them threw me over his shoulder and carried me a short way, his collarbone pressing painfully into my cracked ribs. He slammed me down onto a long flat of cold metal. When I tried to get up, I received a hard chop to my abdomen, causing me to double up in pain. "You want more, like the last time, you keep it up," Steel said. Two of them worked to push my legs flat, then stretch bungee cords tight over my feet, my thighs, my chest, pinning me down.

"But why me?" I yelled through the bag. "Why are you doing this to me?"

"We better gag her, bro." I recognized Short's voice.

"I can't breathe!" I said as they fastened a gag right over the bag, pulling it so tight behind my head that it cut into the corners of my mouth. "I . . . ant . . . ee!"

I heard the engine crank on the UTV and then an arctic blast of freezing air rushed over me as we took off at top speed. My whole body jostled with every dip and turn as we rumbled off-road, the back of my head banging against the cargo skid, a constant jarring vibration shaking my brain like a rattle. The noise of the motor roared right in my ear and exhaust poured out from beneath me, sickening me so that I prayed I wouldn't have to puke, knowing I would choke to death on my own vomit if I did. The air was so cold that I began to shake with chills. For a time I felt biting pain in my hands, my feet, my nose, and then my body began to work hard to survive as it closed down the circulation to my arms and legs, preserving my vital organs. My shivering subsided, my fingers and toes went numb. Speeding through the frozen, dry-desert night created a cryonic mistral that instantly dehydrated me; with my mouth forced open by the gag, it freeze-dried my tongue. My throat ached with thirst and I could not swallow. I knew that delirium was creeping in when—instead of trying to figure a way to escape my bonds—all I could think about was oranges.

The UTV slowed and idled for a long stretch. I could hear the two men talking, but the noise of the engine was too loud for me to make out what they were saying. I worked hard to move my fingers and my toes, at first without any success at all. Then gradually a little movement in the hands, and then pain—such a deep, aching pain in my feet—as I managed to wiggle my toes. And then the vehicle stopped. A gale of frigid air blasted me, and I realized that it was not just the speed of the UTV that had been causing the freezing wind. We were out on the mesa.

When the bungee cord lifted off my chest, I drew in a breath and felt how desiccated my nose and throat had become, the soft tissue at the back of my mouth like parchment, unable to flex without tearing. They picked me up—one at each end—the way they had taken me to the place under the cottonwoods, only this time I didn't struggle. Whatever they were going to do to me now, I was not going to risk another beating. I couldn't. If there was a way to survive, I had to keep what little strength I had.

They dumped me on the ground and I didn't move. Grit and dirt blew right through the bag over my head and blasted my face. I heard them shuffling around, then one of them picked me up from under my arms and dragged me a few feet, sitting me upright against what felt like a post. The bitter wind drove against my chest, and I heard a groaning sound as they stretched a rope around me, making painfully tight loops at my waist and across my chest beneath my breasts. They lashed me to the post, my hands tied behind me, my legs outstretched in front of me, my ankles bound together.

"Want to see what we've got in store for you?" Steel said. He tugged on the bag around my head and I felt him maneuver a knife tip through the cloth, then draw it up, slicing the fabric open with a loud *r-r-r-r-rip*. He pulled the torn bag down around my cheeks, but it remained tied over my mouth by the gag they had placed over it. Above me, the midnight sky was filled with a lustrous array of stars, so big and so bright that they looked like great celestial luminarias placed along the sky paths of the spirits for their journeys in celebration of Christmas. Ahead of me, upslope, stood the high wall of the Pueblo Pena ruin. To my left, no more than a few yards away, stood the smashed gates in the wall of the San Pedro de Arbués Indian School, the shadow of the bell tower rising above it in dark relief against the starlit heavens. I had already known where I was before he removed the bag from my eyes. The groaning sound made by the bell as it strained against its rope restraints had told me I was at the place of sorrow.

"See that meat trail over there? It leads right to you." Steel walked a few feet away and picked up a small chunk of dark flesh, possibly a cube of stew beef, and held it up between two fingers for me to see, replacing it on the ground. He walked a few yards farther and picked up another piece, which I could barely make out at that distance.

Short, who had stayed close by, leaned over me with an open thermos and poured a cold, dark fluid over my legs and into my lap. "Guess who's coming to dinner, man?" he said, and they both laughed. Even though my nose was parched and frostbitten, I caught the game scent of fresh animal blood and thought of the elk in the meadow and her unborn calf.

Just as the two men were making ready to leave, a bolt of white fire soared through the sky, a shooting star so large and luminous that it swept the ground with light and trailed a silvery streak across the heavens that burned blue, then yellow, and then golden before dissipating. "You know what that means? My grandmother told me that means someone is going to die," Steel said. "And that someone is you." The two men chuckled at this as they walked away.

I listened as the UTV chugged away, upslope to the ruin, where it stopped and idled for a few minutes, then drove away. I waited in the blowing cold for the two cougar cubs to find me.

Hungry as they must surely have been, it took the lions nearly an hour to appear. I guessed that they were delayed because they were frightened by having been caged, and were so mistrustful of the sound of the UTV that they cowered in their former den for a while before venturing out. Or maybe the cold wind had dried the meat so much that it had lost most of its scent, and so they had trouble finding the trail. During this hour of waiting, I watched as an enormous full moon rose from behind me and floated high into the sky, pulled upward by the pulsing planet, Mars. The other stars retreated demurely into the background as Grandmother Moon bathed the mesa with her silvery light, as if to spotlight my predicament. But Mars remained—close and large like a brilliant red warning beacon. Momma Anna had taught me that Mars was an ancient elder of her people named Qusayu, a warrior who protected the People. It was my frail hope that Qusayu had brought the moonlight to help me.

But I was not idle while the heavens arranged themselves so gloriously. I spent the whole time wriggling my torso up and down, flailing my bound-together legs against the ground, and trying to sever the rope that pinned my wrists against the pole by rubbing them frantically against it, all to no avail. I had worked my jaw to try to loosen my gag, I had twisted my head back and forth for the same purpose, and the only benefit to any of this was that I had burned enough calories to keep from freezing to death in the howling, bone-penetrating, blood-congealing ice-wind.

After a time, though, I had ceased struggling and had begun to think about my imminent demise. The lament of the ropes that held the bell had commiserated with me, crying out in misery with each gust or gale. I thought of Kerry, his face, his eyes, the wild places he loved, the wild places within him, the way he looked at me, the way he smelled. I thought of Momma Anna and her sweet little, flat smile, the courage she showed in teaching me, her dedication to the rituals of her culture. I thought of Tecolote and her potent medicines, her foreseeing wisdom, and her cryptic way of communication. I thought of Roy, and of Diane, but I tried not to think of Mountain because I didn't think I could bear it. And when I did relent and think of him, my chest hurt so bad that I felt my own heart become the milagro that Tecolote had given me, the one that was cracked in two.

In that same instant, I glimpsed two low, muscular silhouettes in the moonlight—one slightly larger than the other, both of them nose to the ground on the slope above me. No more time to feel sorry for myself; it was time to die. They loped forward from meat bit to meat bit, and the wind carried their voices as they spit and growled, fighting with one another in their hunger over each morsel.

As I saw them coming for me, young and beautiful and starving, I thought that if I had to die, it was perhaps a good thing that it was so that something wild could live. I had worked all my adult life to protect the wilderness and its inhabitants. My body would be my final gift to the wild.

Gift! Tecolote's voice echoed in my mind: *I advise you to treasure every gift you receive. Even if the thing, it seems small or insignificant, you must treasure it.* I remembered Roy's little gift! I rolled slightly onto one hip and began maneuvering the tips of my fingers into the back pocket of my jeans.

One of the cats caught the scent of the blood, raised its nose to the air, and then lowered into a half crouch and began to creep down the slope toward me. The other followed, and they approached cautiously, but clearly hungry. I tried to make a growling noise through the gag, but it came out as more of a groan, which did nothing to dissuade them. My frost-numbed fingers found the seat belt cutter, but I couldn't get hold of it. The larger of the cougar cubs moved cautiously toward my boots, and I flopped them up and down, startling the two youthful predators into a quick retreat. But they were not completely intimidated. They studied me from a few feet away, their tails flipping with excitement, their cat-minds wild with ideas driven by the smell of the fresh blood. They began to sniff the air and cry, their voices still young and high, but threatening enough. And then they began to circle, unsure how to begin, looking for the best avenue of attack. I plunged my fingers deeper into the pocket and caught the small knife between two fingers. I had begun to maneuver it out when the larger cat made another attempt, this time taking my boot into its mouth and biting down hard. I felt a needle pierce my arch and I cried out and flopped my legs again, throwing the cat off. But this time, the cougar pounced, grabbing hold of my boot with its claws. Gripping my boot in its strong clutches, the cat made ready to bite again, when a blur of speeding fur blew by me from behind and struck the cub with a thud, bowling the attacker off of my legs. Mountain stood up and posed over my boots, teeth bared and growling, the hair on his back spiked in a high ridge, his head low and forward, ready for a fight.

If I could have spoken, I might have cried out with joy. If I'd not been sandblasted dry by bitter winds, I might even have cried. But pinned and gagged and parched as I was, my sole reaction was to freeze, unmoving, in a strange mixture of relief and disbelief. In an instant, I recovered and fingered open the seat belt cutter and used the strong, hooked blade to slice through the ropes on my wrists. It was an amazing tool! No knife could have done it that well.

The cougars hissed and growled as Mountain stood his ground, and I watched as the ravenous cats began to evolve rapidly into killing machines, working to flank the wolf, taunting him in tandem with one swipe at his thigh, then another at his neck.

I worked at the ropes binding my body, cutting one strand without gaining any relief and then finally another, which allowed me to pull my torso free. The cats tried a charge, but Mountain charged back and they retreated. Still, they resumed circling. While one of the cougars menaced Mountain from the front, another moved around to attack me from the back. But, no longer pinned to the post, I was a moving target now, and I turned, scooting myself around to keep my eyes on the cub. That was when I saw the man coming at me with the rifle.

He charged toward me and paused at thirty paces, taking square aim in my direction with his gun. At the advance of this intruder, the cubs had scattered, but the gunman made no notice of that and instead raised the barrel of the rifle slightly, adjusted his line of sight, and prepared to fire—on the wolf! I raised up to my knees and pushed my body in front of Mountain's, holding him to me with one arm while I yanked hard on the gag, finally pulling it from my mouth. "Stop! What are you doing?"

"Move out of the way," Daniel Kuwany yelled. A gust of wind caused the bell ropes to wail.

I tried to make myself larger, shielding the wolf with as much of my body as I could. "Stop! Daniel, it's me, Jamaica Wild. This is Mountain, my wolf."

"I know that wolf. I'm going to shoot him. He killed three of my sheep tonight."

"No, it wasn't him. It wasn't him. He's been in my car. He had a full belly, he had goat meat for dinner. He wouldn't have attacked something if he wasn't hungry. And besides, he didn't have time. It's only been about an hour since . . ." Amazingly, Mountain hadn't moved from behind me.

Kuwany moved to one side to get a better shot. "You got company behind you."

I turned to look, and discovered why the wolf hadn't budged. The cubs had regrouped and were stealthily moving toward Mountain and the smell of blood on my boots, which were outstretched under him as I stood on my knees.

The piercing *whhhinnnng* of gunfire startled us all, and we froze in still life for a second. Frightened, the young cougars fled rapidly up the slope. Kuwany dropped his rifle and put his hands in the air. Mountain moved around beside me and peered into the darkness. Still standing on my knees, I seized the opportunity to slice the rope binding my ankles, trying to imagine who this next opponent might be. A gush of wind began howling, nearly pushing me over, and it continued unrelenting. Daniel Kuwany's blanket flew out straight from his shoulders, Mountain's mane blew up like a lion's, my hair whipped out from beneath the bag still encircling my neck and buffeted my face, and the ropes on the school bell started weeping and wailing and ululating and groaning and then suddenly a loud *snap!*

The great iron bell gave a deep, metallic creak, and then it rang—a deep, round, guttural, gonglike tone. Another deep creak, and then another *bong* from the bell. And another, and another. *Bonnng . . . bonnng . . . bonnng.*

I got to my feet as Kerry walked toward us, pushing against the wind, his rifle pointed at the shepherd's chest. He looked at Kuwany, then at Mountain and me, and he glanced up at the bell ringing in the bell tower. The gale subsided, and in a few moments, the bell stopped pealing. Kerry eyed Kuwany with suspicion. "Is he the one who's been—"

"No. But he and I have to have a little talk about wolves and sheep." I grabbed the shepherd's rifle off the ground.

"So, where are the bad guys?"

"Gone," I said.

"They didn't go back through Pueblo land. I'd have seen them."

"Me, too," Kuwany said. "Whoever did this, I didn't see nobody but you and that wolf and those two cats."

"How did you know to come out here?" I asked Kerry. "And how did Mountain—"

"Mountain must have opened the car door again. I found the

Blazer parked in the corral with the door standing open, and I found your cell phone on the ground." He reached in his pocket and then held up the Screech Owl. "I returned the last call, and Lorena Coldfire told me what she had told you. I figured you would be out here."

◂ 43 ▸

Christmas Present

On Christmas morning, Kerry drove me near to the address I had written down on my hand. "Slow down, don't get too close," I said. "Park down the street a house or two."

"Diane's coming, right?"

"Right. We wait for her call."

"She's getting a warrant?"

"As soon as she can find a judge who will answer the door on Christmas morning."

Just then, the Screech Owl sounded off. I checked the display, then punched the button to answer. "Did you get it?" I listened a moment, then clicked the button to end the call. I looked at Kerry as I reached for the door handle. "She's on her way."

"How do we know if he's there?" Kerry asked.

"I'll find out." I got out of the truck and closed the door slowly and quietly. My face ached; it was swollen, frost-nipped, and red every place that it wasn't bruised. I had rope burns on my wrists, and a painful little puncture wound from a cat bite on my foot. I was still bruised, scraped, and sore from the beatings, the avalanche, and the explosion of Diane's gas line. I walked up the street to the house, Kerry a few steps behind me, and I recognized the car sitting out front. "He's here," I said. I glanced down the street and saw two black SUVs coming in our direction. "Here comes Diane. You take the back door."

I burst through the front door without knocking. I did not draw my weapon, fearing how easy it might be to use it. Eloy Gallegos was sitting in a big leather chair in the corner of the front room, celebrating holiday gift-opening with his family, dressed in an expensive-looking plush black robe and pajamas. He looked up in astonishment as I came through the door. "You!" he gasped, his eyes bulging. "How did you . . ."

Heaps of torn colored paper, open boxes, and lavish gifts covered nearly every inch of the floor. I had been cool and determined before that, but when I saw him sitting in his comfort and luxury, I became furious with rage. Ignoring the woman and the young boy on the sofa, I strode fast across the front room and struck Gallegos with a blow to the abdomen and another to the face, which caused me to shriek with the pain to my hand and my wrist. But I drew back to strike again all the same, when Eloy ducked and rolled over the arm of his chair and then raised up and ran for the back door. I bolted after him and caught hold of his robe, pulling him down, falling on top of him. I bashed him again with my fist, this time in the soft flesh of the side, right under the ribs. He gushed air but pushed me off and scrambled to his feet, grabbing a wooden spoon off the counter and smacking me on the shoulder with it as I started to rise. He picked up a marble rolling pin and struck at me, swiping the air as I dodged to the side, smashing the heavy tool through the wood facade of the cabinet beneath the counter. Gallegos grabbed the handle on the back door and yanked it toward him, but once again, I caught hold of his robe. I wanted to smash his head in the door or even take up a kitchen knife myself, but while I restrained myself from either of these, Eloy seized the toaster off the counter, jerking the cord out of the socket along with it, and he swept it in an arc behind him, smashing it into my right shoulder. I was knocked sideways by the blow but I grabbed the collar of his robe again as I went. Gallegos cleverly shrugged out of the garment and fled out the door in his pajamas. Kerry was waiting, as planned, on the porch behind the house. As Kerry moved to grab him, Gallegos faked to one side, jumped the step, and fled across the yard toward the garage at the end of the drive. Both Kerry and I pursued him, flanking him on either side, while two of Diane's men moved in from the sidelines with guns drawn and ready. I pushed Gallegos from behind and knocked him down. I jumped astride him, ready to strike, but Kerry pulled me off before I could punch Eloy again.

"Easy, babe," he said, jerking Gallegos to his feet. "Easy. He'll get his. You don't have to do it."

But I couldn't stop myself. While Kerry held Gallegos's arm pressed high into his back, ready for me to cuff him, I punched Eloy as hard as I could in the gut. "You told Daniel Kuwany my wolf killed the sheep!" I yelled.

Gallegos nearly doubled over with the blow, but drew up again and looked at me defiantly. Then he looked around at the other agents in his backyard. "That's what this is all about?" he said, a venomous grin on his already-swelling lips.

"I don't know all the details of how you did it, or even why you did it, but I know you killed Cassie Morgan. And then you tried to kill me. More than once."

Gallegos spit. "Do you have any evidence to support these charges?"

I whipped a white handkerchief out of my coat pocket and flourished it in front of him.

"That's your evidence?"

"That's your handkerchief. You used it to gag me last night. It smells like your cologne, the same citrus cologne that was on your handkerchief when you supposedly rescued me from the two attackers."

An SUV pulled up the drive to the end, and Gallegos glanced at it, looking less confident as he did so. "Most men have handkerchiefs. Many men wear the same brand of cologne as me. Am I under arrest?"

Diane Langstrom got out of the car and walked toward us as two other armed officers stepped out, their guns trained on Gallegos. Diane unfolded a badge holder. She held it up in front of Gallegos's face and she paused, her head cocked, a smile on her face, relishing the moment. "Eloy Gallegos," she said, "I'm arresting you for kidnapping and assault on a federal officer while in the performance of her duties, reckless endangerment and attempted murder of said federal agent, and"—she paused a moment and glanced at me and nodded—"for the murder of Cassie Morgan."

"You can't prove any of that," Gallegos spit.

Diane waved a hand, and one of the agents came forward from the side with handcuffs at the ready. Diane moved her face within a few inches of Gallegos's ear. "I can. And I will."

After Diane booked Gallegos into custody, we all met at the BLM. I'd unlocked the doors to let us in, and we foraged for breakfast items in the two refrigerators used by the employees. "And you thought there was no place to get breakfast in Taos on Christmas morning," I said to Diane, holding up Roy's new stick of deer sausage in one hand and a package of a dozen homemade tamales in the other. "There's some juice in there, too. And Kerry made coffee."

Kerry got us cups and paper plates as I started the first round of tamales in the microwave.

"When all the clues seemed to be playing out wrong yesterday, I had them run the DNA sample from the rope through the federal database, just on the off chance we'd get a match. I didn't get the results before I left for the pueblo, but they came in last night. Because Gallegos is in the National Guard, his DNA is in the federal repository for the military. The sample from the rope is an exact match."

I pulled out a plate of two warm tamales, sliced off a hunk of deer sausage and put it on the side, and handed it to Kerry. I sliced another hunk of deer sausage for Mountain, tossed it to him, then started another plate of tamales warming. "But, why? Why did Gallegos hate Morgan so much? Because of what she did to Sica?"

"Nothing that noble. As you know, I've been looking into Gallegos's business and financial affairs, trying to build a better case for my appeal in the tenant dispute. I found out that when Eloy's mother died, he and his second cousin, Benny Baca, were the sole heirs to the Baca Land Grant, a tract of land given in the Spanish Land Grants. Eloy used his share of the inherited land to become a Taos slumlord, renting his handful of run-down adobes and failing to provide needed repairs and services. Benny, whose family had moved to California when he was young, had gotten into gangs and afoul of the law. After his parents' death and a short stint of prison time, he returned to Taos to be the strong-arm in the Baca Land Development operations that Eloy was running, which for years was only renting the run-down places and extorting the renters for their rent and deposits. But recently, Eloy Gallegos was courting a developer who wanted to buy the land and put up condos."

"Don't tell me," I said, putting a plateful of warm food in front of Diane. "Cassie Morgan was somehow involved in the development deal."

"Kind of," Diane said. "However, it's more like she *wasn't* involved, and refused to be involved. Gallegos had made an enemy of Cassie Morgan through a series of confrontations over the years because Morgan's fine home was on land adjacent to the run-down Baca houses—over on the opposite side of the land grant from where I rented from Gallegos. Morgan had lodged countless complaints of raw sewage, improper maintenance, noise, trash, and more—but each time, she was thwarted because Gallegos paid off the officials. So, when the Baca Land Development Company needed Morgan to sell them an easement so that the condo deal could go through, Morgan refused."

I poured coffee for each of us, and gave Mountain another hunk of deer sausage. I had a fleeting thought of what Roy would have to say about that, but I shoved it out of my mind. "But what a way to kill someone—not that there are good ways—but this way was really malicious."

"Or maybe that's just his way of being wily and creative. As a child, Gallegos had to have heard countless stories of the child abuse at San Pedro de Arbués Indian School. When Gallegos discovered Morgan's past identity, he figured a way to remove her as a problem and to point the finger of blame for the murder at the Indian school survivors. And besides, he probably counted on the body not being found, or at least not for a long time, at which point the evidence would have been mostly gone and the trail cold."

"But what about the attacks on me? Do you still think it was that ATV chase that started it all?"

"You discovered the body. And the UTV itself was a major clue; it belongs to the National Guard. It's specially made for rugged terrain to transport medics and supplies. He thought you saw it, and possibly him, too. They figure you either knew or could put it together eventually. Gallegos is the keeper of the keys for that fenced federal training facility out there. That's how he'd come and gone without anyone seeing him do it when he left Morgan's body at the old Indian school."

"That's how those guys got back from leaving you out on the mesa last night without me seeing them, too," Kerry said. "Or that shepherd Kuwany."

"But what do you think Gallegos was doing out there, idling along on the UTV a day or so after the body had been found?" I said.

"Like I said, they left something behind." Diane spooned a bite of tamale into her mouth.

"Wait a minute," Kerry said. "Jamaica doesn't know about the knife." He turned to me. "The paramedics were checking you over when Diane arrived last night, and I gave it to her. In all the excitement, I forgot to tell you: I found a knife on the ground about a hundred yards from the entrance to the Indian school. It's a military-issue commando-style knife."

"You found a knife? But how did we miss it? We searched the whole area in a grid pattern the morning after I found the body," I said.

"Probably the winds. Covered it up the night you were trapped in the snowstorm. Could have uncovered it last night," Kerry said. "The blade was glistening in the light of that full moon."

"I sent the knife to the lab," Diane said. "The prints were there, we'll just hope we get a match."

We were all quiet a minute or two while we ate. Then I said, "So we've talked about Gallegos and Baca, but there's a third guy involved. And what about the elk cow? And the cell phone?"

"Let me tell you some of what I found out about Benny Baca," Diane said. "His juvie record was sealed, but the Silver Bullet is going to help me get it opened, now that we have the DNA on Gallegos and see the tie-in. But just look at his adult sheet, and you'll find out that Baca has been charged with two counts of torturing animals—one for setting his neighbor's dog on fire and watching it burn to death, and the other for dragging a string of six cats behind his car down the Santa Monica Freeway. He pleaded down to a lesser charge and did six months of community service. Animal rights don't get high priority in most overcrowded court systems. He's also had a string of arson, assault, and attempted rape charges brought against him, most of which were dropped. He did serve time for assault when he was nineteen, and the victim was a woman who'd been badly beaten. They tried to prove rape, but that charge got thrown out due to a technicality in the handling of evidence.

"And I told you before how Eloy Gallegos has everyone in town on a bribe or a debt. That's one of his number one landlord ploys—if he gets someone in a position where they owe him, he can call in a favor when he needs it. He probably knows someone that somehow got your cell phone number for him. You said it's posted on a bulletin board in here. It could have been anyone—a janitor, a delivery person, even a visitor that he sent in here under some pretext. Or it could be someone who works here, who didn't know what they were doing when they gave it out."

"And what about the third guy?" I said.

"I think I have an idea who it might be," Diane said. "Once we question Baca and Gallegos, we'll know for sure. Baca's got a buddy down in Española he runs with, another winner with a checkered past. I had him picked up this morning just in case. He had a parole violation, so he can spend Christmas in lockup and we'll put him and Baca in a lineup for your viewing pleasure tomorrow."

Just then, Roy peered in the doorway and looked right at me. "How are you doing, kiddo?" he asked, coming forward to study my face.

"I think I'm going to make it now, Boss."

He started to raise his arms, as if he might have wanted to hug me, but wasn't sure if he should do so. Instead, he reached up and tipped his cowboy hat back on his head, then dropped his arms to his sides. "I told you last night when the paramedics were looking you over that I'd come in and file the incident report today so you could get some rest. Looks like you didn't pay a bit of attention, as usual."

I tried to suppress a smile as I reached out and put my arms around Roy, giving him a big hug. "I wanted to be the one to make the bust," I said. "I needed to . . . break the news to Gallegos personally."

Kerry and Diane smiled at this. Roy patted me gently and then pulled away from my embrace. He turned to Diane. "So you got Gallegos in custody?"

"And Baca," Diane said. "And another guy I think was probably involved."

"And, Boss," I said, "I did hear you last night: I didn't file the incident report yet."

Roy pursed his lips. "So, you got the bad guy yourself and left me with the paperwork, huh?"

I just smiled, even though it hurt my cracked lips and swollen cheek to do so.

"So what are you guys doing here, then?" Roy asked, looking around. "Wait a minute—is that my deer sausage?"

◂ 44 ▸

Everything Changes

On the morning after Christmas, I received the best possible gift. Charlie Dorn and his crew returned the she-lion to the Coldfire Ranch. Lorena and Scout had reported seeing the cubs eating at the feeding station east of the spring on Christmas Day, so we all hoped that meant the family would be successfully reunited. I drove out to the ranch to watch the release. The crew kept the cage covered until they were ready to set the cougar free, and the rest of us stayed well back of it and out of her way. The biologist pulled the release and the cage door flew open. A hesitant lion pushed her nose out and sniffed, but she did not move out. We waited, hushed and hopeful, for what felt like a small lifetime; then, she extended her head and looked from side to side. We huddled in our group behind the screens set back twenty yards from the cage. A minute later, she sprang, bounding away toward the foothills without looking back—surely remembering in our scent, and in the cage, and in the vehicle behind the cage, the report of the gun that had pierced her leg and cost her so much. I was excited that she might actually survive because of this fear, and hope purchased a small handhold in my worried, skeptical mind.

Later, I drove the Blazer out to the overlook where I'd gone to monitor the traps. I made Mountain wait in the back while I got out and watched through my field glasses. I trained them to the east, where the cubs had been spotted, and for an hour I waited and watched without a sign. The wolf fell asleep, and I nearly did, too. Just as I was about to give up, I spied the two cubs crossing a flat, and in a few minutes, I saw their mother come in from the west. She lowered in the front, crouching as if to pounce, but stood stock-still and let the little ones approach, her tail high and waving, posed as she might to attack prey. I held my breath and said a silent prayer. Nothing happened for a few minutes, and the wary cubs started to leave. Then suddenly, the she-lion lay down, and the young ones returned—one of them sidling up to lick her face and the other snuggling into her side. She raised her head and closed her eyes, and I could almost hear the sound of her deep, motoring purr. These three great cats of the wild, these few of the last living embodiments of the untamed West, were a family once more.

That afternoon, I stood in front of a one-way glass as six men lined up in a room on the other side of the barrier. The man I knew as Steel slouched casually against the wall and smirked, as if he had secret knowledge that this was all somehow going to go in his favor, and the rest of us had been deprived of that information. He picked dirt from under one of his fingernails with a thumbnail, and when asked, he stepped forward, crossed his arms over his chest, put one hand under his chin, and grinned leeringly at the glass. I felt my insides tighten, and for a moment, I thought I might lose control of my bladder. "That's him," I said. "He's the one who almost raped—"

Diane interrupted. "That's Benny Baca," she said. "Anyone else here look familiar?"

I swallowed and nodded. "The guy on the end, on my right."

Diane pressed a button. "Number six, step forward, please."

Short didn't look confident. In fact, he looked close to panic. His lips were quivering and he kept shifting his eyes from side to side nervously. He shoved his hands into the front pockets of his jeans as if they might fly away if he didn't.

I nodded. "That's the other one," I said.

"Yeah, just like I thought," Diane said. "That's Baca's Española buddy." She pressed the button again. "Thank you, gentlemen, that will be all." Diane turned to me and put an arm around my shoulder. "You okay?"

I drew in a long breath, and let it out. "*Unh,*" I said, as the women at the pueblo had taught me to do.

The following Monday, Diane called to update me. "Benny Baca rolled on his cousin Eloy for the murder, and on his friend from Española, too. He's hoping to plea-bargain his own murder charge down to manslaughter and leave those guys holding the bag. Eloy's fingerprints were on the knife. Baca says Gallegos used it to cut off the victim's hair. We only got prints from the knife, though, no hair fibers. But we have the DNA from the rope, so everything else is redundant."

"I figured you had the right guys," I said. "I haven't been attacked now for the better part of a week."

She laughed. "Yeah, I think we got it figured out. And I want you to know that even if Baca can plea down the murder charge—and I don't think he can—he's still going down for the assault on you."

"Why do you think Gallegos came to rescue me when Baca and his buddy had me under the cottonwoods?" I asked.

"I've been thinking about that. You remember when you said something about recognizing him from before, when we were outside of the courthouse?"

"Yeah. I was talking about recognizing him from the first day I went to the courthouse. He was wearing his army uniform that day; he bumped into me."

"I'm guessing he must not have been sure what you meant—or that he had a sense that *you* weren't quite sure about him."

I was quiet a minute. "You mean, you think he might have set that rescue thing up to sway me away from suspicion?"

"Well, it's all I can come up with. It's not like the guy has a decent bone in his body and would have done it for the right reasons."

"Or maybe Baca was going too far . . . getting out of control . . ."

"Too far? Let's remember how Cassie Morgan was murdered, shall we?"

"Yeah, I guess you're right. You know, the idea that maybe Eloy set up the scene to save me makes a little sense when I remember what happened on Christmas Eve morning."

"Tell me."

"I told him that I was grateful for what he had done, but that I didn't change sides. I said that I knew what he was up to, and I was going to see that he paid for it."

"So, when he hears that, he decides to get rid of you for good, that very night. Maybe Baca's been pushing for it, and Gallegos has either been wanting to just try to scare you off or wait and see. But now that seals it."

"That's probably as close as we can get for now. Maybe we'll never know the whole story."

"Look, Jamaica, there's always a flaw or two in their thinking. There's always some deviation from sound reasoning, that's what leads the bad guys to do the wrong thing in the first place. When what a murderer does starts to seem logical," Diane said, "it might be time for us to go do something else. Like sack groceries or wait tables."

"So is Agent Sterling going to get you a promotion and a new assignment, now that you've solved the case?"

"I can get my own promotion. I don't need Agent Sterling to do it for me."

"But I thought you and the Silver Bullet—"

"Let me tell you something: he may be the Silver Bullet, but I am the gold standard of done. He bores me. He's too full of himself."

"So, what about that new assignment you wanted?"

"I could request a new assignment. But you know, I'm reconsidering."

"You are?"

"Yeah. That procession on Christmas Eve, it was really something. It made me think I ought to stick around, maybe see what else I might have missed."

Kerry came in as I was hanging up the phone. Mountain got up from snoozing on the floor and greeted him with his tail wagging. "That was Diane," I said. "She's going to stay in Taos."

He looked down at me and blinked his eyes but didn't speak.

"And you?" I said.

"I got the job, it's confirmed."

I rose from my chair and kissed him. "Congratulations, Kerry."

He folded his arms around me, pulling me against his chest, into the warm cave of him where I had always felt safe and sheltered. He put a finger under my chin, raised it up, and studied my face. "Come with me," he said, his eyes pleading.

"I can't." I wanted to look away, but I didn't.

I felt his chest deflate. He stared me down. "You won't."

I was quiet a minute. Mountain moved in between us, demanding to be rubbed. "I can't," I said softly, my eyes filling with tears.

"Maybe we can figure out a place for Mountain," he said. "There's a wolf sanctuary in Washington—"

"I won't leave him," I said. "I can't."

Charlie Dorn sent a crew to my cabin to put up a fenced area for Mountain, and the wolf watched warily from the end of his chain as they built it. Once the workmen had left, I propped the tall hogwire and two-by-four gate open and hooked Mountain's chain to the eye-bolt in the gatepost so that he could enter the new confine in his own time and by his own choice. I walked into the nine-foot-high fenced area and pretended to be curious about its construction.

"This isn't how I wanted it to be," I said, looking back at the wolf.

Mountain stood as far away from the pen as his chain would permit, and he watched me with curiosity, his ears up, listening.

I took hold of the fence and gave it a shake. It was solid. I turned to face my four-legged companion. "You just couldn't make it in the wild, buddy," I said, my lip quivering. "First, your mother was shot, and you needed someone to take care of you, or you would have died. Then we tried to get another pack to adopt you, and they wouldn't take you in. You were so tiny, you were all alone. They kept you in a cage for a few days, and then they asked me to help take care of you until we could get you placed somewhere with a pack."

A breeze blew up, carrying the scent of the pines. Mountain and I raised our noses in unison and inhaled the fresh, beautiful fragrance.

I sat down on the ground in the middle of the enclosure. "But we became a pack. You and me." Tears streamed down my face. "I never thought it would come to this, you on a chain or in a pen. I would never have kept you if I had known. Of course, if you were in a sanctuary somewhere, you'd be in a fenced enclosure, but it would be bigger, and you'd have other wolves with you."

Mountain sat down just outside of the gate and looked in at me.

I remained seated on the ground. "This is just for your safety, and I will never leave you in here when I'm not home. I'll always take you with me whenever I can. And we'll still go running together out on the mesa when the weather is nice, hike up through the woods, go out for long romps in all our favorite places."

Mountain got up and walked slowly toward me, his head down. I reached out a hand and he came forward to experience my touch—the touch of someone he trusted, someone he loved, someone who loved and adored him. I stroked the beautiful mane on the side of his neck, and he nuzzled his nose into my armpit, taking intense pleasure in the experience.

Kerry spent his last night before leaving at the cabin with me. As we lay on the bed facing one another in the glow of the candles flickering on the nightstand, I tried to memorize everything about my lover that I beheld: the round form of muscle at his shoulders, the soft down of hair on his chest, the angle of his jaw, the thin white scars under his chin. I savored the fragrance of his skin and realized I could probably go blindfolded into a room full of people and pick out Kerry just by scent alone. Like a wolf, I had imprinted Kerry's pheromonal signature in my sense memory.

The next morning when Kerry left, I gave him the deerskin vest I had made for his camera accessories, and I saw his eyes grow moist. "I love this," he said as he put it on. It fit wonderfully, and looked good on his lean frame. "I love that you made it with your own two hands."

"And by precious little light," I said. "It's a wonder I got the seams straight."

"I'm not giving up," he said. "I'll be back to get you soon, and by that time you will have missed me so much that you'll go anywhere with me."

"Maybe Mountain and I can come for a visit," I said.

"Come soon, babe," he said. "Come for a visit, and never leave."

◂ 45 ▸

The Heart of the Matter

On the last day of the year, Mountain and I went for an afternoon hike. I had a destination in mind, and I'd brought a backpack full of treasures. We came across the high mesa from the northeast, passing by Pueblo Pena and carefully making our way down the slender, sloping path and around the slide debris on the small shelf below the canyon rim. I spread two large squares of cloth, then unpacked food, and plenty of it. I'd brought things that hungry children love to eat: hot dogs with ketchup, macaroni and cheese, corn chips, chocolate cupcakes, and candy. I set out bottles of root beer and boxes of juice, all arranged nicely as for a feast. I put out some unfilled balloons, some marbles, and two slingshots. On one cairn, I propped the Howdy Doody doll; on the other, a child's set of plastic bow and arrows, because Tom Leaves His Robe had told me how much the boys at the Indian school loved to play Wild West. In case these two needed to escape danger, I left the tool that Roy had given me. It had saved my life, and it might just save theirs, too. I clutched my Apache tears that were given me by Sica Blue Cloud, and I choked back my own tears and forced a smile.

As Mountain and I climbed back up on the canyon rim, the sun was beginning to set across the dry back of northern New Mexico, over the vast, empty country that stretched to the west, a land of precious few rivers and high, haunting mesas broken only by more cracked-earth canyons like this one for as far as I could see. Long, shimmering beams of silver sunlight stretched like fingers into the sky, up toward the lone white cloud that floated in the turquoise heavens, to touch it tenderly before leaving. Seconds later, the western horizon was stained with color as an enormous fuchsia fruit ripened atop the soft purple swells of faraway mountains. Behind us, the ancient and enduring walls of Pueblo Pena, the silent house of sorrow, glowed red and gold.

As I stood there watching, with Mountain sitting beside me, a peace and a warmth came over me unlike any I had ever known. I felt a knot of sadness in my chest unraveling, and its barbwire tentacles no longer clutched at my heart. In that moment, I knew that the one true mother who had always been with me, the one that Momma Anna had spoken of—for whom I was a cherished and beloved daughter—was Mother Earth. Her beauty, shelter, and love had always been there for me, had always comforted me and nourished me and provided for me.

Before leaving, I went down the slope to the abandoned Indian school. I passed by the post where I almost became a meal for two hungry cubs. I walked through the gates that had been battered down by my horse, and I went to the chapel doors, which had since been forced back in place after I had stumbled onto a saga of sorrow. They were now sealed with a strong brass lock. I looked around for a pin or a nail, until I found a large cactus thorn. Returning to the chapel entrance, I pushed the cactus thorn into a crack and pinned the milagro—the cracked heart bound with barbwire—to the door of the San Pedro de Arbués Indian School, and I asked for the miracle of healing for all hearts that are filled with sorrow.

◂ Epilogue ▸

Epiphany

Before dawn on the morning of the Epiphany, I drove to Momma Anna's house in the Blazer. We had made plans to go to the home of Sica Blue Cloud Gallegos to pick up the bultos of the Holy Family and return them to their permanent home of veneration in the church. Yohe met me at Momma Anna's front door. "We gathering some few things for Sica," she said. "Sica not feel good. Very ashame her nephew do that terrible thing. And very bad more, he try make look like *Indun* do that. Sica say that like a knife in her heart."

Momma Anna came to the door with a large handwoven basket covered with a cloth. "I make soup for Sica," she said. "She not eat. She wail, they hear her cry in the village. We go church, ask Sister come, pray with Sica."

Sister Florinda Maez, Momma Anna, Yohe, and I went together to Sica's door, prepared to give the old woman comfort, and to transport the Holy Family back to the church. Sister Florinda knocked, but there was no answer. She knocked again, and we waited. The sister pushed open the door. "It's dark, the lamps aren't lit," she said. "Maybe Mrs. Gallegos is sleeping."

Momma Anna and Yohe looked at one another. Neither woman spoke.

Sister Florinda pushed the door a little farther. "Mrs. Gallegos? Sica? It's Sister Florinda, I'm going to come in and make sure you're all right." But she didn't go in. And Momma Anna and Yohe remained fixed where they stood.

But I did not hesitate. I stepped across the threshold, through foot-thick adobe walls into a dwelling that had been built nearly five hundred years before white explorers had come to "discover" this new world—a world in which a vibrant civilization balanced delicately on the rim of a tiny river, celebrating with the movement of the sun and the stars, resonating with the rhythms of the earth. I entered into the abode of a woman who had been lucky enough to have been beaten so badly with a broom that she was permitted to come home from a place that sought to steal the soul of the People through the genocide of its children's spirits.

It took a few moments for my eyes to adjust. A blanket had been tacked up over the window behind the Holy Family on their table, leaving the room in darkness. A large shadow hung in front of me, the shape of it instantly recognizable, and I felt a violent rush of sickness sweep through my chest and into my gut.

Sica Blue Cloud had struggled long and hard to get to a spike that had been driven into one of the vigas that spanned the low ceiling in her humble home. Holding on to a broom for support—a broom, of all things!—she climbed onto a low stool, and then the folding chair that I had seen her nephew bring. From this she stepped off and flew, rising like a Blue Cloud—away from the pain and the sorrow, away from the shame and the incapacity to fathom why, away from the leather belt that encircled her neck, holding her suspended in midair for just long enough to give her spirit time to leave her crippled body behind. She had made a sign and hung it to her chest by forcing the crucifix on her rosary through the top of the paper. The sign read: *I am an Indian.*

I went to the doorway and looked out at the three women who awaited word of what I had found. Their faces looked stunned, confused, and fearful—much like the faces of the children in the photographs I'd seen at the abandoned Indian school. "Sica's sorrow," I said, looking at Momma Anna, "last time."

About the Author

Sandi Ault celebrates her love for the wild west in this series. She loves to write, to explore, to adventure, to research, and to discover. She spends her free time hiking mountains, deserts, and canyons, searching out new sources of wonder and amazement, new places of magic and enchantment. She is at home in wild places, in the ruins of the ancient ones, in the canyons, on the rivers, on cliff ledges and high mesas. She loves to visit her friends and adopted family at the pueblos. She lives in the Rocky Mountains of Colorado with loving companions: a husband, a wolf, and a cat. Visit her on the Web at www.SandiAult.com and www.WildSorrow.info.

COMING SOON:
Another episode in the WILD Mystery series:
WILD PENANCE